PENGUIN BOOKS
Oracles & Miracles

Stevan Eldred-Grigg is a novelist, short story writer, essayist and historian. He has been awarded a Doctorate by the Australian National University, a Scholarship in Letters and other major grants by the Arts Council of New Zealand, an Honorary Fellowship in Writing by the University of Iowa, a Writing Fellowship by Victoria University of Wellington, and sponsorship from the Foreign Ministry of the Federal Republic of Germany. He has three sons and lives in Christchurch.

Oracles and Miracles, published in 1987, was his first novel. In 1988 it was awarded second prize in the Wattie Book Awards and was shortlisted for the fiction section of the New Zealand Book Awards. It was the joint winner of the Asia-Pacific section of the Commonwealth Writers Prize. Stevan is the author of five further novels: *The Siren Celia* (1989), *The Shining City* (1991), *Gardens of Fire* (1993), *Mum* (1995) and *Blue Blood* (1997). His short stories have been anthologised. *My History, I Think*, a postmodern memoir, was published in 1994. He has also written a number of significant works of New Zealand history: *A Southern Gentry* (1980), *A New History of Canterbury* (1982), *Pleasures of the Flesh* (winner of the 1984 AW Reed Memorial Book Award), *Working People* (1990) and *The Rich* (1996).

ORACLES
&
MIRACLES

A NOVEL

Stevan Eldred-Grigg

PENGUIN BOOKS

PENGUIN BOOKS
Published by the Penguin Group
Penguin Group (NZ), 67 Apollo Drive, Rosedale,
North Shore 0632, New Zealand (a division of Pearson New Zealand Ltd)
Penguin Group (USA) Inc., 375 Hudson Street,
New York, New York 10014, USA
Penguin Group (Canada), 90 Eglinton Avenue East, Suite 700, Toronto,
Ontario, M4P 2Y3, Canada (a division of Pearson Penguin Canada Inc.)
Penguin Books Ltd, 80 Strand, London, WC2R 0RL, England
Penguin Ireland, 25 St Stephen's Green,
Dublin 2, Ireland (a division of Penguin Books Ltd)
Penguin Group (Australia), 250 Camberwell Road, Camberwell,
Victoria 3124, Australia (a division of Pearson Australia Group Pty Ltd)
Penguin Books India Pvt Ltd, 11, Community Centre,
Panchsheel Park, New Delhi – 110 017, India
Penguin Books (South Africa) (Pty) Ltd, 24 Sturdee Avenue,
Rosebank, Johannesburg 2196, South Africa

Penguin Books Ltd, Registered Offices: 80 Strand, London, WC2R 0RL, England

First published by Penguin Group (NZ), 1987
This edition published in 2007
1 3 5 7 9 10 8 6 4 2

Designed by Richard King
Typeset in Paladium by Edsetera Book Productions in association with
Typocrafters Ltd, Auckland
Printed in Australia by McPherson's Printing Group

ISBN 978 0 14 300733 3

A catalogue record for this book is available
from the National Library of New Zealand.

www.penguin.co.nz

CONTENTS

PART ONE

1

Our debut in the City Beautiful

Ginnie

Me and Fag was born on the double bed Mum and the old man slept in. The old man had sent one of the boys to run down to the hospital and get a midwife and not long after she turned up on her bike a friend of Mum's, Mrs Palto, turned up too. It was a Saturday night early in 1929. That is, we started to be born of the Saturday night, though we didn't make our final appearance till the Sunday morning. Mum had no trouble at first, till I was born, but then she had a lot of trouble over Fag.

Fag heard about it for the next thirty years.

'And I nearly died having you,' Mum would say. 'Yes, and what I went through having you. I nearly died giving birth to you.'

And so on, etcetera, etcetera.

Mum chose our names. The old man didn't seem to have much say. I got called Janet, Janet Feron, but because I had a lot of ginger hair they called me Ginnie for a nickname and from then on Ginnie was who I always was.

Fag's name was Daphne, but she never got called Daphne, she was always just Fag. I don't know why.

After we was born we was put in a drawer in a duchesse, cause Mum didn't have anywhere else to put us. Mrs Palto cleared the old man's socks and long-johns out of the drawer and put us in. Of the Monday the old man went back to work. He was a labourer and at that time he was in work. Mrs Palto stayed to help look after us.

'Ach, Margaret,' she said to Mum, 'it has been hard for you, but you vill come right now, and your little twin girls vill be your reward.'

3

Mrs Palto was what some people called a 'Hun'. Her husband drove a cab and was an Italian.

'I curse the day my own mother had me,' was what Mum said in reply.

This was something we heard years later from our older sisters, who of course had their ears glued to the bedroom door.

Ginnie

It was in a house in Simeon Street, in Spreydon. Mum and the old man had been living there a year or two, and after me and Fag was born lived there a few years more. It was an old house, what you called a cottage, with a verandah across the front and a dark corridor down the middle. There was four rooms out the front and at the back under a drop-down roof was the kitchen, which was where we lived most of the time. One of the front rooms was what Mum called the dining room, though it was practically empty and according to my older sisters nobody was ever known to eat or even sit in it. Then there was three bedrooms. We had about four people in a bedroom. Outside at the back there was a shed with a copper, and a dunny with a wooden seat and a tin.

The house didn't belong to Mum or the old man, of course. It belonged to people that lived in a big house nearby, people of the name of Moneygall. They were toffs. She had big bosoms and wore yellow cloche hats and a long string of topaz beads. And when she talked she sort of minced words up with her teeth. Her husband wore stiff collars and a gold watch. I thought he was King George but really he'd been captain on a boat. He had farms and properties all over the place, which he rented to people.

Mum hated the Moneygalls, but was frightened of them too. 'Don't touch the wallpaper,' she'd say. 'It doesn't belong to us. The landlord will come and turn us out.'

She always seemed scared of landlords. The rent money was always put away first, no matter how hard up we was.

'You have to have a roof over your head,' she'd say.

4

So even if there was no food in the house, there was a house for there to be no food in.

When old Moneygall came to inspect the place, which he did every now and then, Mum would be in a frenzy. The toilet had to be scrubbed and disinfected, the back steps scrubbed, and that. Mum was always very polite to him, always keeping a few of us kids in the background, cause I think she probably got the house by not saying exactly how many kids there was. When me and Fag was born there was eleven of us, not counting Jimmie who'd died in a motorbike smash. Then after me and Fag there was another baby, then another one a couple of years after that. So in the end there was thirteen kids in that one house.

Not that all of them was kids any more. By the time me and Fag was born some of the boys was already great big slabs. Jock and Eddie were so big they kept banging their heads against the top of the kitchen door.

'Fucking door,' Jock used to say. 'I'm gonna bust the bloody thing down one day.'

Jock busted a lot of things.

'Watch your bloody language,' Mum would say. 'Mouth like a bloody sewer.'

Fag

Ginnie and I often talk about our childhood. Now that we're women ourselves, with houses, husbands, children, mortgages, now that our legs have swollen up with varicose veins and our tits have dropped down to our bellies, we think we should look at our childhood, lift the scab off our memories and have a look at the stuff underneath. It's a long time ago now, after all. Our childhood was a long time ago, those things are over and done with.

Well they're not, of course. The past is still living, it's inside us, making us what we are, whatever that is. But at least the actual things that happened, the things that make the living past, are in a box we've buried, like Mum.

The trouble with Ginnie is that she can't really see much further than her own nose.

She hasn't read much, that's her trouble, she doesn't know enough words. When she left school to go to the factory she just stopped looking at words, she just made do with the ones she had and didn't bother to look for any more. But me, well of course as Eddie used to say about me, I'd read brown paper if there weren't any books. So when I look at the past I can bring more knowhow to the job than Ginnie can.

Not that she isn't good at it. Ginnie looks at something, she looks at it hard, and she says, well now did it happen that way or am I remembering it wrong? Was it really like that? Were those my actual feelings?

But of course she's trapped. She hasn't got enough words to describe things, so she's trapped.

She thinks that if she can just manage to work out exactly what happened and how she felt about what happened, and what sorts of dreams and hopes and smokes and shadows came and went in her head because of those things happening, then she'll understand it, she'll know the past.

Not knowing that a thing is more than just the sum of its substance and shadow.

A trap, for example, is a trap.

I, on the other hand, well I can reach up to my brain and help myself to the words up there, leaf through the volumes and say, oh yes, that throws some light on the thing, and of course, yes, that was what you might expect, given the time, the place, the circumstances . . .

But you need a lot of words.

The Historian

'Oh Christchurch!' is what some people used to say when they wanted to swear. And 'Oh Christchurch!' is also what some people used to say when they went for a drive up onto Cashmere and stopped at the Summit Road and got out of their cars and looked at the city below them.

'Oh Christchurch!'

A little under their breath, a little awed.

'To anyone who takes his stand today on the Cashmere Hills,' said *Sixty Years of Progress*, a book published by the city council not long before Ginnie and Fag were born, 'and looks upon the panorama of a great modern city that is spread before him, it will appear very like a miracle that all this has been accomplished. Eighty years ago, could the onlooker have stood upon the same spot and gazed over the same extent of country, he would have seen tussock and fern and scrub, flax and toi-toi, swamp and sand-hill and fertile level plain, but of town or city there would have been, literally, no vestige or trace. The land then was as it had been for, perhaps, thousands of years previously, and puny man had left no mark upon it, if one excepts the few poor scratchings of the native cultivations. What a change was to take place within the next three-quarters of a century!'

Well.

If Margaret Feron had been rich when Ginnie and Fag were born, and had lived in one of the big houses rambling over the spurs of Cashmere, what would she have seen, looking out from a bay window across the plains?

'Christchurch the Garden City of New Zealand' was what she would have seen according to the city council, the chamber of commerce, the Progress League, and the Industrial Association. 'Christchurch the City Beautiful that enraptures those who behold it from some high spur of the hills.'

Margaret Feron wasn't rich, of course. She only got up onto Cashmere once in her life, when she went in a dray to a works picnic and had a row with the old man about his drinking.

'Gitting himself full as a boot so he couldn't see the road to the dunny if it had red flags on it,' she'd say years later, when-ever Ginnie or Fag mentioned the word Cashmere.

But of course to Ginnie and Fag the word Cashmere was a magic word. It was a sort of abracadabra that opened the door to a fan-tasy land of mansions and chauffeurs, silk and brocade, astrakhan and pearls.

'Remembering the uninviting prairie that the early colonists gazed upon,' said the chamber of commerce, Progress League, and so forth, 'it is apparent that only men and women of vision, working under the influence of poetic inspiration handed on from father to son, could have succeeded in fashioning the City Beautiful. Not without cause the resemblance between Christchurch and Damascus, the oldest city in the world and one of the newest, has been commented upon by those who travel in many lands and have seen the great cities of the earth.'

So that was what it was all about.

Progress. Christchurch was 'the most modern city on earth'.

Continuity. Christchurch was 'firmly rooted in civilised history', a city founded by Pilgrims, 'high-minded, noble, and religious English gentlemen and ladies who hoped to found in the New World a city which would replicate entire the civilisation of the Old World, but leaving behind the vices. A civilisation in which manners, learning and the arts would be revered, where rank would receive its due, but where working people would be freed forever from the poverty, hunger, and fear that so disfigures their lives in the cottage homes and slumlands of the Motherland.'

And . . . Well, they did it, you see.

'How and in what manner the Pilgrims and their descendants, and those who have been imbued with the spirit of the Pilgrims, have "accommodated the shows of things to the desires of the mind", is to be seen in Christchurch on every side. Their desire to transplant a slice of England has been realised abundantly. The beautiful Gothic Cathedral, the many buildings of grey stone, the groves of oak and chestnut, and long lines of poplars, the songs of familiar English birds, are all signs and sounds that testify that the dream of the Pilgrims has become real.'

If Margaret Feron had been up on Cashmere the afternoon before Ginnie and Fag were born she would have seen in front of her the rooftops of houses stepping down the hillside amidst gardens and terraces. Trees. Flowers. And big sparkling windows, stealing the sky.

In the distance she would have seen Hagley Park, the colleges, the cathedral, and the city squares, filled with trees and spires and advertising signs and fountains and department stores and statues of worthies. Beyond that a forest of oaks, ashes, eucalypts, willows, walnuts, poplars – the 'umbrageous precincts of Fendalton and the other northern and western suburbs where the inhabitants enjoy more even than most of the happy citizens of the City Beautiful, the delights and pleasures of modern life.' Then beyond the 'umbrageous precincts' Margaret would have seen the Alps, blue and white and far away. A hundred miles away, people told her. Sparkling and cold, marching across from the east of the world to the west of the world.

But between Cashmere in the foreground and Hagley Park in the distance was South Christchurch.

South Christchurch, seen from the hills, looked as though lava, bursting from the flanks of the extinct volcano on which Cashmere squatted, had flowed out onto the prairie to lay everything waste, to reduce three dimensions to two. A lava of red oxide iron, dingy yellow wood and rusty orange signs, cracked and broken by the black ciphers of railways, factories, chimney stacks and the great stinking towers of the Christchurch Gas Coal and Coke Company Limited. A magma of peeling paint, flaking iron, cracked linoleum, dusty yards. Lean-tos and asphalt, dunnies and textile mills. Middleton and Addington and Spreydon in the west. Sydenham and Waltham and Phillipstown, Linwood and Woolston in the east. A lava baked hard on the surface of the prairie, sealed tight under a lid of yellow gas – the smog of five hundred factories, ten thousand fires, one hundred and twenty thousand human throats.

This was her Christchurch. This was her world.

The Historian

What was happening in the City Beautiful when Ginnie and Fag were born?

On the Saturday night, when the pains first started, a well-known 'high society girl' gave 'a very pleasant little cabaret' in the family mansion in Fendalton. The jazz band at the cabaret were dressed as 'Negroes', so their faces were black and their suits were white. The young men who danced with the flappers and laughingly licked champagne from little manly wrists had faces that were white and suits that were black.

While Margaret Feron grunted and swore on the double bed in Simeon Street, thousands of people danced to jazz.

At the Dixieland Cabaret under a dome by the cathedral a 'BIG BIG JAZZ JAZZ' band played while the fashionable architect Heathcote Helmore talked to the clever Charles D'Auvergne and another fashionable architect, Guy Cotterill, chatted with Maurice Heaton O'Rorke, the sociable landowner, grandson of Sir Maurice O'Rorke, Speaker in the House of Representatives. At the Winter Garden less stylish crowds danced to jazz too, while down at the seaside under the moonlight and Chinese lanterns there was laughing, dancing, and clapping at a 'gala carnival' on the New Brighton pier.

As Mrs Palto told Margaret to 'bear down' for the hundredth time a crowd at the New Opera House clapped the 'Gorgeous Staging' of the latest 'Bright, Breezy, Snappy' revue, 'SNAP-SHOTS of 1929'. In the glamorous dim of the picture palaces other crowds watched 'WICKEDNESS PREFERRED', a spicy sex comedy on the flickering silver screen at the Liberty, 'VAMPING VENUS', a hilarious sex farce at Everybodys, and the siren Janet Gaynor puckering her 'Tempting Lips' in 'SUNRISE', a sex drama about 'The Eternal Conflict of Pure and Illicit Love'.

Margaret Feron, in the meantime, was having trouble getting Ginnie out.

'Ten more big pushes and it'll be over,' the St Helens nurse lied encouragingly.

'Shit, fuck, hell,' said Margaret.

'WORRIES OF HOUSEKEEPING?' said the evening paper. 'The monotonous never-ceasing daily round of household duties, together with the worries arising from the care of children and housekeeping, fray the nerves and have depressing effects on the patience and health of many wives and mothers. A short course of Dr Williams' Pink Pills will give you renewed vigour. So get a three shilling bottle from your chemist today – nothing else will do.'

The evening editorial noted that New Zealanders had more telephones than the people of any country except the United States and Canada.

'The multiplication of such material signs of civilised life is gratifying,' said the leader writer. 'They signify that the country as a whole enjoys a high standard of living. The remarkable thing about New Zealand is the ease with which nearly all classes of the community enjoy a full life. Holidays and recreation give the working class New Zealander a freedom that the English or European toiler can rarely hope to attain. It has been the aim of government in New Zealand, from the first, to win and preserve high standards of life for the people, and the telephone registers of the cities, towns, and country indicate that progress has been real and rapid.'

'REAL DISTRESS EXISTS AMONG MANY POOR FAMILIES IN CITY,' said a headline a few pages away from the editorial about telephones.

'Despite the excellent work being done by the Charitable Aid Board, other organizations, and the generosity of private citizens, to help relieve matters,' the article commented, 'considerable real distress is in evidence among the poor families of the city. Although no cases of actual starvation are known of, there are cases where conditions are almost as serious – homes where food in even actual sufficiency is not available.'

On the middle page of the evening paper the Communist party asked for a basic wage of five pounds a week for each worker. On the front page was an advertisement for a 'DAIMLER LIMOUSINE' which a rich landowner had bought for two thousand pounds.

'The interests of classes,' the president of the Christchurch branch of the Communist party wrote, 'are categorically opposed. Are the underemployed, the paupers, the unemployed, at peace with the wealthy wasters? No, they are at war. Class war is not the outcome of any factitious policy by the poor, it is irresistibly and economically determined. Here lies the crux of the fate of our country: a *prosperous* country full of pauperism, unemployment, anxiety, wretchedness!'

11

As the sun slid behind the Alps and darkness slipped in from the ocean, farmers, housewives, railway workers, society ladies and schoolteachers in the little towns and the big country houses and the fifteen thousand farmsteads between the city and the mountains, leafed through the pages of the evening paper.

'Anything in the rag tonight, Dad?' asked Mother as she turned his leggings and began to stitch patches on them for the second time.

'Usual rot,' said Dad, reaching for the gin.

In the dark and vacant night, punctured with distant stars, the rooms of the province crackled with gramophones, Bible readings, radios, and breaking bottles. In Timaru, the 'sister city', the 'Riviera of the South', people like their cousins in Christchurch danced the charleston, went to bed, boiled blackcurrant jam and drank. Up and down the province could be heard the unscrewing of pill bottles, the popping of beer bottles, the scream of kettles as Mother reached across to the tea caddy and said, giving it a little rattle, shivering with delight at the sound of the dry leaves sifting gently within,

'Another cup, Dad?'

In Christchurch a young drug addict released earlier in the week from Sunnyside Mental Hospital was wandering about 'with glassy eyes' when he was arrested for stealing from a department store. Down at New Brighton the 'GALA CROWDS THRILLED' at the prospect of a suicide when a man in a suit and hat jumped off the end of the pier. In a silent cowshed near the country town of Rangiora an old labouring man 'in a depressed state of mind' tied a rope round his neck, stood on a soap box, and kicked the box away. In Timaru eight policemen raided an opium den and arrested the dreamy occupants. Over on the other side of the Alps, among the forests and mines and storm clouds of the West Coast, punters drowned their failure in ten thousand jugs of beer at the end of a day of racing at the summer meet of the Greymouth Trotting Club.

It was Sunday before Ginnie was finally born. And then, while Mrs Palto wiped off the stuff from the baby and the midwife gave the orders, Margaret started the agony of giving birth to Fag.

12

The Historian

In 1929, when Ginnie and Fag were born, women like Margaret Feron were being bludgeoned with phrases like 'scientific mothering'. It wasn't modern, they were told, to have a baby at home, it wasn't scientific. Women shouldn't be having babies at home amidst dirty socks and old dish rags and slop buckets and *sepsis*. They should take advantage of the clean, cheery, well-scrubbed wards of St Helens Hospital, built with government money on the south side of the railway tracks for the express purpose of making sure 'expectant mothers of the working class' would be provided with 'gratuitous but high quality assistance' when giving birth to 'the future soldiers, workers, mothers and wives of the nation'.

But although St Helens was free, it still cost money to go there. If Margaret went to hospital, who would look after the house? The old man could take time off work, but his pay would be docked and after the baby was born he might find there was no job for him to go back to. Or you could get a woman in to look after the house, but where would you get the money to pay her?

So Margaret, like most women in South Christchurch, was 'confined' at home.

She would get onto the old double bed, nagging and complaining, the springs squealing. The old man would walk off to work every morning and then, after walking back home again that night, would boil up plum duffs in old flour sacks, poking at them with a wooden spoon over the big black range, serving them out in a steaming clatter to the double line of kids at the kitchen table. And Mrs Palto would come as many hours a day as she could, and would wash and cook and clean and scrub and darn.

Then, when Margaret had got better and Mrs Palto had walked off to her place in Waltham again, Margaret would set her teeth.

'Right,' she'd say. 'This place needs a good lick and a root.'

Then there would be the most vicious licking and rooting the house had seen for months. Brushes, rags, mops flying. Kids scattering. Dust fluttering up to the ceiling then dropping back down to where moments before the busy rag had been whisking.

13

Last of all, the straightening out of the mats.

'*And* disturbing all my mats,' Margaret would say with an accusing glare at the invisible Mrs Palto.

The mats would be squared off until once more they divided the floors into measured patches of managed emptiness.

The Historian

The morning after Ginnie and Fag were born was a fresh sparkling Sunday morning, with little puffs of cumulus scudding across a placid sky. The sort of morning that promised a 'lovely day'. Dew on the grass, and people thinking of picnics at rivers, beaches, in the mountains.

'TAKE A MOTOR TRIP THIS SUNDAY . . . AND DRIVE YOURSELF!' suggested the newspapers. 'Take your family out for an automobile run in one of our modern, roomy cars. You drive yourself – and the cost is surprisingly low.'

So the tanks of the shiny Humbers and Fords and Studebakers and Austins were filled with 'benzine' and the boots were heaped up with parasols, hampers, Kaiapoi woollen rugs, portable gramophones, stacks of the latest dance tunes, jazz and ragtime. 'No longer is a Portable Gramophone purchased merely because it is portable,' the newspaper instructed its readers. 'The public now demands as much of a Portable Gramophone in the matter of tone, quality and appearance as it does of large Cabinet Gramophones – and justly so.' And the Humbers and Fords and Studebakers and Austins went for a spin to the Alps and the sea. Parents, children, and Kaiapoi rugs unrolled on the white sand of New Brighton, the golden cove of Corsair Bay, the bleached white crescent of Caroline Bay. Sandwiches and tea cakes, parasols and sun lotion; and the Portable Gramophones began to warble their scratchy good fun to indifferent waves, hissing on the sand.

While the people picnicked at New Brighton and Timaru, while a long train of red carriages filled with 'trainers, attendants, ninety horses and several hundred of the general public' wound through the narrow passes of the Alps returning to Christchurch from the Greymouth trots, Ginnie and Fag snuffled and stirred in the drawers of the duchesse.

Ginnie

When me and Fag was little, Jock and Eddie was mad on motorbike racing. Well it wasn't that they was mad on it, it was just that racing was about the only sport you could make money in, if you rode your motorbike fast enough and didn't get yourself killed like Jimmie. Jock and Eddie had made a dirt track in our yard, to practise on. It went right round the house, so Mum and the Moneygalls had that to put up with.

Mum didn't put up with it, or at least she didn't intend to put up with it without a fight, so she nagged them about it night and day. The usual story.

'Waking the dead,' she'd say, 'and sending the sane to Sunnyside. Tearing round on those bloody machines.'

Of course the boys kept doing it, and of course Mum kept nagging them.

The Moneygalls didn't have to settle for nagging. They evicted us. So one fine day I was looking at our stuff on the back of a lorry and we was walking down the road to Braddon Street.

Our house in Simeon Street had been old, but the house in Braddon Street was older. It was smaller too. That meant a lower rent though, which was a good thing, cause times was harder by then. The old man wasn't in work any more and the older kids couldn't get work either. So it was a good thing it was up sticks. Upping sticks was nothing new anyway. Mum and the old man had always been shifting round from one rented place to another. Always old wooden places with corrugated iron roofs, always places in need of paint, and always in the same districts of South Christchurch that the Feron family had been drifting round for three generations, 'getting nowhere slow', as Eddie used to say.

Braddon Street was in Addington. At one end was railway yards and warehouses and a couple of factories, and at the other

15

end was all these old, old little houses, all squeezed together in dusty little yards.

Our place was a square box with four rooms inside. In the front was three bedrooms. Out the back was a kitchen under the usual drop-down roof. Behind that was the usual shed with a copper, and the usual dunny with a wooden seat and a tin. And that was it. The old iron hand pump over the well wasn't close to the back door like in Simeon Street, it was way down the bottom of the yard, so every time we wanted water it was a trek. And the biggest curse of all about Braddon Street was the gas lights. They hadn't been looked after and always seemed to be going phut. Mum would stand up on a chair, balancing on one leg and fiddling with the gas mantles, and her mouth would be just a thin white line.

'Stupid bloody . . .', she'd say. 'Bloody landlords . . .'

The yard at Braddon Street was just that, a yard, with rusting corrugated iron fences round it. In winter it was just mud and in summer it baked all hard, so Eddie called the house 'Mud Flats'. Eddie was a bit of a dag, he could see the funny side of things. And Mum, if she was in a good mood when he cracked a joke, would manage a sort of grim smile. And if she wasn't in a good mood, which was ninety per cent of the time, she'd bite his head off.

'Cut out your stupid trash,' she'd say.

At Braddon Street the landlords was getting only fifteen shillings a week from us, so we was three shillings up, cause at Simeon Street the Moneygalls was getting eighteen. The new landlords was called Stevenson. They was a family of builders, and one of them lived out Fendalton way in a big house looking over the polo grounds in Hagley Park, while the other one lived on the Esplanade in Sumner, in a big house looking out over the ocean. They owned quite a lot of places in Addington. I think they must of sent some agent round to collect the rent, cause I don't remember ever seeing any of them in Braddon Street. Though one day when Mum was walking with some of us kids down past the Stevenson workshops in Colombo Street a big yellow car flashed past and I saw a fat red face underneath some glass.

'One of them Stevensons,' Mum said. 'Driving on soft wheels to hell.'

Not that Mum believed there was a hell. She liked the idea, especially if it meant there was a place where Moneygalls and Stevensons would get what was coming to them, but she knew it'd be too good to be true.

While we was living at Braddon Street one of the young Stevensons got married and Mum read about it in the society page of one of the papers.

'SOCIAL NOTES,' it said. 'WEDDINGS. STEVENSON-MERBROOK.'

'Tt,' Mum said, screwing up her eyes.

'Many friends gathered at St Barnabas Church of England, Fendalton, on Saturday,' the paper said, 'to witness the wedding of Guinever Virginia, third daughter of Mr and Mrs C. F. Merbrook, to Mr G. W. G. Stevenson, son of Mr and Mrs G. W. Stevenson. The ceremony was performed by the Rev. E. A. Osmers, and Mr Foster Browne was organist. The bride wore a becoming frock of pearl tinted satin with a long oval train and ruched bodice. Her veil of tulle and beautiful old lace fell from a halo head-dress of tulle lilies and silver, and she carried a sheaf of cream begonias. The bridesmaids wore blue cloques with slit bodices caught by silver and pearl clasps. Their plaited coronets were of silver lamé, and pink begonias were arranged in the sheaves which they carried. Mr and Mrs Merbrook entertained their guests afterwards with an elegant breakfast at the Hotel Federal. When the bride and groom left during the afternoon for their wedding tour, the bride was wearing an astrakhan coat and a peach-bloom velour hat. On returning from their tour they will make their new home in St Andrews Terrace.'

'Tt,' Mum said again. 'That's where our rent money goes. Bun fights at the Hotel Federal and houses in St Andrews Terrace. Fine life for some.'

And she screwed up her eyes again.

That wedding sounded like something from fairyland to me and Fag. It was like all the stories about Cinderella and the Sleeping Beauty and that.

'You can be the bride,' Fag said, 'and I'll be the groom.'

We got a dish rag that had been drying on the line, and we arranged it on my head, and we got married in the back yard down by the rubbish heap. Me with my 'veil of tulle and beautiful old lace' falling from my 'halo head-dress of tulle lilies and silver', and Fag standing at attention next to me, like we imagined a toff like 'Mr G. W. G. Stevenson, son of Mr and Mrs G. W. Stevenson' would of stood.

Mum found us getting married down by the rubbish heap but she didn't get mad, she just looked sort of old, and walked away again.

Our fifteen shillings a week can't of been much help in paying off the mortgage on the Stevenson house in St Andrews Terrace, cause we was only paying it for a year or two. Then Mum heard of a place nearby in Kent Street. It had electricity, Mrs Palto told Mum.

'Just think, Margaret,' she said. 'No more of those dirty gas mantles. All you vill need to do vill be to go flick, and there the light vill be shining.'

Mum just growled, but there was a sort of gleam in her eyes, and a week later we were packed up and ready to go.

Us kids thought it was a real step up, going to Kent Street.

'Just think, Gin,' Fag said. 'No more of those dirty gas mantles. All we vill need to do vill be to go flick, and there the light vill be shining.'

Jock went round and smashed all the gas mantles with his fist.

'Bugger the Stevensons,' he said.

So we shifted to Kent Street.

It wasn't very far, just a couple of streets away, but it was fancier than the place in Braddon Street. There was a verandah out the front and a bay window off one of the bedrooms. Otherwise it was the usual story. Dark narrow corridor down the middle, three bedrooms in the front, and a kitchen under a drop-down roof at the back. The kitchen walls was lined with tongue and groove. The bedrooms was covered with scrim, sort of bulging here and there, with old shiny wallpaper, almost like lino, but sort of hanging off in parts. The floors was bare, of course;

tenants was supposed to bring their own coverings. Luckily Mum had her mats.

Houses came and went, but Mum always had her mats. She would put them down, square them off and stand back, resting her chin in the crook of her hand and pointing up her cheekbone with her forefinger, sort of squinting at the mats.

'That's one job done,' she'd say.

They was mostly just sea-grass mats, or else coir mats as she called them, made from coconut string. There was also an old possum skin, really just a bald old thing, but it had drifted with Mum round South Christchurch for years, and it was going to keep drifting round with her.

Beds was in short supply. I don't know how long me and Fag slept in drawers, but we did end up in the family cot eventually. It was a big kauri cot with room for two babies, though not really room for two toddlers, so it got a bit of a squeeze for me and Fag after a while. Fag got promoted to a bed, which she had to share with Peggy and Hock. I stayed in the cot. I was still sleeping in it when I went to school – in fact I was nearly eight before I finally got out of that cot.

We slept on thin kapok mattresses, and the pillows was kapok too. On top was what Eddie called the 'ancestral blankets', which was so thin you kept putting your foot through them.

Our landlord this time was Sir Bert Pelf. We never saw him, of course, though sometimes we found a picture of him in the papers, shaking hands with the new Labour prime minister or Lady Meyers or somebody like that.

'The portrait of a self-made man,' Mum said, but I didn't quite know what she was getting at, especially since she said it in a sarcastic sort of way.

Mum just about went berserk the first two or three days at Kent Street, cause us kids kept going round the house reaching up to the brass switches and going flick, flick. And a yellow light would pop out in a glass bulb. The yellow light was sort of flickery and the glass bulbs was bare and fly spotted, but we thought it was really exciting. Then of course we got used to it, but a battle had started with Mum that lasted for years.

19

'Leave those lights alone,' she'd say. 'Wasting power.'

'Costs thruppence,' Eddie would say, 'every time you switch a light on.' Pretending to back Mum up.

And Mum would glare at him, her mouth a thin white line again, and Eddie would find something else to do.

Eddie liked growing vegetables and that, which was why he hadn't been too happy about the mud flats at Braddon Street. At Kent Street he made quite a good vege garden in an empty section next door between us and the big Shell Oil Company place. The empty section was all overgrown – there was broken concrete foundations where a house had been, the landlord had burnt the house down, the neighbours said, to get the insurance money. So it was a bit of a jungle and us kids built huts and found dead cats and things there, and used to whoop around. There was an old pear tree too. So we had plenty of bottled pears and lots of cabbages, carrots, spuds and that from Eddie's garden.

There was a bit of money in the house too. Work wasn't so hard to find by that time. Eddie and Jock had found steady jobs as labourers at an engineering works. Lindsay had managed to get an apprenticeship with a painter. The big girls, Ruby and Sadie, was in work too, on an assembly line in a textile mill. So there was a bit of board coming in for Mum.

We was still hard up, mind you. And it wasn't helped much by the fact that the old man had cleared out again, and this time he never came back.

2

Standing at the kitchen sink on one leg

Ginnie

Me and Fag never really got to know the old man. He was always sort of drifting in and drifting out. Some weeks he would be around, other weeks he wouldn't. When we was living in Simeon Street he was labouring here and there for a while and then he drove a motor lorry for a transport firm and used to go away for up to two weeks at a time to Timaru and Greymouth and that. And even when he wasn't down south or over on the Coast he was hardly ever at home, he'd have to be out the door before six in the morning to walk to the lorry yard. Then after driving the lorry all day he had to wash it down at night. And then he'd walk home and stop off at the pub. Often as not us kids would be in bed before he got home, and then of course Mum would start up and we'd hear her through the wall.

'Boozing yer life away,' she'd say. 'Coming home all piss and wind like the barber's cat.'

Sometimes she'd end up screaming, but the old man never said anything much. Though I can remember one day when he came home late, not very late, cause me and Fag was still up, and Mum hadn't kept his tea for him.

'If yer so bloody fond of yer boozer,' she said, 'you can fill yer belly with beer and save me the trouble of cooking.'

Well the old man looked sort of tired. He leaned over to the bench where Peggy and Hock was washing the dishes, and he picked up a plate and threw it at Mum. She didn't duck, but it flew past her head and smashed against the kitchen wall. Then the old man walked out.

That was the only time I saw him do anything like that.

Of course once he was out the door Mum's tongue got going
again and he was all the piss brained boozers this side of
Sydenham Town Hall, but I don't think the old man did drink
all that much. He went to the Club Hotel to have a beer after
work, like I said, but I think really that was about it. There was
never beer in the house, and in fact me and Fag can't remember
ever seeing the old man with a glass in his hand.

He was a very clean person, the old man. He'd never go out
with his shoes dirty or anything, and he could cook a good meal,
and he really worked hard, when there was work for him. He
had great big hands and great big feet, like all the Ferons, or so
people used to say. The Feron boys always took about a size ten
shoe, and Eddie used to say, 'Ten with the backs pushed out.'
Not that the old man was a big person. Apart from his hands
and feet he wasn't particularly big. The thing I remember most
about him is his hair, sort of reddy coloured, curly hair he had.
And Mum used to say when I was young that I was the only one
that had his colour hair.

'Much good it'll do you,' she added.

Mum and the old man didn't always fight. I remember, when
times was good and he was in work and the bills had all been
paid for the week, he'd come home sometimes straight from work
without stopping at the pub and grab Mum round the waist.

'Come on Marg,' he'd say, 'we'll go to the pictures and pretend
we're young again.'

Mum would sort of frown.

'And who's going to get these kids to bed and get this mending
done, that the boys need for school tomorrow?' she'd say.

But she'd go anyway, and sometimes when they walked out
the door she'd be smiling.

When times was good he was often quite gay, the old man,
and when times wasn't so good he was sort of friendly and quiet.
The first thing I can remember about him is sitting on his knee
in front of a fire. He used to pick me and Fag up off the floor
and sit us on his knees, cuddling us and talking to us. Which Mum
never did. And one night he plonked me on the bar of his bike
and rode me down to town. There was a circus, he was taking

me to look at the animals and the big top, and on the way we stopped at a fruit shop. The fruit was stacked up in big gleaming pyramids on the footpath, and it was like magic to me, it was all lit up, this shining fruit piled up.

Then we rode on. I can't remember seeing the circus, but I can still remember the fruit, and how it made me think I was happy.

But the old man got the sack from the transport firm, they was laying men off, so he went away to work round the bays, doing work on the Peninsula and that. Then he came back, cause there was no work anywhere, and Mum was pregnant again, and her and the old man was trapped in the house together, snapping and scrapping. Then he was on a scheme they had going, what they called relief work. He was working three days a week building a new road up on Cashmere, and he got twenty-eight shillings a week for it, when just our rent was fifteen shillings.

'And he watches he gits his beer out of it,' Mum would say.

Sometimes me and Fag would think the old man was the worst person in the world. But then other times we'd think, well after all that hard work with pick and shovel isn't he entitled to something of his own?

Mind you, what did Mum have that was her own?

The old man managed to get steady work as a labourer in the yards for the Stevensons. So they was paying him a wage to work for them and we was paying them most of the wage back again for rent.

'Making a profit each way,' Mum said.

Then the Stevensons laid the old man off and money was tight for a while again. Then he got work labouring for the Luneys, another big building outfit, and then Williamsons, they was big building people too.

By this time Mum was pregnant again and never had a kind word to say for him. When he was home they wasn't speaking to one another, and when he wasn't home just about all Mum *could* talk about was how terrible he was, how he was a waster, a boozer, and everything under the sun. She got the big boys and the big girls on her side, and when the old man drifted in Eddie and Jock would swear at him and Sadie would yell and carry on.

She really seemed to hate him, Sadie, she'd sort of get into a frenzy.

'Piss faced stinking old goat,' she used to say.

One day she spat at him, and he didn't do anything, just wiped it off. Another day she picked up a stone from the yard and threw it at him. It hit him on the head.

From then on Sadie used to stone the old man every time he turned up.

Me and Fag would sort of squeeze ourselves into a corner and hold hands very tight.

Ginnie

After the old man had gone for good Mum stopped talking about him for a while, and me and Fag nearly forgot all about him. But then there was trouble about getting money out of him. He went away up north and for a few weeks nobody seemed to know where he was, so Mum wasn't getting any money and things started to get desperate.

'Wait till I find him,' Mum said. 'I'll slap a writ on the bugger.'

Me and Fag didn't know what slapping a writ on somebody meant, of course. Fag had an idea it had something to do with handcuffs. But what Mum really meant was once she'd found out where the old man was she'd take him to court and get the magistrate to make him pay maintenance.

Then she seemed to give that idea up for a while, cause the next thing I can remember is hearing that the old man was back in town and that he was staying in a boarding house off Montreal Street.

'Git round there,' Mum told us. 'And don't come back till he's given you some money.'

So me and Fag walked through Addington and across the railway yards and down along Montreal Street and knocked at the door.

A woman came out. She had greasy brown hair in curlers.

'He's not here,' she said. 'He's out.'

But me and Fag had the feeling she was lying, and anyway we

24

was so scared about having to go home without the money that we crept round the back into a little dingy yard with brick walls and some wet clothes sort of drooping on a line, and as we looked up we saw the old man, just for a minute, his face against one of the windows. We threw some gravel up onto the glass.

'Dad!' we yelled. 'Dad!'

He flung the window up.

'You bloody kids!' he said.

And we said, 'We've come for some money Dad.'

And he said, 'I haven't got any.'

And we said, 'Mum told us to come, and she told us we're not allowed to go home till you've given us some.'

He shut the window and went away. But we kept throwing gravel up, so in the end he flung some silver down into the yard, and me and Fag took it home.

'Well?' Mum said when we got in the door.

We gave her the money.

'That's not enough,' she said. 'Go back.'

But Fag had had enough and she said she wouldn't go back, and that was it. Mum ranted and raved, but Fag wouldn't go back again.

Later on things got so bad Mum did 'slap a writ' on the old man, and that meant instead of traipsing across town to a boarding house us kids had to trek up town to the courthouse in Victoria Square. Me and Fag had to do it a lot of the time, we had to take the babies with us too, Billie and Tots, but it wasn't so bad, it was nice once we crossed the railway and got into the middle of town where there was the river and the big smart shops and the weeping willows and that, it was like the postcards of Christchurch you could see for sale on news stands in Sydenham. The courthouse was like a sort of castle or mental hospital, so it scared us and excited us at the same time.

But as often as not the money wasn't waiting for us when we got inside.

'One thing I'm sure of,' Mum would say when we got back home with empty hands, 'I'm going to outlive that bugger. I'm going to dance on his grave.'

The Historian

The truth was too complex for the Ferons, like all of us, with our formulas, our slogans that come so effortlessly and endlessly, our phrases that divide confusion into order.

Landlords, for example.

To the Ferons they seemed rich, remote. Moneygalls Stevensons Pelfs, they were like a Hindu deity with a thousand arms held out for money, their surnames interchangeable titles for the same brassy god.

'And all so tight,' Margaret Feron used to say, 'they wouldn't know the Brighton tram was up them till it rang its bell and people started getting off.'

But of course the Moneygalls, Stevensons and Pelfs weren't Hindu gods, they were Anglicans or Presbyterians, so they believed in their money and thought they were decent people. They imagined, for example, that people could be rich and still honest. They thought that people like them weren't parasites but benefactors.

They 'provided working people with work'.

When they or their politicians said things like that Margaret Feron assumed they were lying. She would have been startled to have been told they believed it.

Then again, when the Ferons saw topaz beads glittering on the bosom of Mrs Moneygall, and read about the slit bodices and pearl clasps of the bridesmaids at the Stevenson wedding, and saw newspaper photographs of Sir Bert Pelf shaking hands with the Labour prime minister, they thought that Moneygalls Stevensons Pelfs all belonged to a single indivisible world of money where big fast motorcars zoomed along on an endless geyser of benzine and champagne. In reality the Moneygalls and Stevensons were as far from the top as they were from the bottom.

Old Moneygall began life as an ordinary able seaman, and although he ended up with the title 'Master Mariner' he was only captain of a little coastal ship working out of Lyttelton. And although he then bought a bit of farmland down on the plains near Ashburton, it wasn't exactly an estate with porticoed mansion, it was a dirt farm and he ran only seventy sheep on it. In

1923 he sold up and bought 'two acres one rood twenty-six perches' of land in Spreydon, and that was the basis of the Feron idea of him as a great urban landlord. He built a few houses, sold some, and let the rest to working people.

The Stevensons were a little higher up in the pecking order than the Moneygalls. They'd made money in colonial times and by the time Ginnie and Fag came along had a fair bit of cash to jingle.

'Their business was established,' according to the *Canterbury Cyclopedia*, 'by the late Mr Nathaniel Stevenson in 1864, shortly after his arrival in the colony. It is amongst the oldest building and contracting businesses in Canterbury, has progressed steadily ever since its inception, and is at the present time acknowledged to be one of the leading building firms in the province. The sons of the founder of the firm have recently undertaken a very important contract, namely, the building of the Roman Catholic Cathedral in Christchurch, one of the architectural adornments of the city. Their headquarters in Sydenham occupy about an acre and a half and comprise the office, the workshop and a large timber yard where wood is stored and seasoned for the various works undertaken by the firm.'

But though they had money, the Stevensons were persons quite unknown to the hostesses of the Christchurch smart set. A wedding breakfast at the Hotel Federal was something beyond the comprehension of the world of fashion, because although the Feron family saw the Hotel Federal as a glamorous pile of elegance to be gazed at across the lawns of Victoria Square when they walked up town to collect the maintenance, for those who knew about such things it was just a hotel. Respectable, yes. But by no means 'the go'.

The first genuinely big capitalist to find his coffers enriched by Feron rent money was Sir Bert Pelf. When he died, a millionaire, he was held up by top people as an example of the 'self-made man' (as Margaret Feron observed in her Kent Street kitchen), evidence that anybody who deserved to do well *would* do well, the implication of course being that those who didn't do well deserved their fate just as richly as the Pelf family deserved their millions.

The newspapers liked cooing about the Pelf millions.

'In 1908 a young Timaru boy set himself up,' the story went, 'with a set of plumber's tools, a few pounds in the bank, and a boundless store of optimism.'

The land of opportunity, you see.

Bert Pelf 'worked and saved', he 'worked six days a week and every night in the week,' he told a politician not long after the Ferons descended on the dump he owned in Kent Street. 'I put back into the business everything I made except bare living expenses. My wife for years kept the house going on five pound a week, providing out of it all our clothing, making all the clothes for the youngsters herself. I took on men. I went into wholesale and by this time had secured the confidence of my bankers. We built a domestic appliances and engineering factory near Timaru. Within five years we opened up new factories in Dunedin, Christchurch, Invercargill and Wellington. We bought into agricultural machinery, and reduced the price of harvesters. We opened electrical engineering works in Auckland. We have today the longest assembly line for the manufacture of washing machines anywhere in the world outside America . . .'

The Minister of Finance was a Labour politician. Labour had just thrown out what the Ferons called 'them Tories' and had promised to make the country 'a better place for the working class'.

The fact that the Labour government helped make families like the Pelfs get rich by giving them contracts to build and supply state houses, public works, and other government enterprises is something that almost everybody knows about. But who's ever noticed that at the same time as Labour and the Pelfs were holding hands and walking towards a brave new future, the Ferons were doing their bit for the partnership by paying fifteen shillings a week for four rooms and an outside toilet in Kent Street, Addington?

Fag

When we were kids Ginnie and I invested our lives with a sort of dark, eternal significance. We weren't just two little girls with no father and a mother strapped for cash, we were The Poor Girls. We didn't look at the square miles of rusty iron, cracked linoleum, peeling wallpaper surrounding us and say, This is representative housing for families of the unskilled working class. Instead we thought, This is Our Place of Suffering.

Ginnie

Mum was a mixed up person. The main feeling me and Fag remember from when we was little is the feeling that nobody loved us. It was sort of as though we was there in the house with Mum by accident. I can't remember her ever putting her arms round us, giving us a kiss or telling us she loved us. I can't even remember being touched by her, except to be pinched or hit or clipped round the ear. So we was starved of love, and if anybody ever spoke kindly to me, which they hardly ever did anyway, my eyes would fill up with tears. Which I used to hate myself for.

We seemed to spend all our life watching Mum, trying to work out what sort of mood she was in, keeping clear of her when she was fierce, and sort of hanging round her when she wasn't so fierce, trying to get her to notice us and say or do something kind.

Sometimes she did unbend a bit and talk about her feelings, not to us, but to the bigger girls.

'Your grandfather died of la grippe,' she told Ruby one Saturday afternoon when her and Ruby and Sadie had sat themselves down with a cup of tea.

Me and Fag, sitting under the table, opened our eyes wide and wondered what 'la grippe' might be.

'It was because of his work,' Mum went on. 'He worked for one of the big papers. He was a compositor, not just a labourer like the Feron men. But he got screwed down tight all the same, they made sure they got their blood money from him. It doesn't matter whether you've got a skill or you haven't, they'll always screw their blood money out of you.'

Ruby had something to say about that, mainly cause she was going out with a skilled joker and her and him was setting their sights on a bungalow.

'No,' Mum said. 'They'll always screw you down. When my old man pegged out he was only forty and his face looked like a jam tin a tram had run over. Then my Mum had to take in washing. She'd walk across town to the big houses in Fendalton, us kids hanging round her skirt, then she'd have to walk back over the railway yards to Sydenham and wash it. And what did she get for it? A couple of shillings a day. So she starved herself to feed us kids. One morning she was out in the yard scrubbing a load of washing when she went black in the face, fell into a tub and never got up again. She was forty-two years old, Ruby, and the morning she died she didn't have sixpence to jingle on a tombstone.'

Ruby didn't want to hear this sort of thing, so she started talking about something else. But me and Fag had taken it all in. Later that day we acted it out in the back yard. We got the washing tubs and dragged them out and pretended to wash some old rags in them.

Fag made choking noises and clutched at her throat.

'Ooh,' I said to her. 'You've gone all black in the face Mum.'

And Fag, choking and gasping, toppled over into the tub.

'Oh help,' I said. 'We haven't even got sixpence to jingle on a tombstone.'

Another day when Mum was in a good mood me and Fag was helping the big girls do the washing in the wash house out the back. Sadie was holding the poss stick, poking it up and down to stir the clothes in the copper, and Mum came out to inspect.

'Poss those clothes, Millie,' she said. 'Poss them good and proper.'

Sadie looked just sort of stupid, but of course Fag piped up.

'Sadie isn't Millie. Why did you call her Millie?'

So Mum told us a little story.

'When me and my sisters was small we used to help our Mum do the washing she took in,' she said, not looking any of us in the eye, but sort of enjoying herself. 'Your aunty Millie used to

30

do the possing. And our Mum would come out and check up on us, and she'd say, "Poss those clothes, Millie. Poss them good and proper".'

Then Mum went back inside.

Me and Fag sort of gaped at one another. Mum had told us a story!

Another day, a month or two later, when her and the old man had been out on the town and everything was sweet in the house, Mum said something about her courting days.

'I used to work in a factory in Woolston,' she said. 'It was a sewing factory and I was on a machine. I worked upstairs with your aunty Millie and your aunty Aggie. Your old man was a young joker then, he drove a big pantechnicon wagon, six horses in the traces and him up there on the box. He'd drive his team down Ferry Road on the way to the wharves at Lyttelton and as he got near our factory he'd whistle in a special way he had, and the girls who sat by the windows would call out, "Your feller, Maggie", and I'd run across and lean out and wave.'

'Christ,' said Sadie. 'Makes me sick hearing about the old bugger.'

And Mum looked fierce, then bit our heads off for something.

'You kids git!' she said. 'What jer think this is, a mick confessional?'

Ginnie

Mum was a little person, and as me and Fag grew older she seemed to shrink more and more into the ground. She was skinny, with a little round face and two little sharp blue eyes. Her hair was a sort of mousy brown, twisted into a tight little bun with brown shellac combs stabbed into it.

She stood on one leg a lot. It was because one of her legs was ulcerated bad, and she had bad varicose veins too, and when she was feeling tired or a hot norwester was blowing the bad leg would play up. So she'd stand at the kitchen sink, balancing on one leg, murdering potatoes and carrots. Then change legs after a while, like a stork.

'Standing at the kitchen sink on one leg,' Eddie used to say if somebody was in a bad mood.

She spent a lot of time sitting too, Mum, sitting and doing nothing in what we called the yellow chair. It was just a wooden chair, painted yellow, and it had wooden arms and a cloth cushion, and when all the newspapers had been read they was shoved under the cushion. It was always at the bottom of the kitchen table, the yellow chair, and if Mum was sitting in it she'd lean an elbow on the table and hook her thumb under her chin.

'Wait till you get to school my fine lady,' she'd say to me or Fag or somebody else. 'Then we'll see the fur fly.'

Or else she'd just stare, looking into space with her lips closed tight.

When a norwester was blowing Mum would sit there for hours. She'd put her legs up on a form and she'd wrap a bandage round her head, just a wet rag she'd tie round her forehead, and another rag she'd tie round her bad leg.

And she'd sit there, moaning.

'Bloody norwester,' she'd say. 'Bloody headache. Bloody sore leg.'

'Better watch out youse kids,' Eddie would say to us if we was out in the yard and Mum had taken to the yellow chair. 'Mum's got her putties on.'

Eddie called the rags she put on her leg putties, cause they looked like those putties the toffs wore at the polo grounds in Hagley Park.

And if Fag was feeling cheeky she'd go inside and have a look at Mum, all bandaged up and grim on the yellow chair.

'How are your putties Mum?' Fag would say.

I'd sort of titter nervously.

Once or twice Mum laughed, but most days she'd wind up the gramophone and start the usual record.

'There'll come a day when you might have a leg like this,' she'd say. 'And *I* won't be here to say I told you so.'

And on and on.

But she didn't just whinge, she could be really hard on us kids. She didn't actually bash us, she'd cuff us over the head and hit

32

out at us round the legs with a strap and that, but she was never very good at it, it was mostly when she'd reached the end of her tether and, you know, just sort of flailed out at whoever happened to be nearest. So we wasn't scared of her bashing us. It was her tongue that put the wind up us.

Like, I had big hands and feet, like all the Ferons, and of course when we was out in the yard playing they'd get dirty. Then I'd go into the kitchen, which was Mum's lair, and Mum would pounce on me.

'Bloody pig's trotters,' she'd say, knocking my hands off the bench. 'Git those bloody dukes out of the way.'

And I'd put them behind my back and feel as though they was monstrous.

Freckles too. I had a lot of freckles, all of us did, and Mum used to go on and on about them, saying we looked like a pack of Catholic dogs.

'Look at your face,' she'd say. 'Look at those bloody carpets on your face.'

So I ended up thinking I had big horrible hands and a big horrible face.

Me and Fag and the other girls used to try really hard to do things for Mum, partly cause we was frightened of her and partly just cause we wanted to try and make her feel good, cause she always seemed to be feeling so bad, and we sort of thought that if we could do things for her she might smile or say something nice. So of a Sunday morning we used to get up early, just us girls, and take her a cup of tea in bed. And sometimes, when me and Fag and Hock and Peggy had managed to scrape a few pennies together, we'd buy her a little treat. Like, once we secretly bought a cake of honeycomb chocolate and gave it to her. Or we'd pick flowers from gardens along the street and give them to Mum. But it was no good. Mum would just go all sort of stiff and not look any of us in the face.

'What do youse want?' she'd say. 'What are youse crawling round me for?'

So we never seemed to get anywhere.

No matter what we did, we was classed as second rate to what

33

the boys was. It wasn't that Mum liked the boys any more than us, it was just taken for granted the boys should have it easy and us girls should be skivvies. They always got more food than us, the boys, and they got little extras too. Like, every fortnight Mum would buy four mutton chops to give the twelve or thirteen of us for tea. She'd cook them and cut them up and give us each a piece. But we all loved the centre bone in the chop, we liked to dig out the marrow and eat it, and somehow the boys always got it and if me and Fag made a fuss Mum would smack us on the hand with a spoon.

'Stop your whingeing. Wait your turn.'

But it never was our turn, we only ever got a taste of marrow if Eddie felt sorry for us and gave us some off his plate.

Mum would give him a black look.

'Yer brain's going soft like yer old man's,' she'd say. 'You'll spoil them cheeky little tarts.'

The boys always had the best place by the fire too. And there was only ever one fire. Coal cost money of course, and like Mum said, 'Money doesn't grow on trees and there aren't any trees in our yard anyway.' So there was always just the one fire burning, and half the time there wasn't coal in the grate. Mum burned bits of wood and vegetable scraps to sort of eke out the coal. We'd all be sitting huddled over the fire, everybody jostling for a place, and just as a yellow flame started flickering in the grate Mum would come in with a bowl of potato peelings, toss them on, and then sszzz . . . Nothing left in the grate but clouds of white smoke, and potato peelings curling up at the edges, and sszzz . . .

But we fought even to sit in front of that. The boys always won, so it was the back row for us. And if by some miracle there was empty places in front of the fire and some of us girls sat down to enjoy the cheerful hissing of the potato peelings, the boys would soon come clumping in and take over.

'Out of the way youse tarts,' they'd say. 'Shift yer bum or we'll belt ya.'

The boys were allowed to belt us whenever they liked, and Mum would just stand by. She wouldn't say anything unless she was in a paddy, and then she'd say, 'Give them tarts the hiding

34

they bloody deserve.'

The worst one was Jock. Me and Fag hated Jock, really hated
him. He was built like the side of a barn and he had black hair,
so everybody called him 'Black Jock'. And he belted us all the
time. At night time if us girls started playing up and talking and
giggling together in bed and that, he'd call out down the passage.

'Cut it out youse tarts.'

And if we kept giggling he'd call out again.

'Right!' he'd say in his big bull voice. 'I'm coming to give youse
tarts a hiding.' He'd come barging down the passage, bust into
our room, pull up our nightgowns, put us over the bed and whack
us. Not just a bit of a whack, but the real thing. So we'd end up
with stinging bums and eyes full of tears, and all howling with
rage.

'You black pig,' Fag would say. 'You don't own us! You can't
hit us!'

But he did.

To make things worse, we had to fetch and carry and clean
for the boys. The worst job, which we all hated, was emptying
the slops can.

During the night Mum would put an old corrugated iron bucket
in the front passage, and when the boys woke up in the night
they'd pee into the bucket instead of walking outside to the dunny.
By morning it would be brimming full, and the first job of the
day for the girls was to hump it down the passage and empty it
out the back. Mum had been using it for years and it was all sort
of corroded round the sides. I suppose it must of been the acid
in the pee. Us girls had to get a scrubbing brush and scrub it round
and then pour a bit of disinfectant into it and leave it outside till
night.

As we was scrubbing, Mum would come to inspect.

'Call that clean,' she'd say. 'You've left it half claggered up.
Clean it out properly.'

Then the other jobs would follow. Making breakfast for the
boys, washing the dishes, making the beds. The boys didn't make
their own beds, we had to do it for them.

'The men haven't got time for that,' was what Mum said if we grizzled. 'The men have to save their strength for work.'

So we cleaned their shoes and washed their clothes and cut their lunches and all the rest of it. And of a Sunday, after they'd spent the day galumphing round a league pitch or roaring round cinder tracks on their motorbikes, we had to get their muddy boots and scrape them clean with sticks, and put mutton fat on them, and spit and polish them till they all stood shining in a row on the back porch.

For me and Fag the biggest curse of all was getting the coal once a week from the State Coal yard. It was our particular job, getting the coal. We had a cart, and we had to pull it down to the State Coal and fill it up with as much as we could take, for a shilling.

Mum always sent us off with the strictest orders.

'I want it full,' she'd say.

She'd give us the shilling for the coal, then eightpence to stop at the dairy and buy a pie each for Eddie and Jock, cause they was on the night shift at the engineering works. And, well coal day was our nightmare. As the week wore on and coal day got closer me and Fag would work ourselves up into a state and we'd be absolutely terrified by the time we set off down the street, holding the cart handle between us while the cast iron wheels squeaked behind. The problem was that next door to the State Coal there was this row of little brick cottages, and in one of them was a family of Maori kids, who whenever me and Fag went past would come screaming out and attack us. We was so scared when we got near their place we'd lift the cart up and try to sneak past, carrying it so they wouldn't hear the wheels. But then we'd catch sight of their black hair sprouting over the top of the rusty iron fence.

'Ai! Ai!' they'd yell.

And they'd rush down on us, running right up to us with clenched fists and just hitting us, smack on the face. Or sometimes they'd pick up bits of coal and pelt us. We was terrified. One day we even told them that if they stopped hitting us we'd give them the eightpence for the pies, which shows how scared we was, cause it would of meant a hiding from Mum if we came home without the pies.

'Keep your Pakeha money,' one of them said. 'We'll just bash you up.'

And they did.

Other times they wouldn't attack us on the way to the yard, but then they'd charge down on us when we went past with the cart full. Me and Fag would hold tight to the cart handle and try to run for grim death. Sometimes they gave up and let us go, but as we ran a lot of the coal would spill out, so when we got home Mum would look at it and sniff.

'Go back and fill it properly,' she'd say. 'You've lost too much coal on the way.'

So then it was the awful job of squeaking all the way back to the yard and getting bashed up all over again.

Mind you, though Mum was hard on me I had it easy compared to Fag. Fag to Mum was like a red rag to a bull. Fag was always 'the cuckoo in the nest', according to Mum, she was 'the foundling'. Mum really made it sound as though Fag wasn't one of us. She'd say she was going to have Fag put into Nazareth House, which was a great big orphanage in Sydenham. It was built of brick with a big high tower and inside it there was all these nuns like magpies, and me and Fag was always terrified they'd swoop down on us and throw us onto the quicklime pit.

'There's a cellar under Nazareth House,' Mum had told us, 'and it's filled with quicklime, and when the orphans play up the nuns throw them onto the quicklime and it eats into their arms and legs and faces.'

Then as we got a bit older Fag started reading books about religion and that, and one day when Mum threatened her with the quicklime pit Fag answered back.

'That's just made up,' she said. 'The nuns are just ordinary people and all they do is nag the orphans and hit them and say horrible things to them, just like ordinary mothers.'

So the shit hit the fan.

'Let me tell you, madam,' Mum said, 'what happens to nasty deep cats like you, let me tell you.' Etcetera, etcetera, etcetera.

But Fag kept reading books, and that made Mum angrier than ever. Mum hated books.

'Think yer going to git something from books do you?' she'd say. 'Think books are going to make yer something better than the useless idle nasty insolent little slut you are. Think yer going to git somewhere.'

Fag would go and hide herself some place. She'd open her book again and start dreaming. Then Mum would find her.

'Yer just a lazy bloody bitch,' Mum would say. 'Yer think yer a flowerpot cause you've got a hole in yer bum. Yer think yer going to be better than us, but let me tell you my fine lady if yer brains was barbed wire you couldn't fence a bloody dunny.'

And on and on she'd go, ranting and raving. And I could see Fag curling up inside, you know, just curling up inside and her face going pale and still.

Fag

All Mum knew about was 'us' and 'them'. And when Labour came to power in 1935 it wasn't very clear that they were going to do anything to change the status quo.

'Politics, huh,' was Mum's usual comment. 'You haven't got time for politics when yer poor.'

Not that she was going to turn government handouts down, if Labour offered any to her. If Labour was going to build state houses, she'd do her damnedest to get a state house. If Labour was going to hand out health benefits and pensions and family benefits, she was going to be there in the queue. And we knew that if anybody came to the door canvassing for political parties Mum would stand on the step, barring the way with thin folded arms.

'This is a Labour house,' she'd say. 'So you can just git back on yer bike.'

We always thought of ourselves as Labour. We went to the Labour fairs in Linwood Park, we cheered when we saw red banners on election day, and we went to Labour rallies in Sydenham Park. I can remember those rallies mainly as orchestrations of light and sound, slow, powerful waves of light and sound. It would be evening, after the factories and pubs had closed, and there would be that little gothic fountain in Sydenham Park 'erected in honour' of somebody or other who had money, and there would be electric floodlights rigged up on tall steel masts. And on the band rotunda in the middle, fenced in by the high spiked iron railings, would be the Labour politicians, sort of glowing in the footlights, surrounded by a huge dark crowd of working people. And 'our Mabel' would be there too, Mabel Howard. She was the darling of South Christchurch, and she'd be standing up booming out promises.

'New Zealand under Labour will lead the world in social reform.'

That sort of thing.

'I hope all of you will remember in the future, when you all find yourselves living a good life that's only a dream for you now, that it was Labour that did it.'

And so on and so forth.

Mum would applaud a bit, she'd slap the palms of her hands against one another a few times in a grudging sort of way, while Eddie would whistle and cheer.

'Good on yer Mabel.'

But we weren't convinced. Mabel was all right, but she was a politician like the rest of them and most of the politicians in the Labour party had a bit of money and were churchgoers. So we didn't think Labour was going to do much for us. We knew they weren't going to pull the Fendalton people off their high horses. We knew Labour politicians wanted cushy jobs and high salaries and knighthoods and that.

'And while they're getting them,' Mum said, 'we have to keep battling. Bloody government's always against working people, doesn't matter whether it's Labour or Tory. Just watch them sell us down the river when the banks decide to give them loans with strings attached, or when the generals want us to fight another war for them.'

So we didn't expect much from the Labour government, and of course our expectations were richly fulfilled.

Ginnie

After the old man cleared out Mum hardly ever had any contact
with men her own age. There was the dunny man, of course, who
came round once a week to empty the dunny tin, but I don't suppose Mum ever said much to him. The postie biked past twice
a day, but he didn't stop at our gate much cause Mum hardly
ever got letters. The milko would rattle past with his cart of a
morning, but he didn't stop at our gate either, cause we was getting milk through the Charitable Aid Board. Then there was the
rabbit-o, who sometimes talked Mum into buying a couple of his
little skinned carcasses. And there was the German knife grinder,
and the Chinese rag man, and there was some bottle collectors
that came round too, they was called the 'saucy niggers'. I think
they was Indians.

'Here come those saucy nigs,' Mum would say. 'Well it's no
use them stopping outside my door as if I'd have anything to
spare.'

But sometimes we did have a few old medicine bottles or that,
and Mum would take them out to the gate.

'Them saucy nigs would rob you blind,' she'd say after coming
back inside and putting a few bits of copper on the bench.

But she didn't seem very aggressive about it, I think she quite
liked it when she had a few bottles in the house and could go to
the gate and sell them.

And apart from the saucy nigs and the rabbit-o and the postie,
about the only other man in Mum's life was her brother Jim. Uncle
Jim Hay, we called him, so we could tell him from our other uncle
Jim. He was very tall, uncle Jim Hay, and had black hair – quite
a nice-looking joker he was. When he died the undertaker said
his coffin was the longest he'd ever made. But uncle Jim always
used to make us feel sad, not cause of anything he said, but cause
we all knew he'd had an unhappy life. He'd been sent away to
the war, what they called the 'Great War' in those days, and of
course the officers and that had made his life a misery. They'd
made him shoot at people on the other side and that, and then
he'd been shot himself, and gassed, and hurt bad, and when he
got back he found it hard to get a job cause of his wounds. So

that was sad, the war was a sort of nightmare he never seemed to forget. When he dropped in for a cup of tea even Mum would sort of soften a bit. He'd ramble on from one subject to another and get lost, and in fact he was real boring, he could talk a glass eye to sleep, just talking and talking and talking.

Not that we ever got much of a chance to listen to him.

'Say gidday to yer uncle Jim,' Mum would say to us.

'Gidday uncle Jim.'

'Now,' Mum would say. 'Clear out.'

So we'd clear out.

But even though Mum would sit and listen to uncle Jim Hay while he maundered on, he wasn't a very important person in her life. She never talked to him about herself, what she was doing and how she was feeling and that. She'd just let him go on and on and she'd pour out cups of tea for him and that was that. Her real friends was her sisters, aunty Millie and aunty Aggie. And of course Mrs Palto.

Me and Fag didn't like Mrs Palto much. She was a big bosomy person and I don't think she liked kids much. She always seemed very condescending, talking down to us and making us feel uncomfortable and that. Mum was sarcastic about her too, behind her back of course.

'Here comes my bust,' Mum would say. 'My bum to follow.'

Mind you, Mum would bite the head off anybody as soon as they was out the door and halfway down the path to the front gate, and I think she really got on pretty good with Mrs Palto. She knew Mrs Palto would always be there when things went bad with us.

Aunty Millie was a lovely person. She always seemed sort of warm and cuddly, though she never did actually cuddle us, except sometimes she'd give us a sort of pat, which made us think she really would of liked to cuddle or kiss us. And she was lucky, aunty Millie, cause she had a very steady husband, uncle Jim Smithers. He got a good wage and there was always money for food and clothes and that, so we always thought they was rich. Uncle Jim Smithers seemed really important, a real toff.

'He's a very educated man,' Fag decided. 'Aunty Millie told me

41

his father was the headmaster of East Sydenham school. And when uncle Jim Smithers was a boy he went to Christs College.'

Uncle Jim told us all about it one day.

'I had it in mind,' he said, 'to take up the profession of dentistry. But the examiners erred unaccountably in their calculations and failed to award me the requisite mark. I determined not to stoop to the indignity of requesting a recount and consequently looked for a career elsewhere.'

So he went into the railways, which of course was a good lurk if you could get it. Railway workers was like city council workers, they hardly ever got the sack and the pay was good. And he went right to the top too, uncle Jim Smithers. By the time me and Fag appeared on the scene he was in charge of a signal box in Addington. We'd see him when we walked across the railway yards, he'd be high up in his box, with all the levers shining in front of him, and we thought he was something really special.

They had a car too, uncle Jim Smithers and aunty Millie, a little grey Prefect.

Sometimes he'd take some of us for a drive.

'Perhaps one or two of your infants might like a spin down to the beach, Margaret?' he'd say to Mum.

And of course Mum would always say yes, cause she was always glad of an excuse to get some of us out from under her feet. So we'd motor down to New Brighton and get out near the pier. Uncle Jim Smithers would roll up his cuffs to paddle in the waves, and he'd collect sea water to take home and wash in. He'd make us take some home for Mum too, to bathe her bad leg in.

'Most salubrious,' he'd say. 'Has many healing properties, has salt water.'

'Oh,' we'd say. 'Yeah.'

But we hated him really. Mum was sort of scared of him, cause of all the big words he used. She was scared he was making fun of her, and she thought he was a cut above her. And he thought he was too. He was a very arrogant, bullying man. He had all sorts of ideas about what women should do and what women shouldn't do, and aunty Millie had to sit and take it. One day we was visiting at their place and uncle Jim Smithers was laying down the law about something as usual, sitting in his fireside chair, when Peter, one of their grown up boys, came into the room.

'Gidday everyone,' he said. 'Good flick on at the Metro next week Mum. What shift will Dad be on?'

Aunty Millie looked a bit worried.

'The night shift,' she said.

'Put on your glad rags next Monday night then,' Pete said. 'You can come out to the flicks with me.'

Uncle Jim Smithers sort of puffed out his chest. He was wearing braces that aunty Millie had embroidered all pretty colours, red and yellow and green.

'Indeed she can not,' he said. 'I'm not having my wife running round the town like a flapper.'

And that was that. Aunty Millie went red in the face, but she didn't say anything and Pete just looked sort of sheepish and cleared out again.

Our other aunty, aunty Aggie, wouldn't of stood for that. She was a real battler, aunty Aggie, she wasn't all warm and cuddly like aunty Millie and she wasn't a fierce little stick like Mum, she was sort of gaunt and wild looking. A tall person, she was, with very pale skin. Her husband drank and used to bash her up, and then he cleared out on her, so she had to go out working as a char to try to get some money. She was always sick too.

'District nurse was in this morning,' we heard her say to Mum one day. 'Says I've got malnutrition.'

Mum tried to look wise, but I don't think she knew what malnutrition meant, though Fag did, she'd read about it in a book and told me about it later.

'Said I've got to eat more,' aunty Aggie said. 'I told her I'd be happy to eat more but the legs of the furniture aren't too tasty if you haven't got a bottle of sauce to help them go down.'

She had a sort of gaiety about her, aunty Aggie, even when she looked like death warmed up, she liked to have a good time. Early of a morning while it was still dark and her kids was asleep she'd be in Sydenham charring, scrubbing and sweeping and dusting in dingy offices, but then of a Saturday night she'd put

lipstick on her mouth and stick a flower in her hair and bike off
to town and dance.

Mum sneered at that, of course.

'That Aggie's a flighty piece,' she'd say to Mrs Palto or aunty
Millie. 'Rather be widdy giddying about the town than doing her
housework.'

Aunty Aggie didn't care.

'Nothing keeps better than housework,' she'd say.

'Tt,' Mum would say.

'Hard workers die young,' aunty Aggie would say.

She seemed to know what she wanted, aunty Aggie, and she
tried to go out and get it. And she was always very kind to us
kids too. Her and her kids lived in this old house in Linwood,
and Mum would walk us all over there to visit, and aunty Aggie
would be all friendly and cheerful and would make sure she said
gidday to each one of us.

Mum didn't like it.

'Git outside youse kids,' she'd say.

But aunty Aggie didn't seem to care if we tore her house to
pieces. She seemed to overlook a lot of the wrong things that kids
would do, at least things Mum said was wrong. She'd overlook
a bit of whooping and yelling and rowdiness and that, she'd be
smiling and talking away while Mum would be sitting there giving
us . . . looks to *kill*.

But at aunty Aggie's we felt strong enough to defy Mum, we
knew Aggie would be on our side.

The big thing for Mum and aunty Millie and aunty Aggie, the
highlight of their week, was when they got together of a Thursday
night to have what they called 'our powwow'. They took it in
turns to have it at their place, and they brewed up a big pot of
tea, and baked up scones and cakes and pikelets and that, and
it was their one day of the week when they did nothing but just
sat and talked. Mind you, when it was Mum's turn to have the
tea at our place she always made a big to-do about it. She was
always competing with aunty Millie. Not that aunty Millie knew,
but Mum would try to outdo aunty Millie with what she put on
her table. So when the Thursday came round there would be this

big spread for the aunties, but it was absolute murder for us getting it to that stage. It would be days of Mum banging the oven door open and shut and scurrying round the kitchen.

'Don't touch that,' she'd snap at us. 'That's for your aunty Millie and aunty Aggie.'

Mum had this rule that only the aunts could eat during the teas, she hated the idea that aunty Millie would see us gobbling up cakes and think we needed a free feed.

'Don't you dare ask for a cake,' Mum would hiss at us as we walked past the factories and railway yards on our way to aunty Millie's. 'If I catch you so much as hinting that you'd like something . . .'

She left the rest to our imagination, which of course didn't need much help to work out what might happen to us.

Then all through the tea aunty Millie would be peeping at us, cause she knew about Mum telling us we wasn't to eat anything. And me and Fag would be squeezed together on a chair, sitting there hour after hour, hoping that aunty Millie or aunty Aggie would say something to us. And in the end they always did, and Mum would scowl, and me and Fag would leap across to the table and pick up a cream puff or a lamington and then for two minutes . . . bliss.

Then it was a matter of sitting and waiting while Mum and aunty Millie and aunty Aggie talked on and on and on, often till midnight or even later. Me and Fag would drop off to sleep, leaning against the back of our chair.

Suddenly a couple of thin hands would be gripping our shoulders and shaking us. We'd wake up to see Mum's little face peering down.

'Time to git moving,' she'd say. 'Fine life for some.'

And me and Fag and Mum would shuffle our way back past the factories and railway yards and the rows and rows of dark little wood and iron houses, down the narrow streets through the night.

3

Dolly tints

Fag

Mind you, even though we knew we were rough and poor, we weren't above looking down our noses a bit at some of our neighbours. Most of them Mum disliked on grounds of personality.

'That bitch,' she'd mutter, sitting on the yellow chair with her chin in the crook of her hand. 'Talks so bloody much she gives me corns on the ear.'

Or else somebody would be stupid.

'Arr,' Mum would say, 'you could ride to Brighton and back on her brain and it wouldn't be sharp enough to cut yer bum.'

Or a neighbour would be indecisive.

'Can't get her to say yea or nay,' Mum said. 'She's neither yer arse nor yer elbow.'

Then apart from the personality defects which strangely enough almost everybody seemed to be afflicted with, our neighbours had an unfortunate tendency to be Catholic, Irish, dirty, uppity, sottish, and all the rest of it. So in Braddon Street it didn't take Mum long to discover that the Flannery family across the road from us were, as their name from the start seemed unhappily to imply, Irish Catholics from the West Coast.

'Them Catholic dogs,' Mum would say. 'They're a different breed from us. Youse kids keep away from them Irish dogs.'

It wasn't that she cared about their religion, and it wasn't that she had any theory of racial superiority to explain why they were 'a different breed', it was just that Mum knew Irish Catholics were dogs, because she'd heard her own mother say the same thing.

Not that Mum was particularly fond of the word 'because'.

Things were more straightforward than that. It was just: 'They're Irish, they're no good. They're Catholic, they're no good.'

And that was it.

And if the sight of a cobweb caught Mum's eyes as she shot quick glances of inspection into the windows of neighbouring houses she'd toss her head.

'Hmph,' she'd say. 'Irish curtains in her window.'

'We might be poor,' she'd add, 'but at least we're clean.'

Not that we *were* all that clean; it was just that Mum put a lot of energy into a lot of violent scrubbings, scrapings, sandings, and delousings to satisfy her understanding of what cleanliness was. Like, she had an absolute fetish about 'a good line of washing'.

Washing clothes was part of the heavy industry of housekeeping for working class women, of course, but Mum made sure that for every drop of soapy water boiled up in our copper there was an angry or frustrated teardrop boiled up in it too. And it never seemed to end, washing clothes. There was the scavenging of sticks to get the copper alight, the lighting and blowing, the boiling and possing, the wringing and mangling, and then of course the pegging and pegging and pegging. Washday every day of the week, every week of the year except New Year's Day.

'Never wash of a New Year's Day,' Mum instructed us. 'If you wash of a New Year's Day you wash your troubles in for another year.'

On the other days of the year, once us girls had pegged and pegged our way down to the bottom of the basket and lifted the wooden props and got the washing up into the air, Mum as likely as not would come worrying her way out of the kitchen and tell us we'd done it all wrong.

'Tt,' she'd say. 'Washing all over the place like a fowl yard after the cat got in.'

And going across to the props and bringing the lines down again, muttering to herself as she did it, she'd unpeg and unpeg, then peg things back on again the way they were supposed to be pegged. Shirts, for example, weren't to be hung up by the shoulders, they had to go up by the tail.

'Now,' Mum would say at the end of it all, 'that's what I call *a good line of washing.*'

Spring cleaning was another way of showing we were 'poor but clean'. Every year as winter wore on us girls would start to feel a sort of anxious knot growing in our stomachs, and when the first blossoms came out on the trees in Addington cemetery we'd hope that some late frost might come along and wither them in their tracks. But no. Spring always came, and with it came the relentless fate of girls, spring cleaning.

First we had to wash all the blankets in the house. We had to get them into the tub, heat up the copper, then knead them, as she used to say, knead them with our hands.

'Never rub blankets,' the order was. 'Rubbing blankets will make them hard.'

Then, after we'd kneaded the blankets in the hot soapy water we had to bail the copper out and set some fresh water to boil, because:

'Never rinse blankets in cold water, youse girls, if you rinse blankets in cold water they'll *thicken up on the line.*'

Then the blankets had to be wrung. Mum would take hold of one end and one of us girls would take the other, and we had to twist them round and round, wringing out the water. Finally the blankets, still heavy and wet and dragging on the ground, had to be heaved over the line, three or four girls struggling with each of them, before at last the props could hoist them out of consciousness for a few hours.

Not that spring cleaning ended there.

The main idea behind the whole operation for Mum was to completely empty every room, completely turn upside down, inside out every room, purify everything as viciously as possible, then put everything back to where it had been at the beginning.

The curtains, for example, all had to come down.

They were lace curtains, that was all we could afford, 'machine lace' Mum called it, made in factories and sold to working class women who wanted something more than 'Irish curtains' in their windows. And every spring, down they came to be washed and 'dolly tinted'. 'Dolly tints' were another part of the repertoire of

48

cleanliness. They were a type of powdered dye made in factories and sold in little orange bags. Into our wash tubs every spring the dolly tint powder would be sifted, and into our wash tubs the 'machine lace' curtains would be stirred. The curtains would emerge a yellowy sort of orange, ready to hang in our windows for another year, a jaundiced banner of good household management.

And so on and so on.

So as a result of being 'clean', and not being Irish, and as a result of our other virtues and blessings, we were able to set ourselves apart from most of our neighbours, Mum keeping us warm in a few tatty little scraps of self importance.

It was also important that though we lived in rented houses in cheap streets, we always managed to keep just a fraction above the very cheapest.

Simeon Street, where Ginnie and I made our debut, was quite well-to-do for a working class district. Almost every second house was owned by the people living in it, and some of our neighbours belonged to the class of 'them' rather than 'us'. Some went to work every day in white collars, they were clerks and salesmen, they wore suits and ties, and two of them even wore bowler hats, so they were definitely toffs and Mum was very scathing.

'Dressed up to the nines like nancy boys,' she sniffed. 'Strutting off down the road with their little leather bags.'

But she was secretly a bit proud of them too, they gave Simeon Street an edge over 'some other streets I could name but won't.'

A few Simeon Street householders were even capitalists. There was a family of fruitgrowers who had an acre of land and grew apples. There were a couple of shopkeepers. And there was a retired farmer who lived in a villa where out the front was a concrete fish with its fins on a pedestal and its tail holding a silver ball in the air. Nobody else could keep up with that sort of high style, but quite a number of families had a few spare shillings, especially the self employed tradespeople and the skilled workers. There were quite a lot of people in the street like that, glaziers, fitters, turners, joiners, carpenters, bookbinders, brickmakers, electricians, and they all seemed to be tied up with trade unions, the Labour party, the Methodist and Presbyterian and Baptist churches. In their front rooms they had antimacassars, in their kitchens they had wireless sets, and out the back they sometimes had a little car.

Even we weren't at the bottom of the heap, we belonged to a group of families in Simeon Street where the 'heads of the household', which was what people said in those days, were unskilled workers. They were motor drivers, warehousemen, storemen, railway workers, gas company workers, and some like our old man who just described themselves as labourers. They didn't earn big wages, but at least they had wages to worry about. Below them, at the bottom of the heap, were families where there were no wages because the men were unemployed or there was no working man at all. Families where the husband had walked out, families where the wife and kids scraped along as best they could on maintenance payments, taking in washing, the Charitable Aid Board, charring and the rest of it. We felt sorry for those families, but we felt a bit smug too.

'Don't know how she does it,' Mum would say with satisfaction, 'living off the smell of an oily rag like she does. Don't know how she gets herself past Monday.'

Which was tempting the gods if anything was.

When we shifted to Braddon Street it was a definite step down the ladder. There weren't many houses in South Christchurch cheaper than the little wooden boxes in Braddon Street, and of a morning when the 'heads' of the Braddon Street households set out for work, only two wore white collars, only a few were heading for desks where they pushed pens, or workshops where they had skilled jobs. Most were just ordinary workers, labourers, storemen, railway workers, asphalters. And the usual haggard little group of families where the head of the household was just plain 'Mrs'.

So in Braddon Street we were getting near rock bottom. And not only was the whole street poor, we were starting to lose our breadwinner too.

'I hope I never see the bugger again,' Mum said the last two or three times he cleared out.

50

But the loss of the wage came hard and by the time we shifted from Braddon Street to Kent Street, Mum had definitely slipped into the rank of deserted women. This was awkward. Mum had to shift her ideas about who was 'them' and who was 'us'. Instead of being able to look down with some faint pleasurable pity on the 'deserteds' below her, she now saw herself looking up, and fiercely resentful, at women who'd managed to keep the man and the wage more or less inside the house.

Fag

By this time Ginnie and I were 'old enough to know it's not all beer and skittles', which was something Mum said to us when we kept coming to her saying, 'Mu-um, we're hungry.'

This was when Sadie started turning against Mum.

'Old vinegar tits takes all me bloody wage,' Sadie said. 'And all she bloody gives me back is boiled bloody cauliflower.'

Now that the old man had gone and 'vinegar tits' was left unchallenged over the kitchen sink, Sadie's feelings began to alter. Since the old man wasn't around any more for Sadie to hate in person, and since Mum was still very much around, nagging, carping, bitching, pinching, Sadie started to think of the invisible old man as not totally disgusting, not absolutely a boozing old goat, perhaps even sort of shadily attractive.

'He wasn't such a bad bugger,' Sadie would say, sucking on cigarettes and spitting out words. 'Least his heart was in the right place. Least he liked a bit fun. Old vinegar tits wouldn't know a good time if it was halfway up her fanny.'

Ginnie and I didn't quite like it when Sadie talked like that, though we couldn't think of anything much to say in Mum's defence.

'At least Mum stuck with us,' I said to Ginnie one day when we were looking in one another's hair for nits. 'She might be horrible, but she's trying to keep the family together.'

It was something I'd heard Mrs Palto say.

'It vill always fall to the woman,' she said, flapping the sails

51

of fat under her armpits, 'to keep the home together.'

'Yeah,' Ginnie said.

Looking as unconvinced as I felt.

'I wonder what it would of been like if Mum had cleared out and the old man had of stayed,' she said after a while.

Sadie, after another year or two, didn't seem to have any doubts at all on that score.

'Christ,' she'd say. 'I should of gone off with the old man and had myself a bit of fun.'

For the rest of her life Sadie would look back on this as 'the time we bloody lived off cauliflower, with the odd slug or two for meat'.

Things weren't quite as bad as that, though Mum was always in such a hurry that when she washed cauliflowers and cabbages she often did leave small servings of slug or spider or insect protein between the leaves and delivered it up to us along with a not much more appetising heap of pasty boiled spud and carrot. But the real problem wasn't tea, it was lunch. Of a morning, after a breakfast of water and porridge, us kids would ask what we should take for lunch, and Mum would get fierce.

'It's no use asking about lunch,' she'd say. 'I've got nothing to give youse. It won't do youse tarts any harm going without lunch for a change, you'd eat the bum out of a baby if I let youse.'

A lot of kids went to school without lunch, we weren't in an unusual situation, but that didn't make it any easier for Ginnie and I to sit through the lunch hour, our stomachs gurgling while the luckier kids chewed their way through jam or chip sandwiches.

'Do you think kids up on Cashmere go without lunches?' Ginnie asked me one day.

'Yeah,' I said. 'They get fat from eating too many lollies and cakes and that, so their doctors make them stop eating. It's called going on a diet. We're quite lucky really, we might be poor but at least we're healthy.'

But this sounded too much like one of the conventional solaces Mum handed out to us.

'Think I'd rather be rich and unhealthy,' Ginnie said after sucking a dock leaf for a while.

So we'd sit and fantasise about the gargantuan feasts of Cashmere.

'And baked Alaska for dessert,' we'd hypothesise. 'And chocolate cake with hundred and thousand icing, and cream kisses with real cream!'

There were big steel rubbish drums at the school, standing in a row outside the furnace, and the 'school rules' said that kids were to throw their food scraps into these tins after finishing their lunch. A formula for misery, of course. The temptation to us lunchless ones. Ginnie and I, sitting aghast, would see the kids from the better off families saunter up to the rubbish tins and toss in sandwiches, Anzac biscuits, scraps of peanut brownies, casually chewed remnants of apples and pears. And other kids, other lunchless kids, watching and salivating alongside, would duck in. They'd scrabble round in the drum and clamber out again, and they'd show us their pickings. Then, with a quick look to see no teacher had noticed them, they'd start chewing.

'Yum,' they'd say. 'Good tucker.'

For Ginnie and me it was the most prolonged and horrible torture. We could put up with the sight of the well off kids eating their lunches, but it was much harder to sit by and calmly watch the other kids scrabbling in the rubbish drums. Not that we disapproved of scavenging, far from it, what we felt was envy.

'If only Mum would let us do that,' we'd say. 'Some of those biscuits look really nice, just a few bites out of them, and if you grabbed them just after they got turfed in they wouldn't be all that grubby, you could wipe them clean with your pinny.'

But in the end we just kept sitting there, watching, doing nothing. We knew that if Mum heard that some of her kids had been picking food out of school rubbish tins it would make her go berserk.

How would she ever be able to say,

'We might be poor but we keep our noses clean,'

again?

The Historian

Ginnie and Fag by this time were not only 'old enough to know that it's not all beer and skittles', they were also deemed 'old enough to be some use round the house and not just a burden on it', as their mother expressed her understanding of what it meant for a female child to grow into its seventh or eighth year. That meant it was time to do more than just the usual scrubbing, cleaning, washing, and fetching cart loads of coal; it meant it was time for Ginnie and Fag to take over the job of 'getting the sugar bag from Charitable Aid'.

The North Canterbury Hospital and Charitable Aid Board was a committee of doctors, 'society ladies', Labour party worthies, and prominent city businessmen who ran the hospitals, lunatic asylums and poor relief system of Christchurch. The money to pay for the system came from a levy on property owners. The landlords and other propertied people of the city paid rates to the Charitable Aid Board and the Charitable Aid Board handed the money over to the poor – that was the theory, at least, and that was why it was called 'charity'. But of course a good deal of the money went into the pockets of the white-collar workers, tradespeople and skilled workers who administered the system or provided it with services, so the poor ended up with much less money from the Board than the Board collected from ratepayers. And of course a large part of the money handed over to the poor had been paid out by the poor in the first place.

'They talk like they're giving us a present,' Margaret Feron observed. 'But we pay for it in our rents. So as usual, we pay and the landlords make the rules.'

The rules of the North Canterbury Hospital and Charitable Aid Board were that if working class families found themselves financially embarrassed they could present themselves to the Board and ask for charitable aid. If they could prove to the Board that they were 'deserving', in other words that they were not disreputable, uppity, promiscuous and neglectful of the need to dolly tint their machine lace curtains, then the Board would give them 'chits', which they could take to the public hospital, a red brick building designed, like most of the public edifices of Christchurch, to scare the wits out of women and children of the working class. On handing over a chit at the hospital, families of the 'deserving poor' were entitled to have a sugar bag filled once a week with free groceries.

So once a week, dragging their feet and whingeing and complaining, Ginnie and Fag would set out from Kent Street.

Fag

There was one consolation in being chosen to go and get the sugar bag filled by Charitable Aid, it was an important job, so Mum would bend over backwards to rake up a few pennies for us to go on the tram. That was a bit de luxe. We enjoyed that, standing on the kerb, trying to look conspicuous, worried that two unimportant shabby little kids like us would be overlooked as the tram rattled banged clanked its way towards the stop. Breathing with relief when the driver did stop. Handing across two of the pennies. Then sauntering down the aisle.

(Travelling by tram, we do it all the time, shopping at the smart department stores, afternoon tea on bentwood chairs at big windows with little statues of naked gods beside us, looking down onto Cathedral Square . . .)

But then we'd have to get off the tram and start down Tuam Street. Factories and warehouses. Then the hospital smokestack, tall and grim, hanging out a limp desolate banner of soot. Then the hospital itself, its stern dirty walls crowding down on the pavement like an unforgiving landlord.

We'd clutch the sugar bag, we'd shuffle through Outpatients, trying hard not to be seen. But a hundred eyes would follow us.

'The deserving poor.' Us.

At the Charitable Aid counter a shiny red faced woman would yell at us, as though because we were poor we were probably partly deaf and certainly stupid.

'Where's your chit?' she'd say. 'You can't have anything without a chit.'

Ginnie and I would try to *wish* the chit onto the counter.

'Come along, come along,' the shiny red face would say. 'I haven't got all day.'

Then, after the horrible piece of paper had finally managed to get itself onto the counter, the woman would take our sugar bag.

'Bread,' she'd say, and as she said it we felt as though she was cataloguing our humiliation for the benefit of all those ears in Outpatients. 'Five loaves. Flour, two pound. Sugar, one pound. Tea . . .'

I'd try to look defiant. Ginnie would sometimes cry.

Ginnie and I also had the job of going up town to the Salvation Army soup kitchen in Armagh Street. Though Mum rubbished churches she was happy enough to take charity from them. Anybody's charity was welcome in our house, and in Mum's opinion anyway, 'them Christians steal money from us in the first place.' So she'd go along to see what she called 'some high up poohbah in the Salacious Army', and she'd persuade him to put her name on a list. There was no shortage of names on that list, of course, so our turn only came up every so often. The Salvation Army had an arrangement with city bakeries and tea shops to collect unsold bread and cakes left over at the end of the day, and they'd hand it out to 'the needy'. When it was our turn a card would arrive in the post and when Ginnie and I got home from school Mum would be waiting for us, tapping her foot impatiently.

'Hurry up,' she'd say. 'You've got to go up town. The god botherers have got some stale bread for us.'

Milk was another thing we got free. We got it through the Charitable Aid Board, at least till the Labour government started free milk in schools. The Board kept a list of families entitled to 'charity milk' and they organised things so city milk contractors would deliver it to 'the needy' free. After the milk had been delivered the milkmen could get paid for it by going along to the Board every week or so and claiming the cost. The only problem was that most milkmen felt life had burdens enough without going to the trouble of keeping separate accounts for families on charity milk and then hanging round the skirts of the Charitable Aid Board begging for payment, especially when the Board got a name for questioning the accounts and not always being up to the minute when it came to handing over the money.

So a lot of milk contractors wouldn't have anything to do with charity milk, and Mum found it hard to get anybody to supply us.

'I have found somebody who might help,' Mrs Palto reported one afternoon when she turned up for a cup of tea.

She'd got friendly with a family of milk contractors by the name of Lamb, she told Mum. They were good hearted people, she said, they'd listened to Mrs Palto tell them about us, and they'd said they could help us out.

'There is a small difficulty,' she added. 'They vill not be able to deliver to you, Margaret. They are rather a long way away, they keep their cows in Beckenham. You vill have to fetch the milk yourselves.'

'If that's the only problem,' Mum said, 'then it's plain sailing from here. Some of those useless girls of mine can go and get it.'

So every day after school Ginnie and I had to go and get the milk, carrying the empty billy through the little narrow streets of Addington, past the rows and rows of little boxy houses of Spreydon, into the bays and shingled verandahs of Beckenham and finally, near the foot of Cashmere, holding out the billy to be filled by the Lambs. Then, as sunset came on and the sky grew dark, trudging back home, the sharp metal rim of the billy banging against our bare legs, lugging the charity milk home to Kent Street.

Charitable Aid groceries, Salvation Army bread, Charitable Aid milk, these things made us realise we'd nearly hit rock bottom. But even then Mum didn't give up. She was always absolutely certain about the things she believed in; it was just a plain fact of life, for her, that us Ferons would always get less than our desserts while 'they' always made sure they got more than theirs. But now she turned her attention away from the distant toffs of Fendalton and onto the women around us who had 'kept their husbands'.

Seeing one of these women commit some vicious extravagance or other, like giving a kid sixpence for ice creams, Mum would know exactly what to say.

'All right for her,' she'd say. 'She's got a husband to foot the bills.'

Though her memories of the old man didn't grow any kinder, though there was often a sort of exultation at having let him go, her comments, what you might call her routine of social criticism, always started now with the idea that if a woman had a husband, no matter how shiftless he was, the bills would be paid.

'Look at her,' she'd say, 'with her shop-bought jam. I wonder how she'd get on with no husband to pay her way.'

But even when Mum saw herself sinking to the bottom there were still consolations. Even when down to her uppers, she always managed to make sure the uppers at least looked halfway decent. It was important to Mum that shoes and clothes looked decent. It wasn't that she cared about looking attractive or smart or anything like that, in fact she'd tear strips off any woman she saw 'tarted up like a Ballantynes dummy', it was just that Mum knew how a person should be dressed, and she made sure she fitted the prescription.

Other women gave up the ghost. Not only the older women among our neighbours, drifting round their back yards in candle-wick dressing gowns, but the girls too, you could see it happen to them. One year they'd be wearing lipstick and little hats, clicking powder compacts open. Then they'd get pregnant and go away, and then when they came back to visit their mother two or three years later, pushing a battered pram full of babies, they'd be shuffling along in dirty sandshoes and their hair would be screwed up under a hairnet. And, hanging from their mouths, a roll-your-own fag.

'Youse kids stop yer bloody yelling,' they'd scream up and down the street.

And even the screaming would seem to lack conviction, it would just be a habit, like the roll-your-own fags.

'Tt,' Mum would say flicking the dolly tinted curtains back into place. 'Dirty hussies in their grubby Jap sandshoes.'

Mum would never been seen dead in 'Jap' sandshoes, she always managed to have at least one pair of leather shoes, with proper heels and a brass buckle. And she always made sure she could spear some sort of hat onto her head. No matter how hard up we were it was almost as important to her that there be a hat in the house as that the rent money be sitting safely in its jar on the kitchen mantelpiece. A little straw hat, which she'd trim with a bit of 'machine taffeta' or a hydrangea stolen from somebody's front garden.

She'd slip on the leather shoes, and the buckle would wink at her. She'd fix the straw hat on the side of her head. And off she'd go, her little heels scuttling along the footpath, her eyes darting from window to window.

So though we were poor and got poorer, Mum still managed to feel that we were in the right and 'they' were in the wrong. They didn't deserve their money, they'd taken it from working people and we didn't owe them anything, they owed us instead. And even in our dingy little streets in Addington, even among our neighbours, working people, poor people like ourselves, there were families that didn't fit the definition of what was ordinary and human. There were the dirty families, the Catholic families, the families where there was a husband 'to foot the bills', the families where the women 'gave up the show and ended up in the gutter'. In the end, when it came down to it, 'us' against 'them' meant the Ferons against the world.

'There's nothing wrong with us,' Mum would mutter. 'We pay our bills and we keep clean and I say bugger everybody else.'

So she knew how she felt, did Mum, and for the first ten years or so of our lives, Ginnie and I knew how we felt too.

But then the series of little boxes Mum put the world into leaving only us, the Ferons, intact in a hard little cube in the middle, her system for explaining the world and making it manageable, it started to fall apart.

PART TWO

Cinderellas waiting for the ball

The Historian

The Feron view of schools was that they were prisons built by 'them' to turn working people into slaves, to tangle and trick working people with words and numbers and symbols, to let loose a noose of language and send it flying through the air to strangle you.

Kindergartens, for example.

Kindergartens, according to a pamphlet published in the 1930s by the Christchurch Kindergarten Association, had been founded by high-minded ladies intent on offering working class families a chance of getting 'advanced early childhood education' in 'light, airy buildings with pretty gardens and teachers trained in the latest methods'.

'Bunch of stuck up tarts,' Margaret Feron said, 'making themselves feel good by filling our kids with ideas.'

But the stuck up tarts were allowed to have their way because as the hard pressed mothers of Addington slogged away at their cooking, washing, scrubbing, mending, they were glad of the chance to get rid of some of their burden by sending their kids to kindergarten – even if it did mean the kids might come back home again with heads stuffed full of 'ideas'.

So Ginnie and Fag went along to kindergarten and their struggle with 'them' began.

Ginnie

Me and Fag started going to Selwyn Street kindergarten when we was four. We was really worried cause Mum had been talking about it as though it was on a par with Nazareth House, except there wasn't any nuns and they didn't lock you up and make you stay there overnight. We was worried too cause the kindergarten was about a mile from our house and we didn't know how we was going to get there. Then Eddie made us a trike. He got odd bits and pieces from the engineering works and the council dump and that, and put them all together, but unfortunately when it came to a seat he couldn't find one so he tied on a piece of sacking.

Mum didn't come with us to kindergarten, she didn't even stand and watch us go.

'All right youse kids,' she said. 'Time to git going. Make sure you don't cause trouble.'

We'd been hoping she would wave us off, we'd been whispering about it of a night. But when she just opened the kitchen door and shut it behind us we wasn't really disappointed, we hadn't really expected her to do anything different.

So off we went. We took turns pedalling while the other one stood on the back.

We knew all the streets, we'd been up and down them often enough, so we wasn't scared of getting lost. Our big worry was the dogs in the yard of a house in Burke Street. They was Scotch terriers, and we was terrified of them, they was horrible little yappy things that used to rush out at us whenever we went past. If we was with our brothers or one of our big sisters they'd give the dogs a boot, but me and Fag was terrified of having to go past them by ourselves.

Well we solved that problem by going about half a mile out of our way, sort of wending round back streets till we got past the dogs and back onto Selwyn Street.

The next problem was when we got to kindergarten, some of the better off kids started slinging off at us.

'What a latey of a trike,' one of them said. 'Hasn't even got a seat, just an old spud sack.'

Me and Fag sort of looked at each other.

'This trike's a special sort,' Fag said. 'It's um, a special racing model and there's sacking on it to protect it, cause our father thought it was going to rain heavy in the night and he put sacking over the trike to protect it.'

Fag was good at spinning a yarn. So while she cracked up our trike all the other kids started jostling round us looking at it.

'Gee,' they was saying, 'a real *racing* trike.'

The boy who'd said it was a latey, his name was Ronnie. He was a pasty little boy but his parents was well off by our standards and he was sitting on a shiny red and silver trike with a bell.

'Can I have a ride?' he said. 'I'd really like a racing model.'

'Well,' Fag said. 'I don't know. This is a really special trike, and our father said . . .'

Blah blah blah.

'As a special favour,' she said. 'And we'll keep an eye on yours for you.'

Soon all the kids was lined up for turns on our racing model, while we whizzed round on theirs. And I can still remember hearing the tinkle of the loose hub caps on our trike and thinking how queer it was that those other kids could be talked into thinking that a heap of old junk was better than what they had.

That was the way things was for the two years we went to kindergarten. I don't remember much about the actual teaching and that, though I can remember thinking the teacher was a *lady*, and feeling scared of her cause of that, but also thinking she was a bit sort of stupid too, cause she talked and dressed in a strange sort of way, like ladies did. But she wasn't important, the important thing was the other kids, and me and Fag felt we really had to battle to keep our end up with them. They all seemed so much better off than us, though when I look back at it now I don't think many of them can of been, they was all from working families like us, but some of them had a few extras we didn't have, and a lot of them had fathers. One boy whose father worked on a night shift we really envied, cause sometimes the father would walk round to the kindergarten and pick the boy up and take him home, and to us that really seemed out of this world, something really marvellous.

'Oh our father's in the building trade,' we'd say, hoping the other kids would think he was a carpenter or something and not just a labourer.

'He's away right now,' we'd say. 'He goes away to work on the Peninsula. But he'll be coming home next week and he's going to bring us a doll, he's going to bring us a watch. He's gone up north for a big job and when he comes back he's bringing bangles for us from Brighton.'

For a while our main ambition in life was to have gold bangles. It was a fad. One of the big department stores was selling these gold bangles and some of the better off girls turned up dangling them from their wrists at kindergarten. They wasn't really gold of course, they was just some trashy sort of metal with a thin coating of gilt, but they was all the go. They was called 'adjustable bracelets' cause you could make them grow as your wrist grew. So these girls sort of sauntered round the playground flashing these bangles at us, and me and Fag got *desperate*.

One day when we got home we found Mum out and the kitchen unguarded. So we stole a piece of bread and spread some meat paste on it and hid in the dunny and had a feast.

Fag suddenly stopped chewing.

'Meat paste jars,' she said.

She stuffed the rest of the bread in her mouth, grabbed me and ran back to the kitchen.

'Notice the lids?' she said.

I hadn't, of course, so Fag got the meat paste jars down again, lifted off the lids and there, flashing at me, I saw . . .

'Gold bangles!' said Fag.

Next morning me and Fag was sauntering round the playground with brass rings from the meat paste jars on our wrists.

'Oh yes,' we said. 'Our father got us these as a little surprise.'

I don't know who we thought we was kidding, but we was certainly kidding ourselves.

Then we turned six and started school.

Ginnie

We didn't want to go to school of course. Mum had been threatening us with it for years, so it wasn't surprising we was scared when the morning came. We was all sulky and grizzly while

Peggy tried to tidy us up a bit, brushing our hair and washing our faces and that. Mum didn't say anything till the last minute.

'Stop yer bloody whingeing,' she said. 'Yer going whether you like it or not and all I can say is good riddance, two less moaning bloody kids I have to put up with.'

Which she probably felt a bit sorry about, after she'd said it, but of course being Mum she'd never let on.

Hock and Peggy had the job of taking us to school. Me and Fag was still sulking, with our heads stuck down in our chests and our feet dragging.

'Hurry up, come on, hurry up,' Hock and Peggy said. 'If you don't hurry up we'll be late and our teachers will give us the paddywhack.'

In the end they got really frantic, they pinched us and *dragged* us down the street, cause I think they really would of got the strap if they'd been late.

And of course when we got to school it was even more horrible than we'd imagined.

It was Sydenham School, a great big huge ugly old place with wire fences all round it. Inside the fences was grey asphalt and dirty concrete and dirty rust coloured bricks and of course kids, hundreds and hundreds of kids, rushing and shrieking and yelling.

Hock and Peggy dumped us outside a classroom and ran away.

Me and Fag looked round bewildered. A bell rang somewhere. Suddenly all the hundreds of kids hurried up onto verandahs and lined up in queues, and of course we didn't know what we was supposed to be doing, so we just stood there where Hock and Peggy had left us.

A woman came out of the classroom. A fat, dumpy woman, with a face like a clown mask all white with powder, and bright red lipstick slashed across her mouth. She sort of minced out on teetering heels and looked at the queue of kids by the door, then looked down at me and Fag.

'And what, may I ask, are you two girls doing here?' she said.

I started to cry.

'We're Daphne and Janet Feron,' Fag said.

The woman sort of whinnied.

67

'Oh no!' she said. 'Not more Ferons! I seem to have been teaching Ferons ever since I came to this school.'

Some of the other kids snickered a bit, but not really sure whether they was supposed to or not.

'Smarmy fat bitch,' Fag muttered.

'What did you say young lady?' the woman shrieked. 'What did I hear you say?' Etcetera, etcetera, etcetera.

So we didn't start off our scholastic career with what you might say was an ideal introduction.

The woman yelled at us for a while, calling us stupid and impertinent and sly, 'like all the Ferons'. Then she changed down gear and carried on for a while longer about the stupidity of kids in general. Then in the end she seemed to sort of lose interest in it all.

'Any child with their wits about them,' she said, 'would have seen five minutes ago that the first thing to be done in the morning is form a queue outside the classroom door.'

Me and Fag stumped up onto the verandah and joined the queue.

'Enter, class,' said the woman.

And we all shuffled through the door, out of the sun and into this big grey room crammed with desks and a big dark map of the British Empire.

'You Feron girls,' the teacher said. 'Sit here.'

She clutched us by the shoulder, steered us to a desk, then went and sat up on a sort of platform.

'Writing,' she said. 'Get out your slates please.'

Me and Fag looked round desperately as all the kids dragged slates and bottles of water out of their desks.

'Just do what everybody else does,' Fag said.

So we looked in our desks, but of course they was empty.

Fag shrugged her shoulders. Two big tears rolled down my cheeks.

'Hands up high,' the teacher said. 'Write in the air what you see on the board.'

She wrote Bb Bb Bb Bb on a blackboard.

'Easy,' Fag said. 'We can do that no trouble.'

Me and Fag spent a fair bit of time looking at newspapers and magazines at home and we'd sort of picked up some idea of letters, though we didn't understand any words. So we stuck up our hands with all the other kids and started writing Bb Bb Bb Bb in the air, feeling quite proud of ourselves.

But that was a mistake.

'What do I see?' the teacher bellowed. 'Left handed Ferons?'

Her face had gone all pink from excitement and all the other kids turned round to stare at us. Some of the kids sniggered, but most of them just looked sort of stupid, just a sort of glazed look, like they were glad it wasn't them and that was about all they could manage to think about.

The teacher seemed to burst through all the faces and pounce on us. She had a wooden ruler clutched in one hand.

'We don't use the left hand, Janet and Daphne Feron,' she said, 'we use the right hand. What do we call left handed people, children?'

'South-paws-Miss-Mitchell-son,' the kids all chanted.

'Cack handed,' Fag said.

Miss Mitchellson looked at Fag in a state of shock for a minute, then started to enjoy it even more.

'In this classroom you will not use such disgusting language, Janet and Daphne Feron,' she said. 'And in this classroom you will soon discover why I like to keep this ruler handy at all times.'

She whacked it down on the desk, then bounced back to the front of the room.

Fag poked out her tongue but then a little tear started to squeeze its way out of the corner of one eye. I was really scared, cause if that woman could make Fag cry then things looked black all round.

And things *was* black all round.

It turned out that after writing in the air we had to write the letters on our slates. And of course we still didn't have slates.

'Where are your slates, Janet and Daphne Feron?' the teacher shrieked.

'Haven't got any,' Fag said.

'We haven't got any, *Miss Mitchellson*,' said Miss Mitchellson.

And so on and so on.

69

Well that was the start of years of sitting and sitting and sitting on hard wooden benches listening to big bullying women reefing off at us. They all seemed to be big buxom creatures, those teachers, big well fed buxom women who all seemed to wear cardigans and blouses and woollen skirts. And their main job seemed to be finding ways to pick on you. Which wasn't hard to do, of course. We soon learnt that the way to survive at school was to just try not to be noticed. We would try to sort of shrink down into our benches, hoping and hoping at the start of each year that we'd be given a desk at the back of the room, where we wouldn't be so easy to see.

I can't seem to remember my teachers as individuals, they just seem to have been a procession of bullies with powder on their faces and big chunky rings on their fingers.

Mind you, I do remember what particular torture each one specialised in.

Like, with Miss Mitchellson it was the ruler. If ever you stepped out of line – whack. And the whacking started first thing each morning. Each morning we had to write letters in the air, and each morning of course me and Fag did it with our left hands and Miss Mitchellson would nag and nag us and tell us southpaws never got anywhere but Sunnyside. Then in the end, when she'd worked herself up into enough of a paddy, down would come the ruler on our knuckles.

'That is not the way to do it, Janet and Daphne Feron,' she'd say. 'We use the other hand.'

Then afterwards, the horrible slates would come out and the screeching would begin as fifty kids tried to scratch Bb Bb Bb Bb or Ff Ff Ff Ff fast enough to avoid the flying ruler.

Our next teacher kept going berserk about homework. She'd load us down with all this work to do after school, then next day the first thing was to sniff and snuffle through us all to find out who to strap.

'What do you mean, Janet Feron?' she'd say. 'You didn't finish your homework because you couldn't understand it! Well you know what happens to impertinent little misses who think they can get around me!'

70

I can still see her knee. I think it used to be lifted nearly as high as her face as she brought the strap down on my hand.

The next teacher loved to get a kid up in front of the class to torment and display her authority over. If you broke a slate pencil or said three times three was six, it would always be, 'Janet Feron, up to the front of the class.'

And if you tried to take your time about it she'd be down from her platform, lugging you by your shoulder.

Getting us up in front of the class was horrible in another way too, cause it was part of the humiliation of 'getting clothes through the school'. It was this scheme they had at Sydenham School, where people who had money would give their old clothes to the school and parents who was poor could ask to be given some. The school would make the clothes up into parcels and every so often would hand them out to the kids from the poor families. Mum had her name down for free clothes, of course, and of course we hated it. We'd be sitting on our bench, trying as usual to merge with all the other kids, when the school secretary would walk in with some brown paper parcels and me and Fag would look at one another and have this horrible sinking feeling.

We'd put our heads down even lower, hoping the teacher would forget we was at school that day.

But of course it was no good.

'Daphne and Janet Feron,' she'd say, 'your clothes are here.'

We wasn't the only ones getting free clothes, there must of been as many as a dozen or more kids in each class getting clothes through the school, but we only thought about ourselves as we slunk up to the teacher to be handed these lumpy parcels wrapped up in old brown paper with string. And they was always horrible clothes. I can remember once I was given a horrible pink velvet dress with a pair of red, horrible, shiny leather shoes to go with it, and I had to clitter clatter round for a year or more in those shoes with that dress and I must of looked like something from a sideshow at the A & P.

It wouldn't of been quite so bad if Mum had of been able to alter those clothes to make them fit, but she couldn't, she didn't have a sewing machine, so it would of meant hand stitching and

71

Mum was long sighted and couldn't do hand stitching any more. She could of bought glasses I suppose, but where was the money going to come from?

Things got worse when we left the Primers.

At first we thought Standard One was going to be a real step up cause we was told we was going to be leaving slates behind and from now on was going to be writing in ink. Then we discovered we was going to be 'getting books through the school'.

It was like the hōo-ha about clothes. Kids whose parents had money could just buy their books and pens and that, on the first day of the new school year. There was a stationery shop round the corner from the school and on the first day the well off kids would turn up jingling silver coins in their pockets. The teacher would hand them a list, it was called the 'stationery requirements' list, and off those kids would go to the shop while in the meantime me and Fag and the rest of us had to just sit writing words in the air. Then back the other kids would come, they'd slap their piles of shiny new books down on their desks and look round triumphantly.

It always took a long time for our books to 'come through'. Mum had to apply to the school in writing, saying she was poor. Then the school would check up on her to see if she really was poor. Then our names would be put on a list. And then finally, after weeks and weeks of waiting, our books would turn up.

And in the meantime the kids whose parents had money would open up their glossy new books and start to write, while we made do with what bits and pieces of paper we could find.

Mum had an old dog eared exercise book at home, it had been Eddie's when he was at school, so every morning she'd pull out a couple of pages and hand them to us.

'There's no point making a meal of it,' she'd say. 'You'll have to use this.'

Then, if the teacher had had trouble swallowing her eggs and bacon that morning, there would be the usual inquisition.

'Janet and Daphne Feron, why haven't you got your books yet?'
We'd have to stand up to answer.

'We're sorry, Miss Soandso, we're still waiting for our books to *come through the school*'.

Then when they did come through there always seemed to be one book or other missing. We'd leaf quickly through the pile, checking that everything was there. And it never was. So Mum would have to write another note and the whole business would have to start all over again.

Mum was quite good at writing notes. We found that out because school was so horrible we started to pretend we was sick. We'd tell Mum we had things wrong with us, things it was hard for her to check up on. Like earache. And if Mum did get taken in, or if it was one of the rare times we really was sick, she'd write a letter for us to take next day to the teacher. It was always the same letter, she wrote it year in year out. It went like this:

'Please excuse Janet Feron from being absent from school.
And oblige,
M. Feron.'

That was *the* letter. And it was always written on a little scrap of paper, never a whole sheet, just a corner torn off the old dog eared exercise book.

But me and Fag soon discovered that staying at home wasn't any better than going to school, cause Mum made us work.

'Lie in bed and the poison goes to yer head,' she'd say. 'Git up and about and you'll be right in no time.'

This wasn't the cure she prescribed for her own 'bad leg' of course, but Mum knew better than we did that rules was made to be broken.

So between school and home it was a case of frying pan and fire and me and Fag didn't see how we was ever going to escape back to just being kids again.

The Historian

There was no hope, according to Feron wisdom. If you hoped for anything you were kidding yourself; there wasn't any hope. You were doomed to be whatever the impersonal, eternal forces of the universe said you should be.

The universe, of course, was Christchurch.

Feron wisdom was the exact opposite of what businessmen and lawyers and landowners said in the newspapers. According to them this was the land of opportunity, the land of hope and freedom. You only had to look at Parliament, where Labour had just got hold of the Treasury benches. Or the chambers of commerce, where people like Sir Bert Pelf who'd started off life with the obligatory sixpence in their back pocket were now puffing cigars and telling everybody all about it. Or 'the comfortable cottages and bungalows' of South Christchurch where 'even working people now enjoy wages and conditions that would have astonished their parents or grandparents'.

You only had to look at the department stores and office blocks in the city, where workers 'no longer had any cause for complaint regarding the lighting, ventilation, and general comfort and convenience' of facilities. Even a Fendalton matron happening to do a pee in the staff toilets of Hallensteins or Calder Mackays or the DIC would feel at home when she found herself enthroned on a rimu seat over a flushing porcelain bowl between polychrome vitreous tiles. The bad old days had gone, workers now were 'looked after with a solicitude that was very rare indeed in the old days'. In the 'modern factories' of Christchurch the matron from Fendalton, if she peeked around the shop floor door, would see a place as clean and smart and attractive as her own kitchen, where of a morning she'd find cook busy amidst winking steel and copper. 'The day of the gloomy, poky factory has definitely passed,' the City Council observed, 'and now the workers carry out their tasks under improved conditions that add greatly to their general efficiency. Nowadays no industrial building is erected without the most careful attention being paid to the health and comfort of the working men and women to be employed within it.'

Businessmen and lawyers and the rest of them had been saying that sort of thing to people like the Ferons for generations. But it was water off a duck's back to the Ferons, they never swallowed a bar of it.

'Things will get better one day,' Margaret Feron would say, 'and pigs will fly.'

But things were different for Ginnie and Fag. They were born in the Jazz Age, the Age of Electricity, the Age of Progress. Things were changing.

Newspapers and magazines riffling their way into the Feron kitchen fell open on promises of love, money, happiness. Cinemas, enclosing Ferons in plaster and chrome, flickered dreamlike images of optimism before their eyes. Schoolteachers chanted the slogans of education. Clergymen crooned about salvation. Department stores dazzled them with shimmering plate glass, armies of slender young papier-mâché ladies drooping under voile, georgette, crêpe de Chine . . .

So Ginnie and Fag came to the knowledge that things had changed for working people; things weren't as bad as they used to be.

Cars, for example.

'Motoring is no longer the luxury of the rich,' one newspaper declared the day Ginnie and Fag were born, 'but within the reach of every industrious citizen.' Working people could save up their wages and buy themselves flivvers or baby Austins or natty little Prefects and tool about the town. There were more cars in Christchurch in proportion to population than in any other city in the world, 'with the single exception of the city of Detroit'.

And electricity. Things had really changed with electricity. Grandmother in the old days had 'puddled out in the rain to cut wood for a smoky stove and took a whole day to do the washing', the Municipal Electricity Department told the Ferons in one of its publicity brochures. But now housewives in the city got 'perfect cooking heat in a moment, on a range of cleanliness undreamt of in those far off days'. And they heated their homes with electric radiators, they swept their floors with 'electric sweepers', they found that with the help of their wonderful new electric washing machine 'modern washing hardly requires the wetting of the hands'.

Well it was true that the Ferons didn't have a car, and it was true that in Braddon Street and Kent Street none of their neighbours did either.

And it was also true that they didn't have a vacuum cleaner

or an electric stove or an electric washing machine or an electric radiator, and although the Municipal Electricity Department and General Motors and the Zealandia Gramophone Manufacturing Company were telling them every day about 'Modernity Cleanliness Progress', if any of them had had the time to look at the statistics they would have found that when Ginnie and Fag were born fewer than three out of ten people in the whole of the City Beautiful had access to electricity.

But of course most working people didn't have time to look at the statistics and anyway they knew that a few years ago nobody had owned cars or vacuum cleaners or gramophones or washing machines, so it was obvious there was progress, wasn't it? And that meant it was just a matter of time before some of the progress reached the Ferons.

And it already had. After all, there were electric lights in Kent Street.

And although the lights were the only thing in Kent Street that were electric, and although the Feron women like most working women everywhere in South Christchurch continued like their grandmothers to scald their hands to a corned beef red as they boiled up their washing in the copper out the back, and burned the skin off their knuckles with lye soap as they scrubbed dirt off the linoleum in the front, and singed the tips of their fingers as they poked sticks into the cooking range in the kitchen, Ginnie and Fag knew that things were *getting better all the time*, that 'the City Beautiful at this moment, although already offering its fortunate citizenry the most advanced and most abundant goods our wonderful era can offer, is but a foretaste of the future of affluence, freedom, and opportunity that awaits us all'.

Fag

What happened was we got on a treadmill of dreams, Ginnie and I. We got talked into hoping for things, and talked into thinking we'd be happy if we got them. And of course we weren't going to get them, most of them didn't even exist, they weren't even there to be got.

School started it. Because although it was horrible and we hated it, and though we were so unhappy at school that we counted ourselves lucky when we were just sort of quietly bored, just stupefied, school made us want to 'do well'. Part of the problem was we turned out to be quite clever, Ginnie and I, so because of that, and because we were scared of the teachers, we ended up being very sort of diligent and sedulous. We learnt quickly how to do what they wanted us to do, make neat rows of numbers and words on paper and say the right things about the words and numbers at the right time. So we not only ended up wanting to 'do well', we actually *did* well, as far as they were concerned.

As far as we were concerned too. We started to get tickets on ourselves.

Once school had given us literacy it started to open up other things, it started giving us access to the whole world of words. And that was really something. That really excited us, especially me. Because before starting school when we'd looked at books and magazines and newspapers we'd thought they looked very interesting but also very esoteric, very remote. When you can't read, language on a page just seems like an endless stream of letters, but once you've been taught to look at it the 'right' way and you start to see that it can be made to form pools or lagoons of meaning, well it's dazzling.

All of a sudden we were yanking newspapers out from under the cushion of the yellow chair and reading.

The headlines, the words inside the cartoon balloons, the movie and love magazines scattered with cigarette ash on our big sisters' beds, the big fat words of the advertising posters from one end of Colombo Street to the other – Self Help Stores, YOU PICK UP THE GOODS WE PICK UP THE BILL, Come in Now and BUY BUY BUY – all these words became a bewildering promise of vicarious sensation.

Shops were wonderful places. Ginnie and I would drift down Colombo Street gazing into the windows, reading the slogans, dreaming of a universe of rayon stockings and steel cash registers.

Even more wonderful were the movie magazines. Movies, the flicks we called them, we'd been brought up on them. From the time we were five years old we'd been watching Ruby or Hock or Sadie hand threepences to the glamorous goddesses who sold tickets in little glass booths outside the Metro, the Majestic, the Mayfair, and the Plaza. And then inside, in chairs of plush or leatherette, we'd gaze up at the thousand loops of satin or taffeta and the footlights would play all their colours – azure, crimson, sea green, gold. By the time we turned seven our entire conception of beauty amounted to the interior decoration of cinemas and the faces of the 'stars' projected onto the screen. Jean Harlow and Carole Lombard, Greta Garbo and Marlene Dietrich, they were our vision of womanhood. They were a sort of mirror we looked into and dreamt that one day, perhaps, we might see ourselves.

Then, once we found we could read the movie magazines as well as sit in the movie theatres, the impressions became almost overwhelming.

Lives of the Stars, Hollywood Gossip, Stellar Nights, we leafed through their crackling, importunate pages, gazing and gasping and going bananas.

In our bedroom at Kent Street the big girls had already started to turn the walls into a montage of Hollywood faces and now Ginnie and I attacked *Lives of the Stars, Hollywood Gossip, Stellar Nights* with scissors, hacking out photographs of our heroines and pasting them all around us, so as we woke up in the morning or went to bed at night the teeth of a thousand smiles flashed down on us.

'What I like best are *suave* women,' I said to Ginnie one day.

We were sitting on the floor busy with the scissors.

'Suave women who don't change out of their dressing gowns till it's time for them to put on their diamonds for dinner.'

Dressing gowns were a particular obsession. Dressing gowns meant luxury, leisure. The idea that we might one day actually be able to wear a dressing gown of our own seemed too fantastic to think about for more than one – or at the most two – delicious moments, but we could always try pretending. So we'd creep into our brothers' room and pull an old coat or two off a nail on the wall. Then we'd borrow a tube of lipstick from the paraphernalia of beauty Ruby and Sadie littered all over the window ledge in our room. We'd slip down to the bottom of the back yard and search about in the weeds till we found some dock. Then we'd roll dock leaves and newspapers into cigarettes, we'd slash lipstick across our mouths and we'd slip into our brothers' old coats, and all of a sudden we became Harlow or Lombard or Garbo and the back yard became a poolside terrace on a hillside in Beverley Hills or Cashmere. And Ginnie and I, hunching our shoulders and pouting, would slink about as we thought suave women did.

Love magazines too. We became feverish about love magazines.

Right from our earliest childhood there were always stories about beautiful princesses, peasant girls, orphans. They were always miserable and poor and unloved, and of course our hearts bled for them because – well, they were us. Then the handsome prince . . . And then, well it was only a matter of time, there would be distractions and complications but in the end the prince would kiss her, and up onto the white horse she'd go, and away they'd gallop up and over the hill.

And Ginnie and I would let our jaws drop and our eyes glaze over.

Goose maidens, yes that was us, Sleeping Beauties, yes that was us too, but most of all we were Cinderellas, poor, sad, sweet Cinderellas, bullied and beaten by cruel unnatural relatives, thrust amidst ashes and slop buckets (didn't we have to clean slop buckets?).

'Cinderella, though fair, was poor and unhappy.'

'Ginnie and Fag, though fair, were poor and unhappy.'

Then as we grew older and our big sisters got older still, the contours of the heroines in the stories started to change. The goose maidens and princesses grew bosoms and false eyelashes, they shaved their legs with safety razors and slid them into 'art' silk stockings, they carried powder compacts, and turned up in the pages of *Living Love, Young Romance, Miracles and Oracles*, which were magazines our sisters would buy for a few pennies at news stands and dairies outside the factory when at the end of a working day they stepped onto the pavement and checked to see if they had change for the tram.

Miracles and oracles. A literature of dreamland.

79

And the dreams came true.

Love, love which conquers all, love which takes goose maidens and factory girls and school kids and Cinderellas and carries them off to . . .

Happiness, of course. Marriage and that.

But if the destination was a bit shadowy it was clear enough that love was how you got there. The journey would be long but the traveller, once she'd finally arrived, could sort of slump into the arms of the prince and slide, drift, slip into bliss. First the unhappiness and the waiting. Then the love and the happiness.

Well, waiting was something Ginnie and I were good at, waiting was something that was second nature.

'Just wait till I git my hands on youse two,' Mum had shouted at us a hundred times or more.

'Just wait your patience,' she'd said a hundred times more.

So we knew about waiting, Ginnie and I. And in the meantime, waiting, we read. And dreamed.

'Wasting yer time with trashy romances,' she said. 'If you think words will pay the rent you've got another think coming.'

'Aw, Mum,' we'd say.

'Only words worth reading are printed on a one quid note,' said Mum.

Fag

Religion started to fit into the picture too, now that we knew how to read. Religion, it turned out, could offer promises and visions of its own.

Mum had always sneered, of course, she'd never in her life been known to kneel to 'that god they're always yabbering on about'. The idea of 'christening' us kids had never occurred to her, and when the time came to celebrate what the parsons in their fancier flights called the birth of 'the Lamb of God', we identified it with the piece of roasted grey flesh which, soused in mint sauce, steamed in the middle of the kitchen table. And when Mum, having made the supreme effort to scrape together a few stray sixpences and present us not only with the roast lamb but also dates, oranges, and even, if the boat was in, a toy, she'd say,

'And you needn't think it was anything fo do with any Father Christmas. It was Mother Feron. Now git out from under me feet.'

But when we found ourselves trapped in the airless classrooms at Sydenham School we discovered that not everybody agreed with the Feron line on religion. In fact although state primary schools were supposed to be secular, the teaching staff at Sydenham were all very pious, all very keen on the thing they called 'God', and they took advantage of their authority in the classroom to do a bit of illegal proselytising. So there were sonorous mooings about 'little baby Jesus' and chirpy chantings of 'Jesus loves the little children'. And once a week a parson with scurfy shoulders would talk to us in a strange filleted accent, which we guessed was the way people talked in Fendalton. He'd lisp stories about the Christ child, and camels through the eyes of needles and so on, and hand out what he called:

'Christian literature'.

On hearing the word 'literature', Ginnie and I were on the alert. Now that we could read, we were eager to read everything.

Mind you, the little limp books the parson passed round the room didn't seem up to the standards of *Miracles and Oracles* at first. The pictures of Christ sort of simpering under long blond waves of what looked like peroxided hair seemed familiar – they reminded us of Harlow and Lombard and Garbo and Dietrich – but after opening the covers and dipping into the text we nearly gave up on religion for good.

'Not one of us, yea verily, not even the artless child who seems all innocence as she bends her dimpled knees before the altar of the holy mysteries, not even this small mote in the miracle of creation, shall be saved unless it be by FAITH. For what is faith? Why, faith is unto us as breezes and the sunshine are unto the bird, it is . . .

But there were juicy bits too if you looked for them, and we did. Like it turned out there was this Mary Magdalene, who was a flapper. We could just imagine what Mum would have said to Mary Magdalene.

81

'Yer a lazy tart, you just want to git into yer room and git some warpaint on yer face and git into town.'

Then we discovered Christ.

'Imagine, if you can, the sensations of our Saviour as the blade pierced his side, adding new sufferings to the already over-whelming delirium of pain in which he hung, white, naked, crucified and alone on the bare rough boards of the cross, impaled on the cruel nails for our sins, *for your sins*, child, that you might be saved. Christ the Saviour, Christ Jesus the Redeemer, suffering indescribable agonies of pain and, yes, fear, the red blood of his wounds coursing down the white skin of his body, that you might be saved ...'

Ginnie and I were riveted by this. It was really quite something to discover that this hero, this actual god, had let himself be nailed on a cross to save Ginnie and I.

'Thank you, Jesus,' we said in our private little sessions of wor-ship, reading the religious 'literature' in the back yard and smoking dock leaf cigarettes.

'Thank you for saving us.'

It added new dimensions to the movies and the love magazines and the plate glass windows of the department stores. In the past we'd often pretended that our father was 'away to do work on the Peninsula' or 'up north for a while', or even that Eddie was our father. But now we actually had a god for our father, and his name was 'God the Father'. This was an unexpected bonus because though God the Father seemed a rather distant and high handed sort of individual, still, fathers were like that, kids were always turning up at school with cuts and bruises and saying:

'Me old man did it.'

It turned out that there was also a 'Mother Mary', though we weren't too keen on her. We were inclined to think that one mother was enough.

But it was clear that we were related to a sort of heavenly royal family. There was Mary our 'Mother', who we thought of as a sort of queen, a sort of misty, nodding replica of Queen Mary. And there was God the Father, who we imagined as a bit like King George and a bit like old Moneygall of Simeon Street. And that was exciting, it gave us a sort of aristocratic genealogy. It seemed to support our idea of ourselves as princesses, Snow Whites, Rapunzels trapped in towers of corrugated iron.

'Rapunzel, Rapunzel, let down your hair.'

More interesting still was the idea of being 'saved'.

Sin was a stumbling block. We weren't too sure what sin was actually supposed to be. But being saved was something we did go for in a big way, it fitted in just right with all the fairy stories and the movies and the love magazines. They disagreed with one another on points of detail, it was true, but they all made it clear that the thing that did the trick, the thing that took Cinderella or the sinner or the princess from poverty, sadness, loneliness, unhappiness to bliss was love. 'God is love,' the little religious pamphlets told us. 'Only true love can bring true happiness,' sighed the heroines of the silver screen.

So we felt we'd made a great discovery, Ginnie and I, and by the time we were eight years old we knew that it was only a matter of waiting, that in time we'd be saved by Jesus or Clark Gable, who would lift us up in their strong capable arms and search our eyes with their penetrating yet gentle gaze, and would whisper:

'I love you Janet and Daphne. Come with me and be happy.'

5

Let the masque begin

Fag

'There vill be a place up for rent in Phillipstown,' Mrs Palto reported to Mum over a cup of tea one afternoon not long before Ginnie and I turned ten. 'It is a good big house Margaret, a bathroom and a gas stove and three bedrooms, and the rent is only eighteen shillings a week.'

Mum fingered her chin, screwed up her eyes.

'What's the catch?' she said.

'No catch,' Mrs Palto said. 'The thing is, there vill be no landlord. It is a Public Trust house.'

And, catching the sound of those magic words, Mum was in like a shot.

Fag

'No bloody landlord,' she said as we turned through the gate and looked at the new house. 'No bloody landlord to make our lives a misery.'

And in we walked.

Not that Mum really had hopes that her life would be anything but a misery.

The house we walked into had advantages above and beyond being owned by the Public Trust. Even more important, as far as Ginnie and I were concerned, the new place was a villa.

It's difficult, looking back now from a world of ferro-concrete and glass and vinyl, it's hard to remember what the word 'villa' meant to us then. 'Cottage' was a word we knew well. A cottage was the natural habitat of Ferons, a cottage was where we'd always lived, and in South Christchurch a cottage meant a box of two or four rooms and a lean-to at the back. But a villa meant something different. It meant six or eight rooms, it meant high ceilings and verandahs, it meant cast iron curlicues and fancy french cuts. It meant bay windows, bow windows. It meant, it almost meant – *toffs.*

From the moment we saw Mum decide she wanted it, we were in a frenzy.

'Things are looking up,' Ginnie said to me.

'Let the masque begin,' I said.

'Eh?' said Ginnie, but I preferred to leave her wondering.

My love affair with words was reaching its peak by then. I was getting feverish for words, for new words, bizarre words, fabulous words and especially *long* words. I loved to look at them, to listen to them, to hunt them up in their hiding places in thick books and let my brain sort of lovingly caress them.

I'd discovered the Sydenham Public Library.

It was one of those places built in colonial times for 'the improvement of the working class', partly paid for by ratepayers and partly by charitable benefactions, but by the time I discovered it, it was just a dusty heap of architecture near Sydenham Park. Inside there were these stupendously lipsticked women in grey cardigans who guarded the books. If you came in and looked as though you were going to disturb the books 'shelved' in rows, if you looked like you were actually going to take down a book and read a few pages, these women would sort of flash their glasses at you and let out little hisses.

It cost money to join the Sydenham Public Library, and that was a problem.

'Eight shillings a year for females,' I told Peggy, 'so that's quite cheap really, it's ten shillings a year for a man. It might sound as though it costs a lot, Peggy, but it's really a bargain, they've got ten thousand lending books, it says so on the notice board. Just think Peggy, ten thousand books.'

Peggy wasn't over excited by the idea and didn't seem to think eight shillings was exactly bargain basement either, but I knew my only chance of joining the library was to talk her or Eddie into giving me the money. There was no hope Mum would ever let me have it. So I started a campaign of wheedling and nagging till in the end Peggy took me along to one of the women in grey cardigans and bought me a yellow membership card.

'You realise it's cost me a fortnight of fags,' she complained as we walked back home, me with my arms full of history and poetry and novels.

'Knowledge is priceless,' I said.

'Fags are getting dearer too,' said Peggy.

And as I ransacked the shelves of the Sydenham Public Library in my search for truth, excited at the prospect of our new house, our new villa, I found that there were some books about Phillipstown. Phillipstown, which to me had always been just another stretch of asphalt and soot and iron, it turned out to have a history, Phillipstown, a romance, a meaning.

'It was called after the Phillips family, see,' I told Ginnie. 'They were toffs. In the old days they owned all that land over there, and they had land up country too. They had servants and carriages and that. And Lady Barker visited them, she was another toff, she wrote books and that, and she went to a ball at their house. Listen.'

Ginnie, slowly sucking on a dock leaf cigarette, closed her eyes and smiled dreamily.

'"White muslin was the universal costume," this is what Lady Barker wrote. "White muslin was the universal costume," and blah blah blah. "I covered mine almost entirely with sprays of light-green stag's-head moss, and made a wreath of it also for my hair. I think that with the other ladies roses were the most popular decoration, and they looked very fresh and nice."'

Ginnie sighed.

'They had a big house in the country, the Phillipses,' I said. 'Fountains and peacocks and that. And they had a house at Phillipstown too, it was called Phillips Town then. They'd stay there near the city so they could go to balls and dinners and that, they called it "the gaieties".'

Ginnie sighed again, then had another suck on her dock leaf fag.

'White muslin the universal costume,' she said.

'Course that was the old days,' I said closing Lady Barker. 'Not modern times, like now.'

It was hard, closing a book and looking at the rusty iron alongside us, it was hard to believe there had ever been that dewy improbable time, 'the old days', 'colonial times', a time when Phillipstown was Phillips Town, when it was paddocks and trees and big houses, and carriages rumbling up gravel drives, and maids in the kitchen, and ladies in crinolines drifting across lawns looking 'very fresh and nice' on their way to 'the gaieties'.

Mum was no help. I made the mistake of letting her hear me tell Tots about the old days.

'Hmph,' she said stripping the skin off some parsnips. 'While them Phillips tarts was mincing round in hoops my grandmother was scrubbing their floors for seven bob a week. Then she got up shit creek and married a labourer and had sixteen kids and three of them died before their first birthday and she died herself giving birth to the last one.'

Well trust Mum to see the worst side of everything.

I kept dreaming about old Phillips Town, with its mansions and its whist, its croquet and its masked balls.

And there were other good things to think about too. Not only were we in Phillips Town, we were on a big wide street too, Moorhouse Avenue. Moorhouse Avenue was lovely, it was a boulevard, a beautiful long broad boulevard with great big whispering trees, and it sort of streamed eastwards from Hagley Park to Phillipstown. At least it streamed eastwards until it got to Fitzgerald Avenue, then it stopped being a boulevard and turned into just a wide stretch of black asphalt, and that was where our house was, alongside that last naked stretch where lorries and motorbikes and cars and buses and trams roared along like an assembly line in a factory. The air at that end of Moorhouse Avenue smelt sort of poisonous, not just from the cars and lorries, but the gas works too, and the factories and railway yards and bus depot, all sorts of fumes and smells. So even inside the villa, even with the windows shut and the dolly tinted curtains drawn, the place stank, everything was always sooty.

Still, it was Moorhouse Avenue, and it was Phillips Town, where the Phillips ladies had once worn white muslin and been 'very fresh and nice'.

And the house was a villa.

To us it was luxurious, that villa, we thought we were going to a palace when we went there. It was really just a run of the mill place of course, really just a big wooden hulk with a hipped iron roof and verandah. But everything in it was on a scale half as much bigger as what we were used to. At the back the kitchen was so big we thought it was like a farm kitchen, not that we'd ever seen a farm kitchen of course, but it seemed so big and roomy. And in it, a *gas stove*, enamelled yellow and green; Mum only had to flick a little black bakelite lever to have an obedient blue flame leap playfully up at her.

'Just think of it, Margaret,' Mrs Palto said in her usual sort of sing-song on her first visit of inspection. 'Heat at your fingertips.'

And of course Ginnie and I, and Tots too, mimicked her for days afterwards.

Tots was turning into quite a smart kid. She was eight when we turned ten and Ginnie and I had started including her in our games.

'Now you go round and knock on the front door,' we'd say to her. 'And we'll open up.'

It was a nice big solid front door, the villa style of things, big kauri panels opening onto a big wide verandah that according to Eddie you could 'ride a bike in'.

Tots was very skinny, very quick, and sharp. She'd run out the kitchen door to go round to the front and Ginnie and I would saunter up the passage.

Tots would knock.

'I say,' Ginnie would say. 'There seems to be somebody at the front door, Pamela,'

'So there does, Diana my dear,' I'd say.

We thought Diana and Pamela were lovely names, they sounded very aristocratic to us. We could imagine some of the young Phillips ladies being called Diana and Pamela.

We'd turn the big scalloped brass doorknob and swing the door wide open. We loved that, the feel of just swinging the door open onto the big airy verandah.

'Do come in,' we'd say. 'How very nice to see you.'

Though Tots usually spoiled it by sniggering.

Apart from the gas stove ('heat at your fingertips') the villa wasn't much of an advance on Kent Street as far as mod cons were concerned. The wash house was the usual shed out the back with a copper on a dirt floor. The toilet was the familiar dunny squeezed between the wash house and a broken down fowl yard. Inside, in the kitchen, the agent from the Public Trust went to a lot of trouble explaining to Mum all the hoo-ha about how you could get a 'permanent supply of hot water for kitchen needs by taking the requisite steps, like so'. And that sounded very promising. But the whole trouble was that Mum and Eddie and Jock just about blew their guts trying to get it to go 'like so' and in the end Jock, getting a bit steamed up as usual, pushed something too hard.

'Busted for bloody good now,' he said. 'Stupid fucking thing anyway.'

'Serves you bloody well right,' commented Mum. 'Going at it like a bull at a bloody gate.'

But the way she said it was almost philosophically calm. It was as though she'd never really believed in the first place there could ever be such a thing as hot water on tap.

But there was one dazzling advance in technology which for Ginnie and me outclassed everything else the villa had to offer.

There was a bathroom.

'When we go there,' Ginnie and I rhapsodised to one another as the family junk was being loaded onto the back of a lorry in Kent Street, 'we'll be able to put on our dressing gowns and have a bath every morning, just turn the tap on and have a bath.'

Though we still didn't have any dressing gowns, only the boys' old coats, and as for turning the taps on, well once Jock had busted the gas stove connection you could turn the tap till you were blue in the face and all you'd get in that bathroom was cold water.

So we were back to the old routine of boiling water on the stove to carry in buckets to the bath.

But but but, it was still a villa.

And one further refinement; opening off the kitchen through two glass doors was a big bare room with a bay. When Mum clapped eyes on it she saw something she'd lost and now intended to have again.

'This,' she announced with a gleam in her eye, 'will be the dining room.'

Into it went two or three old chairs covered in brown moquette which Eddie had managed to pick up cheap along with a couple of wooden jardinières at a repossession sale. The jardinières impressed us all, even Mum, though none of us really knew their name properly till I went to the Sydenham Public Library and looked it up in a dictionary. Then when I got back Mum wasn't interested in the result of my researches. She kept calling them 'jardinnies' and her way of taking possession of them was not with words but by drooping 'machine lace' doilies over their polished totara lips.

Fag

The family could afford to buy the odd moquette armchair now. Times were good. A war was coming, so business was booming. Of a pay day the boys and big girls handed over bulging pay packets and Mum, subtracting allowance to hand back to them, would hide the money in a tin and hold her lips tight with satisfaction.

There was plenty of food in the house too, sausages and mince and mutton shanks and the rest of it, meat every day. And bread, and potatoes, and rice pudding and sago to fill in the gaps.

And lunch.

Lunch every day. Walking out the kitchen door on our way to school of a morning, Ginnie and Tots and I felt safe, protected, confident as we clutched our little newspaper parcels, knowing that inside them, under the headlines 'INDECENCY CHARGES DROPPED' and 'COMMUNIST THREAT GROWING', nestled lunch.

Sandwiches and biscuits and meat paste.

The knowledge that we had lunch helped get us used to the idea of our new school, Phillipstown School, which at first we hated. Sydenham School had been horrible, but at least it was a place we'd got used to. We'd found out the ways of 'doing well', and also, after four years of standing in assembly listening to the headmaster bash our ears about the 'school spirit' and the rest of it, we'd come to believe that Sydenham was a bit better than other state schools.

But as for Phillipstown. Phillipstown was rock bottom.

The Historian

Sydenham was the oldest school in South Christchurch. In 1933 its official historian described it as 'a school composed of a curious mixture of buildings old and new', a school that had 'a long and honourable record of teaching right from the old Provincial Government days'. A history 'rich in tradition'.

Sydenham wasn't really 'rich in tradition', it was just old. Like all working class state schools it functioned mainly as a sort of army camp, turning children into disciplined labourers and factory hands. But as the service industries of the city grew, as department stores, banks, real estate offices and commission agencies spread, there was an increasing demand for white collar workers, polite, meek, grateful people who would push pens, sell garments, add up numbers or subtract truths. This meant that there was a chance for some of the more bookish children of working class families to 'get on', to get salaries not wages, to ride a tram to Cathedral Square instead of a bike into a factory yard. And getting bookish children on was where Sydenham School came in. Sydenham School was particularly good at identifying likely candidates for social promotion. Its leading teachers were skilled at picking such children out from the ruck, teaching them the appropriate formulas, and lifting them out of the back streets of Addington into such elevated places as the lingerie counter at Ballantynes department store or the accounts department at the Bank of New Zealand.

Sydenham was good at that. Sydenham was proud that it set

the standard for working class schools.

But Phillipstown . . .

There was no 'curious mixture of buildings old and new' at Phillipstown, no 'long and honourable record of teaching'. Phillipstown was a rough, poor school and its main building came raw and hard from the 1920s, a big blank block of brick which Education Department architects called Georgian but which to Ginnie and Fag, standing on the asphalt in its shadow, was just an arid and empty rectangle.

Part of the problem was that Phillipstown kids were poorer even than Sydenham kids. In 1935 when a Health Department doctor visited the state schools of South Christchurch she commented that Sydenham was a good working class school in 'an average working class area'. But Phillipstown, in spite of the Feron villa, in spite of having once been Phillips Town where the ladies looked 'very fresh and nice', was probably the poorest aggregation of housing in Christchurch. So the classrooms inside the Georgian box of Phillipstown School looked like specimen cabinets of malnutrition, scarlet fever, tuberculosis, polio and child abuse. It was, the Health Department doctor noted, a 'notoriously poor school'.

Fag

'It'll be hopeless,' I groaned to Ginnie. 'How are we gonna be able to get on?'

At Sydenham we'd been deciding we had it in us to win a scholarship or something, that we were going to do well in our best 'subjects' and end up at the Technical High School or even, dream of dreams, take a 'professional course' at Christchurch Girls High School.

'The teachers won't be any good at Phillipstown,' I said. 'It's not a school, it's a borstal.'

'Well,' Ginnie said. 'We'll be big fish in a small pond.'

Which was a consolation I grasped at eagerly.

So for the first few weeks Ginnie and I went round Phillipstown thinking we were superior to the other kids there. Our superiority seemed confirmed by a big to-do about lunches. At Phillipstown the scrounging in rubbish drums was worse than at Sydenham, and I don't suppose the teachers thought there was anything much they could do to stop it, since at least half the kids in the school turned up each day with no lunch bag. But not long after we started there was a scandal. A girl got her head split open in a fight over some food scraps near the rubbish drums and the infant mistress, a big bustling officious woman she was, started up a sort of witch hunt which ended with a Health Department nurse coming to the school, visiting each class, and talking to us all about 'adequate nutrition'. Each person had to go up to the front of the class and unwrap their lunch, if they had any, so the health nurse could see what was in it.

When it came to our turn Ginnie and I all of a sudden stopped feeling smug and started panicking. It always seemed to happen to us when we'd been getting a bit cocky, suddenly all our confidence would shrivel up and all we'd want was just to be left alone.

But when we unwrapped our bits of newspaper and exposed our sandwiches to the health nurse she actually looked up at us and smiled.

'Excellent,' she said.

Ginnie and I sort of gaped.

'Two of the best lunches in the class,' she said. 'Bread for starch, meat paste for protein, butter for fats, and home made plum jam for sugar and minerals. Much better than the crusts and cold faggots so many of you children are eating.'

So Ginnie and I, smirking our way back to our seats, started to feel there was something to be said for Phillipstown School after all.

We always 'did well' in 'Health', thanks to the way Mum had drilled us and thanks to the way Peggy and Sadie kept attacking us with toothbrushes and combs and hairbrushes. And our nails were always clean. Mum was forever ordering Peggy to 'git onto those fingernails', telling us they looked like 'spades from an Irish spud farm'. Peggy, seizing a kitchen knife, would pare them right down to the quick.

At school in the morning there was always an inspection of fingernails and noses. If your nails were clean, a nod of approval. If they were dirty, a frown. If they were dirty two days in a row, a crack over the knuckles with a ruler.

We always got the nod of approval, Ginnie and I, we were almost the only girls in class who always did.

So our heads started to swell and we started to 'have tickets' on ourselves 'both ways', as Peggy commented once or twice when we started giving her instructions on how to behave.

'You shouldn't say "somethink", Peggy,' I told her one day when she was dicing up some mutton with Mum. 'You should say "something".'

Peggy just laughed and kept on dicing.

'Youse two shut yer big mouths,' Mum said by way of re-inforcement. 'We was talking to the butcher not the block.'

Ginnie

One of the problems me and Fag always had when we sat in the fleapit at the flicks looking up at the stars with our mouths open was that by the time we shifted to Moorhouse Avenue it was obvious that neither of us was exactly beautiful. There was our big feet and hands, our 'bloody big dukes' as Mum still called them, and our freckles, and for me the biggest curse was my hair. It was red, of course, or ginger really, a sort of mop of frizz. And my eyes was a sort of muddy green. Scarlett O'Hara had green eyes, so that was something, but hers were 'as green as the hills of Ireland' and mine looked more like the green at the bottom of a sump. And I was pudgy too. Me and Fag had read about 'puppy fat' in some of the love magazines and we decided that was what was happening to me, it was 'pubescent puppy fat'. But it didn't make me feel any better. When I looked at myself in the cracked mirror in our bedroom all I seemed to be able to see was my flaming ginger hair, my muddy green eyes, my big dukes and blotchy brown freckles, and all the bulges and bumps on my body.

Fag had her problems too, of course. She was really skinny.

'She's jake,' Eddie said to Mum one day when Jock busted the clothes prop. 'We'll use Fag instead.'

Fag hated her hair even more than I hated mine, cause she used to say at least my hair had a colour, even if it was red, cause hers didn't have any colour at all, it was just a sort of pale mousy colour and it was all straight and lank.

'My hair's horrible,' she used to say. 'My skin's awful. I'm never going to get bosoms. I might as well enter myself in a freak show in a circus.'

This was Fag in one of her moods. One day she'd be all up in the air and skiting and giving Mum cheek, then the next day I'd find her huddling in a corner over a book and saying she wanted to die.

'I'm just ugly,' she'd say, 'and that's it.'

It was hard to know what any of the boys at school thought about us cause they was always made to sit on one side of the classroom and the girls over on the other, and there was one playground for the boys and a separate one for the girls. And though some of the girls talked about sex and that, me and Fag was always too scared. We never used to go behind the bike sheds with other girls, though we used to hear some of them tittering among themselves and I used to think, I'm missing out on something. Doreen Flett, she was in our class, one time she tried talking to me about babies, sort of testing the water like, but me and Fag thought she was a horrible person so I didn't say anything much back and in the end she gave up and went away.

There was one or two girls, Doreen Flett was one of them, they was what we called 'boy conscious'. We called them that so we could feel superior to them. They was pretty, they got on good with boys and, well we used to envy them really.

Of course we didn't know anything about sex, what it was all supposed to be about. Fag tried to find books about it but the Sydenham Public Library wasn't the best place to look cause she only managed to find one book there that had anything at all to say about it, and it was really hopeless. It was called *Motherhood and Female Hygiene* and it kept talking all the time about 'the wonderful secrets of reproduction' but never actually got round to telling you what the wonderful secrets was. And there was these diagrams showing 'genitalia of the male and female'. Fag was too scared to get a book with diagrams like that out of the library; she just hid herself behind some bookshelves and tried to copy the diagrams onto some bits of paper, terrified that one of the librarians would see her.

When she got home with the bits of paper we took off our pants and tried to see if we looked like the diagrams, and of course we didn't.

'There's something wrong with us,' Fag said.

'Why not see if you can find another book,' I said. 'There must be other books about it.'

But there wasn't.

We had a vague idea that some of the other girls in our class was starting to get periods, there was all this whispering and that in the cloakroom. Girls would come up and say, 'Did you know Jessie Keegan's got you know what?'

Me and Fag would try to look worldly wise.

'Oh, is that right?' we'd say. 'It's about time isn't it?'

But of course we didn't know what they was talking about.

Then another time, one day at home, Mum had been cutting up potatoes and gravy beef to make a stew, she bent over the fire to turf the potato peelings in, and we saw blood on her skirt. We thought it must of been from the gravy beef.

Fag piped up of course.

'Look what you've got on your skirt,' she said. 'Do you want me to get a rag?'

Mum turned round and really bashed Fag on the head.

'Don't be so bloody cheeky,' she said, and she was going to bash her again but then looked down at the blood stain and sort of tried to cover it up with the potato bowl.

The words 'blood' and 'rags' came up together again a month or two later when we overheard Hock saying something about it to Peggy.

'Time to get the blood rags on,' she said.

So we sort of put two and two together, me and Fag, and decided it had something to do with that day Mum had blood on her skirt. We did a bit of snooping round one afternoon after school while the big girls was still out at the factory. At that time me and Fag was sharing one bed and Peggy and Hock was sharing the other bed in our room, and under their bed we found a pile of old rags that had been screwed up and stuck under some dirty pants. They was all sort of dry and crusty.

Me and Fag got them out and started throwing them at one another.

'Here's another blood rag in your face,' we was saying.

And we got all sort of excited.

Other funny things was going on too. We didn't really know what, but me and Fag just had the feeling that something was happening between some of the big boys and girls in the house that we didn't understand, something really sort of exciting and secret, and it had something to do with blood rags and that. It was mainly of a Sunday morning. The big boys and girls would be at home and Mum would be having a lie-in late and the girl whose turn it was to do the housework in the boys' room would go in there with a broom and bucket. And if it was Sadie or Hock that went in, Jock would shut the door.

Sometimes of a night, quite late at night after Mum had gone to bed and me and Fag was supposed to be asleep, our bedroom door would open and Jock would come in. He'd sort of pad his way across the lino and get into bed with Hock and Peggy and then there'd be lots of creaking and whispering. Me and Fag would lie there in our bed nearly suffocating with excitement, giggling and tittering and hissing at one another to be quiet.

Jock was always bringing girlfriends home too. He wasn't supposed to take them into his bedroom, but he did. He'd sit Mum out of a night then take the girl into the boys' room.

'He needn't think he's pulling the wool over Mum,' Hock said to Peggy one night when me and Fag was supposed to be asleep. 'Mum knows all about it if you ask me, she just doesn't want to get Jock fierce, cause she knows if she does he'll just belt her.'

Well that might of been right, Jock did belt Mum a couple of times.

He belted his girlfriends too. I remember one night after tea there was a knock on the door and Fag opened it and this girl Patty was standing there. She'd been going with Jock but he'd finished it and now she'd come round to try to get him to go back with her. She had thick black hair and they used to call her the 'Black Bike'.

Jock yelled at her.

'Bugger off,' he said. 'And don't bloody come back.'

She started crying, she had a lot of powder and that on, and it started to get all streaky.

Jock and Eddie grabbed hold of her and threw her out the back door, really threw her so she fell on the concrete path and banged her head on the slops bucket. Then they slammed the door. She never came back after that.

Eddie wasn't as rough as Jock. He could be rough when Jock was egging him on, but most of the time he was an easy going sort of a joker. He didn't go out much with girls, he spent more time with his mates, drinking with them at the pub. Of a night he'd bring them home and sometimes they'd sleep in the boys' room. After a while me and Fag sort of had an inkling that those big boys was getting up to something together too, something to do with sex, and that made me and Fag even more mixed up, cause we hadn't really worked out all the other stuff yet and now there was this added complication. We was starting to think we wasn't ever going to get it all worked out.

Listening to the big girls talking was sometimes a help. Like, we'd lie awake in bed listening to Ruby and Sadie and Hock and Peggy talking about their boyfriends and what they'd been getting up to.

'So I said, "Think yer gonna go fishing?" And he said, "Nah, what yer talking about?" So I said, "That rod you've got sticking up in yer trousers".'

And so on and so on.

The big girls sometimes brought their boyfriends home of a Saturday night if they wasn't going to the pictures or a dance, and there'd be Jock and Eddie and Sammie and Bobsie with their mates too, so the house would be full of all these lanky young jokers with fags and big grins and bottles of beer. And things would feel all sort of different in the house. Mum especially. It was funny, a funny sort of change would come over her, she'd start to sort of sparkle, she'd laugh and smile and really get quite gay. All the boys would call her Ma, they'd sort of joke and jolly her along.

'Come on, Ma,' they'd say. 'Have a shandy.'

And sometimes she'd pick up a glass and hold it out to them.

'All right,' she'd say. 'Don't mind if I do have a shandy beer with you this once.'

She always called it a 'shandy beer' and me and Fag would be watching, amazed, cause before those big boys started coming round to the house we'd never seen her touch a drop of beer. Drink was what she'd always blamed for having been the ruin of the old man.

But there she'd sit, drinking her shandy beer. And one day she even gave me and Fag a glass each. It wasn't much, it was really just lemonade and a faint cloud of beer in a couple of meat paste jars, but me and Fag thought we was off on another planet.

Then Mum would start singing.

That was even more of a miracle than the drinking, we couldn't believe our ears the first time it happened. Mum had been drinking a shandy beer and somebody had put a record on the gramophone and Mum had started singing. And Fag turned to look at me and her eyes was like saucers.

The gramophone wasn't much of a gramophone, somebody gave it to us not long after we shifted to Moorhouse Avenue. They gave us a heap of old records too, a lot of them was all buckled and bent and they was all badly scratched, but we put them on the turntable and sang along with them. It didn't take us long to get through the little tin of gramophone needles we'd been given with the records and the rest of it, but that wasn't too much of a problem, we started using tacks. We found some tacks in the wash house and screwed one into the arm of the gramophone. And it worked all right, it was cheaper than a new needle.

And while Mum tapped her feet and sang along with the records, all us young ones would jive.

It was sex, me and Fag decided, that was what it was all about.

That was why Mum started smiling when all these gangly young jokers was round the place. She was sort of excited by them, though she didn't really know what was happening. And for us to see Mum in that sort of light was, well it was a bolt from the blue.

So sex seemed to be quite a good thing. The problem was, was there ever going to be any for us?

My interest in the whole business packed up for a while when I started having periods.

Peggy had done her best to prepare us; she was always trying to help us a bit, Peggy. As we started getting older she showed us how to look after our hair and skin and that, and she'd get us at night time before bed and make us do exercises to 'strengthen' our eyes. Not that she was friendly all the time. Sometimes something went sort of snap, she'd lose her temper and really go mad. There was something sort of wild about Peggy, she reminded us of aunty Aggie. She had the same sort of gaunt wild look in her face sometimes, the same kind nature but that same streak of something wild in it too. Well anyway, she tried to give us an idea of what to expect.

'You'll be getting your monthlies soon,' she said. 'They're . . . Um, and you . . . But when you get them, you have to have some rags.'

So there was that word again, and suddenly we saw what she was driving at.

My first period started one Sunday morning. I got a bit of blood on my pants and felt this horrible cramp in my stomach, so I sort of hobbled outside to the toilet and looked down between my legs and saw it all bloody and sticky. So I sat down and started to howl.

Peggy had seen me go and after a while she turned up, she tapped on the toilet door.

'Have you got your period Gin?' she said.

And I said 'No,' cause I just didn't want to talk about it to anybody, I just wanted not to have to even think about it.

'I'll let Mum know,' Peggy said.

Which of course was the last thing I wanted.

After a while Peggy came back. She talked me into opening the toilet door and she handed me something.

'Here,' she said. 'Mum said to use these.'

They was some old tatty rags.

'You'll be getting your period every month now,' Peggy said. 'There's no need to worry, you just use these.'

So I went off to school next morning with a hunk of rag between my legs. My 'blood rag'. And it was torture, I couldn't run round the playground and I had to stay sitting on a bench when it was time for Swedish drill, and all the girls knew and whispered about it. 'Ginnie Feron's got hers,' they said. The rag was really rough too, really rough and scratchy, so by the time I got home the tops of my legs was all red and raw inside, really hurting. I used the one rag all day and by night of course it was filthy. Peggy had said, 'at the end of the week you wash them.' So when I went to bed I took out the dirty one and shoved it under the bed, the way Hock and the other big girls did. And after a few days there was this heap of dusty dry blood rags there.

On the Saturday morning I went out the back to wash the rags. Sadie and Hock was doing the wash that day, and when they saw me coming with my bundle of blood rags sort of screwed up small as I could manage, Sadie got really fierce.

'Take those away,' she said. 'Don't you dare put your blood rags in with the rest of the things. They have to be washed separate.'

Later on I went out the back again and by that time Sadie and Hock was gone and the fire had gone out under the copper and all the hot water was gone. I knew there wasn't any point asking Mum if I could relight the fire, it would be 'wasting good kindling'. So instead I just put the blood rags in a tub and rubbed soap on them and washed them in cold water. It was horrible. I was terrified one of the boys would come in and see me with my rags in a tub full of bloody water.

I started to peg them out on the line. Mum saw me through the kitchen window and came rushing outside.

'What're you putting those filthy things on the line for?' she said. 'Put them on a string in your room.'

It was like a nightmare.

When my second period started I got bad cramps in my stomach again, horrible dragging pains in my stomach. They went away the next day, but when I got my third period it happened again.

In the end I went to Mum. She was working in the kitchen. 'Oh,' she said.

She didn't turn round to look at me, she just kept rubbing some fat into a bowl of flour.

'Mix up a teaspoon of baking soda and water and take that,' she said.

And that was that. That was all the advice she ever gave me about my periods, or about sex, or about babies or marriage or anything. Except one other time, one day when I was having my period and had got out the tub and started to wash my hair.

'Don't you *dare* wash your hair when it's that time,' she said the minute she saw me. 'If you wash your hair at that time of the month your brain will be turned.'

When I talked to Fag about all this she wasn't as sympathetic as she might of been. She was starting to worry, Fag was, cause she hadn't started her own periods yet and there wasn't any sign that they was ever going to start at all.

'There *is* something wrong with me,' she said. 'I'm a dead end in the evolution of the species.'

6

The South in danger

Ginnie

One night me and Fag was listening to a lot of yelling down the passage. Then Hock came into the bedroom all worked up.

'Sadie's up shit creek,' she said. 'Jock says he's gonna belt her. Mum says belting her won't do no good to nobody. Jock says he doesn't give a bugger about doing good to nobody.'

Well even me and Fag knew about shit creek. We'd heard other girls talk about going up that creek and we knew they usually came back down it with a baby and, if they was lucky, a husband.

'Who's the father?' Fag said.

'Bugger if I know,' Hock said. 'Buggered if Sadie knows either.'

Next morning Sadie was gone.

The air in the kitchen was that thick you could of cut it, but nobody said anything till in the end Fag just had to ask.

'Where's Sadie?' she said.

Mum turned round to let fly, but Eddie cut in quick.

'Gone away for a while,' he said. 'Needed a holiday.'

And of course Sammie and Bobsie started sniggering and nudging one another.

A few days later when me and Fag got home from school we found Sadie sitting in the kitchen with a curtain ring on one finger and a little black haired joker like a weasel sitting at her side.

'Say hullo to your new brother-in-law,' Mum told us.

'Gidday, kids,' he said. 'I'm Curly.'

Curley Siemens was a labourer, he came from a family round Waltham way, and after Sadie and him had finished their cup of tea they went away and rented a couple of rooms in Addington. Sadie had given up her job at the factory and the next time we

103

saw her she was knitting bootees. She came round for cups of tea. Me and Fag watched her stomach getting bigger, till one day she came with a baby, just like all the other girls who got up shit creek.

Well, it was exciting. But it worried me and Fag a bit.

We was glad to get rid of Sadie, she'd always been a stirrer in the family. But marriage we'd always thought of as something glamorous, sort of an escape to something. With Sadie it just seemed sort of dingy and depressing, she was just the same person, and Curly Siemens was just an ordinary working chap like all the rest of them. And Sadie would come and bitch about him to Mum, then go and bitch about Mum to Ruby. And Curly and Sadie was holed up in these poky little rooms right next to the wool stores in Addington.

It didn't seem to fit in very well with our idea of getting married and living in a bungalow and growing flowers.

Jock got married too.

'No useless tart's gonna tie me down,' he always used to say.

But he was wrong. This time it was him who got a girl up shit creek and her brothers and father came to see Jock and fix things up. They was a Maori family, and they was making sure Reina was all right, so they took Jock away with them to Kaikoura, which was where they lived, and Jock got a job up there labouring with the Public Works.

About a year later they came down to stay with us for a week. Reina came. She had a little boy by then, he was a lovely little chap, but Jock was just the same. And so was Mum.

'Ar, that Maori bitch,' she said when Reina had her back turned. 'Got her hooks into my boy.'

The crunch came when Reina's mother landed on the doorstep one day, a sack of crayfish under one arm and a bunch of puha under the other.

'I've been missing my Reina,' she said. 'And I've been missing my little mokopuna, so I got onto the train this morning to come and see them.'

And she sat down. On the floor! On one of Mum's mats!

She stayed two or three days, and all the time Mum went round with jaws clenched and eyes blazing. Then Reina and Jock and the baby and Reina's mother went back to Kaikoura, and the moment the kitchen door was shut behind them . . .

Well Mum didn't actually say anything she'd never said before, but she managed to say it more times than ever before. Ending up, of course, with the worst offence of all.

'*And* disturbing all my mats,' she said. 'The useless, lazy, black tarts.'

So the first two marriages in the family wasn't exactly good advertisements for wedlock, as Fag said to me one day. But then another day we was sitting round in the kitchen listening to a thriller on the wireless Eddie had just bought as a present for Mum, when Ruby came in with Frank Morgan.

'Mrs Feron,' he said, 'I've come to ask permission to marry your daughter.'

Frank Morgan had been going out with Ruby for years. Him and her had always said they was 'making plans together', but we'd got so used to the idea that we'd sort of stopped thinking about it. And Frank Morgan wasn't exactly dreamboat material either, at least me and Fag didn't think he was. He wasn't very tall, he was a little nuggety looking joker with little wee eyes. Sadie said they looked like pissholes in the dirt. But in other ways we quite liked him, me and Fag. He was very sort of solid, you felt as though you could trust him, and he seemed to have lots of energy too, he always seemed to be busy and enjoying himself and cracking jokes. He was two or three cuts above us Ferons, but he never behaved as though it made any difference to him. Just cause he was a trained motor mechanic didn't mean he thought he was too good for us. He was a nice joker.

'Ruby and I weren't able to see our way clear till now,' Frank was saying.

Mum wasn't looking at him. She was looking at the knobs on the radio.

'What with having just started out on my own,' Frank said. 'But things are moving with the war, Mrs Feron. Ruby and I can see ourselves sitting pretty in another two or three years.'

Well of course Mum was never gracious about anything.

She just sort of grunted.

'Hope yer know what yer taking on,' she said. 'She's got a sharp tongue and a high hand.'

Talk about pots and kettles. But Ruby didn't say anything and Frank just laughed.

Ruby and Frank did everything the right way. It was the real thing, just like the stories. There was a wedding at a church, it was St Mary's Church in Addington, a real old colonial church. Ruby starched herself up to the nines in white tulle. Frank wore a grey suit. Peggy was the bridesmaid, dressed up in yellow, and they even managed to get Eddie into a black jacket to 'give the bride away'. Afterwards there was sausage rolls and cakes and that at the Club Hotel in Sydenham.

It made me and Fag think about the Stevenson-Merbrook wedding.

'Veil of tulle and beautiful old lace,' Fag said. She remembered it all by heart. 'Bridesmaids wearing blue cloques with slit bodices caught by silver and pearl clasps.'

Well it wasn't really high society of course, it didn't exactly get in the papers, but it was still a real wedding, and me and Fag sort of hugged ourselves for days afterwards.

From then on Ruby never looked back.

Her and Frank Morgan went away on a honeymoon to the West Coast and when they came back they rented a cottage in Sydenham. But that was only for a few months.

'We're having a place built for us in Avonside,' Ruby announced to Mum one day. 'Frank bought a section a couple of years ago. It'll be a bungalow, just two bedrooms and a sunporch and that, but it's a nice street Mum, it's got trees down both sides and all the other houses are nice and at the end of the street you come to the Avon. It'll cost us nine hundred pound all told. That's not much these days Mum, and that's including all the fences made and the paths laid.'

She ended up almost apologising cause it was clear from the way Mum was looking that something was wrong.

'And I suppose the money's coming from the man in the moon Mum said, stabbing a scone.

'Well we've already got three hundred,' Ruby said. 'The bank will give us the rest. We won't have any trouble paying it off, Frank's making good money now. They need motor parts for the war.'

Mum slashing butter onto the scone.

'You wouldn't catch me with a monkey on me back like that,' she said.

After the bungalow was built Ruby used to invite me and Fag over every now and then for the weekend. Of a Friday afternoon she'd turn up in a car, only an old English make they'd bought for fifty pound, but Ruby got about in it and me and Fag thought it was wonderful. We'd jump in, and Ruby would whizz through Phillipstown, then on through Linwood, the usual dirty houses and narrow streets, but then all of a sudden we'd be rolling along Avonside Drive and beautiful big trees would be sort of arching over us and speckling us with shadows, and on one side big houses with balconies and lawns would be slipping past and on the other side would be the river all soft and smooth. Then after the big houses came the little houses, streets and streets of bungalows. And they all looked so nice and new and sparkling, with little porches and stone fences.

Frank and Ruby's place was painted pink, with green window-sills and a green roof. There was a little square lawn out front and a trellis with a painted wooden butterfly. Inside it was even nicer, it was just lovely, everything was really nice, really cosy and bright and new.

There was even a pink tiled bathroom.

Of a night we'd have a bath together, me and Fag. We'd turn on the sparkling chrome taps and we'd watch the water gush into the bath. Then we'd slip off our clothes and just loll about in soapy water.

'Our sister's built a bungalow in Avonside and she's got an electric stove and a pink tiled bathroom,' we used to say to the girls at school. 'And she's got a vacuum cleaner, and she's got a refrigerator, and she's got a chesterfield suite.'

One of the things that really amazed us was how Ruby seemed to have her whole kitchen filled with stacks and stacks of food.

You'd open a cupboard and there'd be tins and packets and jars and bottles. You'd open the fridge and there'd be meat and eggs and milk and butter. And every afternoon she'd bake. She'd turn out cream puffs and pikelets and lamingtons and we'd have them for afternoon tea.

'Feast after famine,' Fag said. 'Ruby's trying to make up for all those years living off the smell of boiled cabbage.'

Ruby really was cooking enough for two families. Of a Sunday she'd roast a great big piece of lamb or hogget for dinner, and of course her and Frank and me and Fag wouldn't make much of a dent in it. Then she'd send it home with us.

'Tell Mum it might come in handy for sandwiches for you kids,' she'd say.

But of course Mum would eke it out. She'd give it to us for Monday tea sliced cold, and on the Tuesday she'd mince up what was left and make shepherd's pie or stew.

It was Ruby's way of trying to help Mum out, but Mum resented it. She'd take the lamb, but she wouldn't feel grateful. The trouble was that though Ruby was generous she was starting to behave like a toff. In winter she'd buy woollen suits and in summer she'd buy linen suits, and gloves, and even a string of pearls, which she'd wear in the middle of the day. And high heeled shoes, which Mum had an aversion to.

'Prancing round my kitchen on stilts,' Mum would say after Ruby had come round for a cup of tea. 'Grinding her heels into my lino.'

It wasn't that Ruby put on side, it was just that she sort of oozed confidence. She started taking it on herself to make plans for us all and to organise us all and tell us what we should be doing and what we shouldn't be doing. And of course that only made Mum fiercer.

One day she got so fed up with Ruby and Frank she even stuck up for Fag. That was really something out of the book.

It was of a Sunday afternoon. We'd been visiting Jimmie's grave and Mum had been pottering round a bit, like she always did, pulling out weeds and putting flowers in an old jam jar and that. And she said what she always said.

'When I'm six feet under I don't want any of youse coming here and weeping over my grave.'

Well afterwards we all got back in the car and Frank was just starting to drive us out of the cemetery into Linwood Avenue when Fag started fiddling with the car door handle, just sort of twisting it backwards and forwards the way she always fidgeted with things.

'Don't do that,' Frank said. 'The door might fly open.'

Fag didn't seem to hear him, she just kept twisting it backwards and forwards.

Frank leaned back and gave her a light smack on the hand.

'Don't do that,' he said. 'It's dangerous.'

Mum took offence.

'Don't you lay fingers on my kids, Frank Morgan,' she said. 'Just cause yer making money and think yer sitting pretty yer got no rights over my kids, and let me tell you . . .'

And her jaw was away wagging.

Before Frank had a chance to say anything to quiet Mum down, as no doubt he would of, cause he was a really easy going joker, Ruby turned round.

'I won't have you talking that way to Frank, Mum. I won't have anybody talk to him that way,' she said. 'If you think he's in the wrong you can go on thinking it, I don't care, but you can keep your mouth shut. Frank's my husband and I'm sticking by him.'

Mum opened her mouth. Then shut it, and kept it shut.

Till we got back home.

'That bloody Ruby,' she said after Frank and Ruby had dropped us off and driven away down Moorhouse Avenue. 'Gitting so bloody high and mighty she wouldn't show a blind widow a short cut to the dunny. She's so far up her nose she can't see the bloody ground.'

We heard about it for hours.

'Trouble with working people,' Mum said, 'is the minute they git themselves one step up the ladder they forgit they was ever down at the bottom.'

Fag

Though Ginnie was clever at school, she wasn't up to me. She was sort of plodding and pedestrian and literal, she was good at 'getting the answer' when 'the answer' was something you just got by memorising or adding or subtracting. But she didn't have the extra something I knew I had, the extra bit of flash and sparkle, that extra thing that meant I'd end up a movie star or a writer or a millionaire. I was brilliant, that was what I was. I was going to make them sit up and listen. Ginnie would do all right, she'd end up being a – well, a clerk, or a typist, or perhaps she'd even turn out a schoolteacher. But my future was going to be written on a wider page than that.

'Daphne de Feron, the celebrated novelist, put her lips to a daiquiri and smiled while our correspondent began his inquiries by asking, "What is your opinion, Miss de Feron, of . . .?"'

Halfway through the second term in our first year at Phillipstown we were called to the headmaster's office.

The door screamed at us as we crept into a big square room. In the middle sat 'the Head', with his puffy white fingers knotted on a shiny desk.

'Janet and Daphne Feron?'

'Yes, sir.'

We were terrified, of course, wondering what we were supposed to have done.

'Splendid,' he boomed.

He was the first person to ever tell us we were splendid for being Janet and Daphne Feron.

'Miss Blight is so pleased with your progress,' he said, 'she has proposed that you be promoted instantly to Standard Four, without completing the rest of the year's work in Standard Three.'

Well of course we were over the moon. Though in some ways more terrified than when we'd first seen him sitting there with his puffy fingers on the desk. Would we be able to keep our end up among the big kids in Standard Four? Wouldn't we just end up struggling nonentities somewhere near the bottom of the class?

But Miss Blight was 'so pleased'.

Somebody had recognised us for what we were.

Cinderellas, goose maidens . . .

So we spent the second half of the year in Standard Four, and though we had to struggle a bit at first, we soon started getting 'good marks' and by the end of the year we were right up there with the smartest kids in the class. Success, fame, wealth rushing to embrace us.

Then came Standard Five and Six, two years when our delusions got more unreal than ever, two years under the tutelage of the famous Miss Lightowler.

When we first heard we were going to join Miss Lightowler's class we felt a bit scared. She had the reputation of being the most intellectual person in the school, very clever and very hard. And because Ginnie and I had got used to the usual type of teacher, the usual sort of bossy, blundering bully, we felt nervous, we didn't want to expose ourselves to somebody we might actually feel obliged to admire. Looking down on a teacher was a way of giving ourselves a sort of dignity. Looking up to a teacher – well we weren't so sure about that.

Ginnie actually cried after our first day in Standard Five.

'I can't stand it,' she said. 'She seems to see right through my head.'

Miss Lightowler really was a paragon. Miss Lightowler *believed.* She believed in education, she believed in language, she believed that working class girls could be lifted from the slumland of Phillipstown and she believed that they should be trained to see themselves not just as future wives and mothers but as 'career women', women who could be useful, creative, intelligent. Nurses, secretaries, educators, artists. And she believed that the way to do it was to be 'hard but fair', to get girls grinding away not just at the 'syllabus' but also to work on their imaginations.

For Ginnie and I this was something new. We'd listened to Mum, we'd listened to aunty Aggie, but we'd never heard anybody ever say that work could be satisfying.

And more than that, Miss Lightowler seemed to be hinting that work could even be better than getting married, that it could make a girl happier and more satisfied than marriage, that girls could do what Miss Lightowler had done, forget about men. We already knew from our observations of Mum that life without men was possible, but nobody had ever told us it might actually be something desirable, something you might go out of your way to find.

'So that woman Lightowler is teaching youse, is she?' Mum commented at the end of our first day. 'That bluestocking bitch.'

But there was a faint hint of respect in the way Mum called her a bitch, so Ginnie and I got more interested still.

Though also a bit mixed up, because we knew for a fact that Miss Lightowler's stockings were actually a very thick brown lisle, or occasionally battleship grey, never blue.

She was a big, imposing woman, Miss Lightowler, a person who liked to fix us with very stern eyes. She was the sort of person who might say, 'I have no nonsense about me', but never in fact did say it because she had so little nonsense she didn't even need to. No nonsense, which of course with our Standard Five sophistication we knew was an example of two negatives cancelling each other out to mean 'sense'. And that was what Miss Lightowler was all about. Sense. Order. Knowledge. Truth. A big woman, tall and wide, grey hair in a bun, shining glasses on a blunt nose.

Within a week we were meeting her at the bus and vying for the honour of carrying her briefcase to the classroom.

'Music is my only passion!' she cried to us one afternoon in autumn when a norwester was filling the classroom with hot yellow air.

'Pure form, pure symbol,' she told us.

She started explaining to us the basis of music in mathematics.

'Music isn't like words,' she said. 'Music is never narrative, never pictorial. You must never be literal about music but nor must you be romantic. What you must be is emotional. Music is the most beautiful and the least meaningful thing we have.'

Now I didn't quite get all that, and I wasn't too sure that I liked what I did get, but Miss Lightowler was so carried away that in the end I just sat back and let her take over.

'Pure form, pure symbol,' she said again.

That autumn the popular songs we were listening to at home

on our second hand radio were all about love and kisses. The rhythm was 'swing'.

Miss Lightowler didn't mean swing, of course, she meant Schumann and Schubert and Brahms, Liszt and Chopin and Rachmaninov. She taught us the proper way to listen to music, she called it 'music appreciation'. She'd put a portable gramophone on her desk and the person who was in her good books for the day would be allowed the privilege of choosing a record from a wood and brass record case. Inside the record case there'd be a green velvet cloth. The favourite of the day would slide a record onto the velvet cloth and carry it across to the gramophone, where Miss Lightowler would take command. She'd slip the record onto the turntable and turn the switch.

'Heads down!' she'd cry.

We'd bend our heads over the desks, ready to listen, ready to 'appreciate'.

'What instrument has just taken up the melody, Daphne Feron?'

'The flute, Miss Lightowler.'

'Very good.'

Miss Lightowler was active outside school in what she called 'musical circles'. She was on a committee that organised subscription concerts and entertained visiting musicians. Like when Jascha Heifetz came to give a violin recital in the Theatre Royal.

'We shall need special invitation cards,' she said, 'to be presented to our patrons. Not job printed cards; we must execute cards for them by hand. The four with the neatest hands shall perform the task.'

Ginnie and I were among the elect four.

We were solemnly presented with pots of indian ink and a little stack of yellow cards, and then we spent an hour hunched over our desks, scratching black spidery words onto the cards.

'Excellent,' said Miss Lightowler.

Then she wanted props for the stage.

'The committee hopes to fill the stage with flowers,' she said. 'If any of you can assist, the committee will be very grateful, but more to the point the great artiste himself may be inspired to new heights of virtuosity.'

'The jardinières,' I whispered to Ginnie.

'Daphne Feron,' said Miss Lightowler. 'We either speak out clearly and honestly, or we do not speak at all.'

'Yes, Miss Lightowler,' I said.

After school, finding Mum in the kitchen on the yellow chair, I started my campaign.

'Mum can we borrow your jardinières to put on the stage for Jascha Heifetz?'

'No.'

But of course Mum always said 'no' to anything, half the time it was just to give herself time to think, so I wasn't particularly disappointed. I asked her again after tea, then again next morning, and so on. At first all I got was the same 'no', sort of blank and aggressive. Then she started to get irritated; once she let fly at me with the jam spoon. But even Mum could be worn down. Two or three days later, when her baking had gone well and she'd just opened the pudding bag to show off a big puffy white dominion pudding, I asked her again.

'You could talk yer way out of yer own bloody grave,' she said. 'Take the bloody jardinnies for all I bloody care and while yer at it take my whole bloody house, I'm sick of hearing about Jascha bloody Heifetz.'

So Ginnie carried one jardinière and I carried the other, and a member of the committee picked them up from school and took them off to the Theatre Royal.

On the night of the recital we were given free seats. We dressed up in our navy blue school gym frocks and walked up to town through a beautiful warm evening, the air sort of velvety and sparkling with neon and electricity. When we got to the theatre we stopped for a moment to look at the crowd. They seemed sort of impossibly elegant, all shimmering and gleaming and glowing, laughing and chattering and waving to one another.

'Things are starting to come true,' I said.

I don't actually remember the music, all I remember is the 'occa-sion', as people called it. Sitting amidst fairies and princesses. Light and music and sequins and lamé under chandeliers, velvet cur-tains, an enormous high ceiling. And the ceiling was painted, the most wonderful thing I'd ever seen outside the movies, a huge fresco of Shakespearean heroes and heroines all sort of cavorting in greenery and drifting clouds.

The world was doubly glamorous at that time because of the war. Not the boring old 'Great War' but a new war, a modern war, a war of our own.

We'd grown up hearing Mum give us our catechism about war.

'The toffs have their fun playing soldier,' Mum would say. 'But who gets left carrying the can? Well we know the answer to that without asking.'

Mum had always made us go to the Anzac parade when we were kids. She'd 'tidy us up' and she'd march us all out the door. We'd walk across the railway yards into town to High Street. We'd find a possy in the midst of all the rest of the huge black gloomy crowd, and we'd watch the war veterans march past. Men who'd been gassed, men bent up in wheelchairs, men who were blind, holding white sticks while little kids led them along. Uncle Jim Hay would stumble past with the rest of them and give us a wave. But we hated it. We'd always end up crying, Hock and Peggy and Ginnie and Tots and I.

Afterwards uncle Jim Hay would drop in for a cup of tea. And he'd talk about the war.

'All the people who went away,' Mum would say. 'And where are half of them now? Sunnyside or six foot under. And what was it for? Nothing.'

But Ginnie and I knew better than Mum, we'd been listening to our teachers and the radio and the Movietone news, so we got the story right.

'It was to make the world safe for democracy Mum,' we said. 'It was a war to end war. It was to defend civilisation against barbarism. It was to safeguard our homes and our way of life.'

You can imagine how well that went down.

But we didn't care any more what Mum said or what she thought about things. We knew that she knew nothing, or next to nothing, about all the big things in life. She might know the 'right' way to hang shirts on a clothesline, and she might know how to save on butter when it came to making scones, but as far as war and music and literature and that went, well Mum just wasn't in it.

So we stopped talking about the war to her. We talked about it among ourselves.

'It's like Scarlett and Ashley and Rhett isn't it?' Doreen Flett said all excited the day after the Labour government declared war. 'I can't wait till the film comes out.'

Ginnie and I let her rabbit on.

'It's real exciting,' she said. 'Gee I hope them Nazis don't drop bombs on us.'

Ginnie and I had one brief moment of doubt.

'WAR DECLARED ON GERMANY.'

We read those big black words wired down on a newspaper placard outside a dairy on Moorhouse Avenue. We both burst into tears. We didn't know why, but we cried and cried and cried.

'Too bloody late to blub,' Mum snapped as we came through the kitchen door.

And she was right, of course, it was too late to blub. But next morning things seemed different, we didn't feel like blubbing; the war was too exciting and Doreen Flett was right, it was Scarlett and Ashley and Rhett all over again. And we didn't even have to wait long till the film came out. *Gone With the Wind* appeared on the screen almost at the same time as the first newsreels of World War Two. Soon their luminous images merged and met, flickering and gleaming. Images prepared for us ever since we first sat down with a 'true love' magazine, first heard a teacher order us to 'form a queue', first sighed about Garbo or swooned about Jesus.

The South in danger! The bombardment of Atlanta, the radio playing swing, the barbecue at Twelve Oaks, the jardinières sprouting rubber plants on the stage of the Theatre Royal. Our gracious courtly civilisation of white columned mansions, veils of tulle and beautiful old lace, 'white muslin the universal costume', Lady Barker and the young Phillips ladies and the guests from the Stevenson-Merbrook wedding 'very fresh and nice' as they drifted across lawns and carriage drives. The red earth of Tara, the red rust of Phillipstown.

Janet and Daphne de Feron, the belles of old Phillips Town, eyes moist with tears and excitement and fear, lips parting breathlessly with passion and hope.

'Janet and Daphne Feron,' Miss Lightowler said one afternoon at the end of Civics, 'and Ethel McWhirter and Nola Brass, I want you to stay behind when the rest of the class is dismissed.'

Ginnie and I were instantly terrified.

'Some friends of mine,' Miss Lightowler told us after the other kids had left the room, 'are fortunate enough to enjoy the comforts of a large house on Cashmere. Their name is Grace. It is, of course, a name well known in Canterbury. Mr Grace is a barrister and solicitor. Mrs Grace is prominent in several well known city charities. They have offered to let four well conducted girls from my class spend a weekend with them. They live in a manner which to you girls may seem somewhat opulent, but you are my most intelligent pupils and will, I am sure, rise to the occasion.'

Ginnie and I gabbled excitedly to one another all the way home.

'And fancy her saying we're her most intelligent pupils,' Ginnie said.

'Well of course,' I said.

It was a battle getting Mum to agree.

'No sense sticking yer nose in butter if yer going to have to eat dripping the rest of yer life,' she said, drawing breath for a long oration. 'No sense gitting fancy ideas from fancy fat tarts like old lady kiss-me-bum Grace. No sense . . .' Etcetera etcetera etcetera.

But in the end, after a week or so of wheedling:

'Oh all right then. Go and make fools of yourselves and see if I bloody care.'

On a cold still morning a big black Rover rumbled us away from Phillipstown to Cashmere.

It was too overwhelming, that weekend with the Graces. I can't seem to picture it very well in my head. All I seem to be able to remember is a big white house, a great big place surrounded by bare wintry trees, bare black branches reaching out into the air, sort of grasping at a cold blue sky.

It was the movies, it was Lady Barker, it was Tara and Twelve Oaks there was no doubt about it. There was a drawing room,

117

and a dining room, and a 'music room', and a library. Big high pale rooms where we crept around, whispering. There was a silver cigar box on a polished table. There were dragons and lotus flowers twining up the necks of glazed vases. There were golden mirrors reflecting images of us back at ourselves as we stumbled about from one room to the other, clumsy and shabby and awkward and looking forward to ecstasy.

Mrs Grace was 'very kind', very powerfully kind, very overwhelming and solicitous and oppressive.

'We hope you'll make yourselves absolutely at home, my dears,' she said. And she creased her powdered face at us, and ogled her eyes. They were a little bit fishlike, she ogled them round the room.

Mr Grace was rather vague and absent, though he used a lot of courteous words.

'Delighted to have you as our guests,' he murmured at the dinner table on Friday evening as Ginnie and I sat staring in terror at what looked like a set of surgical instruments laid out on the stiff white linen in front of us.

Ecstasy was slow in coming.

'*That's* for thinking you can make a fool of me,' a maid said next morning as she gave Ginnie and I a sudden sharp pinch in the neck.

'Get back to the gutter you came from,' she hissed.

Then she walked away, her grey and white uniform making neat crisp noises.

The other two girls didn't feel much happier.

'I hate it,' Ethel said.

'I want to go home,' Nola said.

'You're just being morbid,' I said. 'It's a dream come true, this place. The Graces must be really rich.'

But Ginnie and Ethel and Nola weren't convinced.

That night, while the Graces were in the dining room 'entertaining' some dinner guests, Ginnie and I stood on a balcony looking out into the night. We could see the lights of South Christchurch scattered across a sort of black emptiness.

'I'm homesick. I want to go home,' Ginnie said.

'That dump down there isn't our home,' I said. 'You think Mum cares about you being homesick? She'll be sitting in the yellow chair down there by the gas works where that cloud of smoke's blocking out the lights. She'll be sitting there bitching and nagging and complaining. And if you think that dump down there is home you're stupid.'

At school next week, back down on the flat in Phillipstown, Ginnie and I kept our mouths shut about the angry maid and the way the reflections in the mirrors had seemed to make fun of us. Instead we got busy fitting the weekend into our catalogue of fantasy, snipping out the best bits and gluing them in between all our other pictures of beauty and love.

'You should of seen the music room at the Graces,' Ginnie kept saying to bored and envious classmates. 'The walls was covered with yellow silk.'

But we felt a faint sort of dismay.

World War Two was disappointing too. It still seemed exciting, but the excitement got a bit complicated.

The soldiers, for example. At first it was something that took your breath away, seeing packs of slouching pimply South Christchurch boys get whisked off to army camps and come back smart young emissaries of death. Not far from us, on the rugby field at Lancaster Park, an army camp was set up and soon thousands of soldiers were lined up there in tents between the grandstands. All the best looking young jokers in Phillipstown seemed to be joining the army. Two of the Coker boys from next door went into camp, and three of 'them Catholic dogs' from the O'Neill family on the other side went into camp too.

One day our brother Lindsay came home early in the afternoon.

'I've chucked me apprenticeship Mum,' he said. 'Went and joined up.'

Mum clenched her fists over the kitchen sink so tight her knuckles turned white.

'Yer a stupid little fool,' she said.

Then she walked into the 'dining room' and wouldn't talk to him again.

But Ginnie and I thought he looked really nifty in his uniform, we were really proud of him. We started skiting about 'our brother Lindsay' when Doreen Flett and the rest of them started going on about their brothers. And sometimes when the soldiers came marching out of Lancaster Park past the school, Ginnie and I would look at the rows of young jokers in khaki and see him.

'Lindsay!' we'd call out. 'Give em hell, Lindsay.'

He'd flash a grin at us from under his khaki hat.

Miss Lightowler was very patriotic; she was like all the teachers when it came to war, very 'loyal' and determined and indignant.

'A war for democracy,' she told us.

Mind you it was a bit tricky sometimes, sometimes Ginnie and I couldn't quite get it straight. A war for democracy: yes, that was true, all the important people kept saying that so it must be true. But it was hard to reconcile with what they also kept telling us about 'defending the King and Queen' and 'defending the Empire' and that, because you didn't have to be too smart to see that kings and queens didn't fit in all that well with democracy. And the Empire bit was even trickier. The word 'Empire' meant white people in Christchurch and Cape Town and London bossing round black people in India and Africa. It sounded more like Scarlett O'Hara and slaves and 'the red earth of Tara' than democracy and freedom and the rest of it. But no doubt our teachers knew how to reconcile these things, because right from our earliest school days the words 'Empire' and 'King' and 'democracy' had been more or less interchangeable – they meant the same thing.

So that was all right. It was tricky to work it out, but Ginnie and I felt all right about it in the end. It was a 'just war', Miss Lightowler told us. Another 'war for peace'.

But that didn't stop us feeling it wasn't as exciting as we'd thought it would be. France might fall and Norway might crumble and Poland right from the start had been bombed into dust, but there wasn't much we could do about it, Janet and Daphne de Feron, the belles of Old Phillips Town. Our job was to do nothing, the usual job of females in war. Do nothing. Hang around. Wait.

'It'll probably get more exciting later on,' we said to one another after the Battle of Dunkirk.

It galled us that none of our brothers were 'going away' to 'do their bit' and provide us with some long distance glamour.

Lindsay was a corporal, it was true, but he was in something mysteriously called 'Supply' and ended up spending most of his war in South Christchurch. Sometimes he even turned up at Moorhouse Avenue for Sunday dinner. So that was a bit disillusioning. Instead of hurling hand grenades and digging foxholes in North Africa, he was placidly chewing mutton in our kitchen while Mum reefed off at him from the yellow chair.

Eddie and Jock were even more useless. They were really scared by the war, they didn't want to go. When in the end the Labour government started calling everybody up, Eddie and Jock made sure the military doctors found they were 'unfit'. It turned out their legs were badly varicosed like Mum's, and their feet were flat, and so on, and so forth. So Jock went back to Kaikoura and Eddie joined the Home Guard.

The other boys were too young to join up and in any case didn't exactly hand out prizes when Ginnie and I came along talking about 'a war for democracy'.

'Do you want to go into the army or the air force or the navy when you get old enough?' we asked Bobsie.

'I wanna go in the army,' he said. 'The Salvation Army.'

Sammie snickered and gave him a nudge.

So we felt humiliated at school, our brothers weren't 'doing their bit'. And when some of the other kids' brothers started getting killed and that, well it was too much for Ginnie and I to bear.

The first person in our class to 'lose a loved one' was Doreen Flett. She came to school one morning all weepy.

'It was very brave of you to come to school, Doreen,' Miss Lightowler said. 'But there are times when we can be too brave. I think you should go quietly back home again. But first we'll bow our heads in silence for a minute and think of your brother. Silence class. Think of Doreen's brother who gave his life for us.'

'Jesus the only begotten son of God, who gave his life that we shall live,' I thought grimly pursing my lips and bowing my head. It was like a church, it was like 'music appreciation', but instead of Schumann or the Holy Trinity it was patriotism and the Empire.

I sneaked a look up to the front of the class where I could see Doreen standing, tears smudged over her face, straw coloured braids over her forehead.

'Ooh,' she seemed to be thinking. 'I'm important.'

So it looked as though World War Two wasn't necessarily going to be the best thing since sliced bread.

PART THREE

7

Working girls

Fag

One afternoon late in our Standard Six year I waited behind in the classroom till Ginnie and the others had all gone, then I went up to Miss Lightowler.

'I want to go to high school next year, Miss Lightowler,' I said. 'I want to learn languages and that. I'm going to be a novelist.'

The minute I said it I felt this horrible sinking feeling in my stomach, as though by putting my dream in words I'd shown myself how impossible it was.

Miss Lightowler didn't seem to notice anything very particular about my feelings. She just gave me a quick glance then looked back at her papers.

'Nonsense,' she said.

But I didn't give in straight away.

'I think there's something a bit special about me, Miss Lightowler,' I said. 'I think I need to be a writer.'

'Don't be silly, Daphne,' she said, not even looking at me again. 'You'll go to Tech and you'll be a typist. You've got a good command of words, you've got nimble fingers. It'll be no trouble for you to pick up typing and shorthand. There's no reason why someday you shouldn't end up somebody's secretary.'

The light in the room was very glaring at the end of the day. I had to screw up my eyes against it, a sharp white sunlight reflected off iron roofs.

'I don't want to be somebody's anything, Miss Lightowler,' I said. 'I want to be somebody myself.'

Well she must have heard the note of desperation, because she looked up at me, a dry sort of look, and I think I saw a little bit of sympathy in it, though it was mostly just dry, very adult and sure.

'You'll get more satisfaction out of a skill than any number of fantasies, Daphne,' she said. 'You'll find as you grow older that the best thing about fantasies is that they're not real.'

'Talking stupid riddles like I was a stupid kid,' I said to Ginnie on our way back home. 'Stupid dried out old tart. What would she know about anything?'

Then I shut up. I was a bit shocked at myself.

Ginnie was a bit shocked too, but didn't say anything.

'Well I'll show her,' I said. 'Wait till I'm rich and famous.'

A couple of days later the Japanese attacked Pearl Harbour.

'The Japs want to be on top,' Mum said. 'And the Yanks want to be on top. And the only difference is the Yanks are gonna do it.'

But the battles in Asia and the battles in Europe and all the big questions about where I was going and what I was going to do and what it was all about soon got pushed into the background by the need to tackle Mum. While I made airy assertions about going to high school and being a writer, Mum had different ideas. As far as she was concerned I was going to leave school at the end of the year and get a job in a factory. All the other girls had done that; nobody in the family had ever gone to high school. So there was going to be a fight.

I waited till the afternoon Ginnie and I came home with our school reports. Ginnie had an A for mathematics and a lot of Bs for the other subjects. I had a C for mathematics and science and an A for everything else.

'Hmph,' Mum said after she'd flicked through them. 'Now we'd better do something about gitting youse a job.'

'I want to go to Tech next year, Mum,' I said. 'Miss Lightowler says I should.'

I didn't bother to lead up to it gently – there didn't seem much point since I knew what Mum's reaction would be.

'Over my dead bloody body,' she said. 'You've wasted enough time already, it's time to git out and do something useful for a change. Me and Eddie and the rest of them have been giving yer free board and lodgings long enough, my lady, it's time to start

126

pulling yer oar. This isn't a charity, it's a family.'

But that evening while Ginnie and I lay side by side in bed complaining about the world we heard a woman's heels click across the verandah. Then a knock on the front door. Then a voice.

'Mrs Feron?'

'What's it to yer?'

'I'm Miss Lightowler. I've come to have a little talk with you about Daphne.'

We heard the front door shut and two sets of feet, Mum's in old slippers and Miss Lightowler's in hard heels, go down the passage past our door.

Ginnie and I whispered to one another till we heard the feet go back up the passage, the front door open, Mum mutter something, and Miss Lightowler say,

'Thank you so much, Mrs Feron. I'm glad we see eye to eye. Good evening.'

The heels clicked briskly off the verandah.

Ginnie and I leapt out of bed and found Mum standing in the passage with her chin in the crook of her hand, stroking her jaw.

'She says a year or two at Tech and you could be a first rate typist. I said where's the money to come from, and she said if I'll support you another couple of years you'll come out of it being able to earn good money. I said so I have to keep feeding you like a kid just so in the end you can go out and have money to spend on nylon stockings for yerself. And she said . . .'

The upshot was that Mum had been talked into saying yes.

'But you'll bloody well git yourself a job over the holidays, madam,' she wound up, 'because I'm telling you now I don't intend to be out of pocket for you while you loll round the place with yer nose in a book. And I don't intend to spend a penny on a new uniform for you either.'

Monday morning I started work at a hosiery mill.

It was Lane Walker Rudkins, a factory in Addington. It seemed a monstrous place to me that morning as I walked along Montreal Street and saw it sort of crouching there in wait for me. Then when I got inside there were lights everywhere, long glaring neon lights. And noise, everywhere noise.

My job was in the packing room. There were about six hundred people working in that factory and over a hundred of them were in the packing room, a great big room like an aeroplane hangar. Up above the workshop floor were lights hanging down on metal frames, pipes and wires, brackets, and snaking rubber hoses. Down on the shop floor were benches and conveyor belts and machines. And *noise* and *movement* and *heat*.

I thought I was going mad. It was like nothing I'd ever seen before.

The forewoman put me at a table, a long table, with ten or twelve other girls in a row folding underpants into cellophane packets. A moving belt took the packets down the line to the end of the bench.

'Your job's to seal the packets,' the forewoman said.

She showed me a sort of soldering iron.

'Be careful you don't press it down too long,' the forewoman said. 'It burns a hole. And be careful you don't take it off too quick, or it won't be sealed.'

I started to work.

Lifting the handle, sliding in a packet, pressing the handle.

Hiss, hiss.

A hot rubbery smell, a little curl of white smoke.

Lifting the handle again, sliding out the packet, sliding in another packet, pressing the handle.

Hiss, hiss.

Another hot rubbery smell, another little curl of white smoke.

And on and on. Four seconds for each packet of underpants. 'A good worker can cut it down to two and a half,' the forewoman told me. Thirteen hundred and fifty packets of underpants before morning tea. Six thousand four hundred and fifty packets of underpants a day. Thirty-five thousand four hundred and seventy-five packets of underpants a week.

When it came to morning tea I went down to the toilets and sat on the dunny and thought, I'll stick it, I'll stick it.

When the lunch break came it seemed incredible that the day was only halfway through. I felt as though I'd been living in a nightmare for days, but I was only halfway through the first day

128

and the whole afternoon was still ahead of me.

The other girls shrieked at one another about boyfriends and lipstick and movies, and stuffed themselves with cakes and soft drinks.

'How yer gitting on with the soldering?' one of them said to me.

'It's frightful,' I said.

Which was a mistake, of course.

The girl stared at me for a minute.

'Fraightful is it?' she said. 'Think it's fraightful do yer?'

She walked away to join two or three other girls in a corner. They turned to look at me and started screaming with laughter.

In a matter of days I was a social pariah.

'That's Lady Daphne Feron,' they said when a new girl came on our table. 'Yer wouldn't know what piss bucket she was brought up in if yer just listened to her talk.'

The more they picked on me the harder I found it to be natural with them. In the end I stopped trying. I ignored them, I hid from them, I spent every morning and afternoon tea break sitting alone in the toilets, and every lunch time I took sandwiches wrapped in newspaper and sat outside on the street alone.

'Those girls are so trivial and stupid and dirty,' I said to Ginnie. 'Fancy working in a madhouse like that. I'm getting out of there as soon as I can.'

But Ginnie didn't seem to like me much when I talked like that.

'They're just ordinary working girls like us,' Ginnie said. 'You aren't making the effort to get to know them.'

So I shut up.

Of a morning I'd sit down at the machine and feel incredulous that I was going to have to go through another day like the one before, and then another one after that . . .

Lifting the handle, sliding in a packet, pressing the handle, lifting the handle, sliding out the packet, sliding in another packet, pressing the handle . . .

The machines roaring and hissing, the conveyor belts rumbling, the loudspeaker system calling up forewomen and managers, and announcing the prize winners in the works lottery.

I spent a lot of time thinking about my pay, how I'd be asked to walk along to the offices, which would be all gleaming and airy and clean, and inside them would be the office staff busy with their typewriters and I'd ask for my wages and I'd be handed a pay packet and the office girl who gave it to me would think I was just an ordinary worker, when in fact one day I was going to be an office worker like her, in high heeled shoes and a smart tailored suit and fingers with long lacquered nails.

'Them bitches in the office,' the other girls in the packing section said. 'Think they're a race apart.'

In the end our pay packets were brought to us by the fore-woman. She came to our table and handed them out to us. We had to sign for them, then they were ours.

Ten shillings, that was the wage for my first week. Ten shillings, which I handed across to Mum. She opened it, counted the money, and gave me a shilling.

'That's for you to spend as you like,' she said.

I was quite excited about that; I'd expected Mum to take it all and here she was giving me something back. It almost seemed like a gift.

'That's for you to spend as you like.'

I'd never heard Mum say anything like that to me before, it was as though she was recognising my new status. A worker. An adult.

I spent the shilling on chocolates for Mum, which she took from me the usual way.

'What yer trying to crawl round me for?'

Fag

By the time I started my 'Commercial' course at Christchurch Technical High School I was full of hope again, optimistic, looking forward to the years ahead when I'd learn new skills and go out into the world and sit in an office like the typists at Lane Walker Rudkins. One day I'd become a personal secretary, as Miss Lightowler had said I might, and my boss would fall in love with me, and I'd find myself living in a big house on Cashmere, with maids who wouldn't be able to pinch me.

I'd write novels.

Once or twice I had visions of even going to university. I knew about the university. I knew it was a big grey stone place near the museum, and I'd seen girls in tweed and linen walking in and out of it. They looked like they were at least fifteen rungs higher up the social scale than me, but sometimes I thought, well I could do that, I could go there. I've got the brains.

Not realising that the only academic future for me after I'd been taught to type and take shorthand in a 'Commercial' course at Tech was to graduate into what one of our teachers called:

'The great school of free enterprise'.

As far as I was concerned even Tech was a 'great school'. As I walked into the main entrance off Barbadoes Street I thought it looked wonderful and I felt so proud of myself, the first Feron ever to go to high school. I looked round for the assembly hall and found it, a huge brick building with a flight of wide steps soaring up to it. And as I filed up there with the other students it seemed to me that I was a young intellectual, I pretended my gym frock was an academic gown and I was walking into the Great Hall of Canterbury College. A prefect showed me where to sit. I sat. Up in front of me I saw a stage, big and empty and important. Some doors were flung open. A row of teachers came up the aisle, parading through the hall in their gowns, the headmaster leading them up onto the stage.

Gee, I thought. It's better than Christmas.

The assembly was silly, of course, the headmaster talked and we sang hymns, and the hymns were ridiculous and the headmaster said stupid things. The whole business seemed quite strange really, very tight and controlled and regimented. But I liked it. It was nice to be bored and ordered about because it seemed to make me part of something real, something that was done because it was supposed to be done. And after a while even the boredom became marvellous, it became a sort of transcendental boredom as my legs went numb and my jaw started aching with suppressed yawns.

I belong to all this, I thought. It's wonderful.

131

My form mistress was Miss Shepherd. She was a friend of Miss Lightowler's and like Miss Lightowler believed in education for girls. She was tall and thin and wiry, and full of confidence and energy.

'Class,' she said, 'I expect nothing but the best from you this year. You're the top Commercial class, and I expect top grade work.'

It was queer being there without Ginnie.

I'm lonely, I thought. They'll all make fun of me.

But the girls in the class weren't like factory girls, they were friendly and serious and quiet. One of them singled me out.

'I'm Nancy Wand,' she said. 'I'm from Spreydon.'

Soon we were cobbers, Nancy and I. We sat together in class and she invited me to go to her place after school and have afternoon tea with her mother. One day I went. Mrs Wand turned out to be a kind sort of person who looked like Aunt Pittypat in *Gone With the Wind*.

Her house was lovely too, at least I thought it was. A little bungalow full of nice things, armchairs and rugs and knicknacks. Mrs Wand brought afternoon tea on a shellac tray heaped high with scones and jam sponge. And after a while Mr. Wand turned up.

'Nice to meet you,' he said. 'Heard a lot about you from Nancy.'

Which made me sort of glow inside.

A real little home, I thought. Just like in the stories.

Mr Wand worked behind the counter at some tearooms in Colombo Street. He got a good wage and he and Mrs Wand owned the bungalow. Nancy looked down on them a bit though.

'The trouble with Mum and Dad,' she said one day, 'is they don't know how far up you can go. All they can see is the next layer up above them. They think that's as far as it goes. But I want to get right to the top.'

She wrote wonderful stories, her stories were the ones that were read out in the class because the teacher approved of them. They were what Miss Shepherd called 'imaginative', like mine, but unlike mine they stuck to all the rules about grammar. Nancy knew how to keep her words in a cage and at the same time make them seem to prowl around inside it, growling and showing their teeth.

She was pretty too, with lovely dark hair.

So I had a 'best friend'. She was no Ginnie, but in some ways she was better than Ginnie; she was one of the cleverest and prettiest and most well off girls in the class.

But while things went well at school, there was a fight to the death at home. Mum nagged me all year. How much it was costing her to keep me, how it was time I started doing my share, how she missed the money I'd been getting from Lane Walker Rudkins. How I was putting on airs.

'Smarming up to schoolmarms,' she'd say. 'No bloody use to anyone.'

Sometimes Mum seemed really beside herself, and she'd go white in the face, screaming with rage.

'Yer the laziest bloody bitch from here to the Club bloody Hotel,' she'd say. 'Think we've got nothing better to do than find money to keep you in books. Think we should be bloody shitting ourselves with thanks if you so much as bloody talk to us.'

One thing that interested me was that I didn't feel unhappy about that sort of thing any more, I just felt calm and hard and cold.

One day during a visit at Nancy's her father came home early from work and gave me some butter left over from the tearooms.

'Might find some use for this at your place,' he said.

Butter was being rationed, Mum was desperate for it, so when I got home I dumped it on the kitchen bench.

Mum picked at the paper suspiciously.

'Butter,' she said. 'More than two pound by the look of it. And where did you get this, madam? Been flogging it I suppose so the bloody flatfeet will start banging on the door making trouble for us all cause a lazy bloody tart wants to crawl round me so I won't give her the decent bloody hiding she needs.'

I picked up the butter, walked over to the rubbish tin, and threw it in.

I'd never seen Mum look shocked before and it was something worth waiting for. Her jaw just seemed to hit the floor.

'Good butter,' she said struggling for words. 'Good bloody butter.'

She started scrambling into the rubbish tin.

'Can't believe me bloody eyes,' she said, clutching the butter to her bosom once she'd got it out of the tin. 'Must think we're bloody made of money, throwing good butter away like it was last week's jerry can. Must think we can eat dirt for bread and drink piss for beer, throwing away good butter. She must . . .'

By the end of the year Mum and I were at such daggers drawn there was no hope asking her to let me stay on a second year at Tech.

'Right,' she said on the last day of school. 'Come Monday yer to find yourself a job.'

I tried to fight her on grounds I thought she might understand.

'I won't be able to get a good job if I don't go back another year,' I said. 'My shorthand and typing aren't good enough yet. If I wait another year I'll be able to get better money.'

It was no good. Mum didn't understand, or didn't want to understand.

'Come Monday,' she said, 'yer to find yourself a job.'

Ginnie

I felt really bad at the thought of leaving school. It wasn't that school had been good, it had always been awful – even those last two years with Miss Lightowler. But I felt terrified of going out into the workforce, into a factory. The thought of it was something I dreaded. I pictured a factory as – well, just how it turned out to be, a horrible place, rows and rows of machines, crowds of people, and everybody bossing me. And that's how it was.

It was Ruby who jacked up a job for me.

'There's a clothing place in Lancaster Street,' she said, all sort of brisk the way Ruby always was. 'It belongs to some people I know. They're making uniforms for the war and they want a junior.'

I felt absolutely terrified. And just for that moment I really hated Ruby, I wished the floor would just open up and let her drop through it.

'I want to go to Tech with Fag next year, Mum,' I said. 'I don't want to work in a factory.'

'Jobs are hard to get,' Ruby said. 'When a chance turns up you have to get in and take it.'

'We need more money coming in,' Mum said. 'With Jock and Sadie and that gone I need you bringing something in to help keep us all.'

'And you'll need to take a pair of scissors,' Ruby said. 'When you start there you'll need a pair of scissors.'

So I tried making a fuss about that, cause we didn't have any scissors in the house, Jock had busted the last pair. In the end Mum got fierce.

'Shut up about them bloody scissors,' she said. 'You're starting tomorrow morning and you can borrow some scissors from somebody there.'

Next morning Ruby marched me down into Lancaster Street past the great big Kaiapoi woollen mill and up some brick stairs into a high dark room full of girls and women bent over whirring sewing machines.

'Here's my sister I was telling you about,' Ruby said to a woman. 'She'd like the job and she's ready to start now.'

A few minutes later Ruby was gone and I was all alone in that place. I started to cry again.

'Where's your scissors?' the woman said. 'I thought I told Ruby Morgan about the scissors. Every junior who starts here has to bring her own scissors.'

'I haven't got any, Mrs Eisenbaum,' I said, sniffing and sobbing and not knowing what to do.

Mrs Eisenbaum scowled.

'You'll have to have a pair from out the back then,' she said. 'But you'll be docked sixpence a week to pay for the use of them.'

Then she stalked away.

A forewoman showed me what to do. I had to sit on a stool and trim loose threads off the seams of shirts. Then after trimming the seams off I had to lift up a big iron, a really huge iron

135

it seemed to me, cause I was still just a kid really, and I had to press in the seams and the epaulets on the shirts. I did that all day till my arm ached from lifting up that iron, and my knuckles was sore from the scissors, and my back was aching from being on that stool, cause there was nothing to lean back on. Then at half past four the forewoman came over to me.

'Knock off that now,' she said. 'Next you have to sweep the shop floor.'

An hour later I found myself walking home alone down Moorhouse Avenue, sore and tired and dirty and filthy, and I felt like I was just nothing, and I was howling, the tears just pouring out.

'I'm not going back there, Mum,' I said. 'I don't care what you do to me but I'm not going back there.'

Mum didn't say anything straight away, she just looked at me and I suppose I must of looked like a dog run over in the road, cause for a minute she looked as if she felt sorry for me. And she didn't say anything.

Hock came home then.

'They need a hand at United Footwear,' she said. 'Gloria Hitchings left today, she's got a bun baking at moderate heat so she's heading up north to see if she can find the joker that did it to her.'

'And pigs'll fly,' Peggy said, starting to peel some spuds for tea.

'She was working on the rubbing down machine,' Hock said. 'That's just an unskilled job, Ginnie could do it. I'll take her along tomorrow and jack it up.'

I made myself not think about that. What was a rubbing down machine? It sounded terrifying. But anything had to be better than that place in Lancaster Street.

Next morning Hock dubbed me on her bike to United Footwear, a great big place on FitzGerald Avenue, a big concrete and glass place.

'The most modern footwear factory in Christchurch,' the forewoman told me. 'Three hundred workers all told.'

Her and Hock took me into a work room. There was about forty girls and women there, sitting in lines, waiting for the machines to start running.

136

'This is the machine room,' the forewoman said. 'It's all women in here. Over that dividing wall is the making room, that's where the shoes get put on the lasts. It's all men over there.'

'Cheeky bunch of buggers too,' Hock said.

The forewoman looked sort of disapproving.

'Now,' she said. 'You'll be starting at the bottom, Janet, but there's no reason if you work carefully and pay attention you can't end up a qualified shoe machinist like your sister.'

So that's what there is to look forward to, I thought.

Hock went away and the forewoman took me to the rubbing down machine. It turned out to be a big heavy machine fixed onto the edge of a bench.

'Sit yourself here,' the forewoman said, 'and the belt will bring shoes down to you after the lining machinists have sewed up the linings. When the shoes come to you, pick them up and rub down the backs of the linings.'

So I sat down and started to work.

Well it was what I'd expected, it was horrible and I hated it. It was like when I first started school and everything seemed terrifying. After a few minutes something seemed to go wrong with the machine, and I was too scared to speak up and tell anybody, I just sat there and my eyes filled up with tears.

Then when the machine did get going again it was horrible too, because it was so tiring. It was hard work, really hard work, but boring work too, struggling with that great big juddering machine, rubbing down the backs of shoe linings all day long.

I cried myself to sleep every night. I felt like I was just a machine myself, a machine that had to clock itself in at eight o'clock in the morning and then keep working till clocking out time at quarter to five of an afternoon. And all that time just juddering and juddering my way through shoe linings at the rubbing down machine. Ten minutes break of a morning, half an hour for lunch, ten minutes more in the afternoon. Overtime of a Monday, a bit of a break for tea then working on till eight o'clock.

You had a choice about doing overtime. The first time they offered it to me I turned it down. Last thing I wanted was to be trapped at that machine any longer than I had to.

'Turning down good money,' Hock said.

'Next time there's overtime you make sure you git some,' Mum said. 'Or there'll be trouble.'

So from then on every Monday I stayed at my rubbing down machine, juddering into the night.

Clocking in was something I hated. Each worker had a number, and when you walked in of a morning your number was sticking up. You had to pull on it and clock it in. And if you turned up just a couple of minutes late you lost a whole quarter hour of pay. That used to really nark me, and as I started to make a few cobbers among the other girls we used to talk about it. One day one girl said she was fed up.

'If they're gonna dock me fifteen minutes for being two minutes late,' she said, 'I'm gonna make bloody sure I get my fifteen minutes worth.'

Next day she clocked in exactly fifteen minutes late.

We was all quite impressed by that, and for a week or two if one of us found we was running a bit late of a morning we'd just take our time and make sure we turned up right on quarter past eight. But the bosses found out what was going on. They started docking pay by half an hour if anybody turned up on the quarter hour.

'Trust them,' Hock said. 'They'll always get something out of us for nothing.'

So we gave up.

The trouble was that we was getting such poor money we couldn't afford to lose any of it. When I started at United Footwear I was getting nineteen shillings a week. Then after six months it went up five shillings, then five shillings again after another six months. Most of us in the machine room was only getting half what the men in the making room was getting, and the women who was married and had kids and whose husbands had gone away to the war had a hard time just getting by.

It took me a while to make a few cobbers, cause though all the machinists were really good to me, really helpful and friendly, we didn't have much of a chance to talk. The noise from the machines was too loud for us to be able to talk easy, and we was all under pressure to get as many shoes through as we could. There was a quota system at United Footwear so if you made over a certain number of shoes a day you got a bonus. It wasn't much of a bonus, but most of us was so desperate for that bit extra that we was hunched over our machines all day. But during tea breaks there was a chance to yak. We wasn't allowed to leave our machines, but we was allowed to switch them off, which most of us did. A tea woman would bring the tea and biscuits on a trolley. The tea and biscuits was 'free', the factory paid for them, or at least that's what the forewoman told us, but of course the cost was taken out of our pay. And it was horrible tea, all stewed, you wouldn't pay good money for it if you had a choice. But at least it was warm, something to drink while we talked.

There was lunch time too. We was allowed to leave the work benches at lunch time, though there wasn't a staff cafeteria for us to go to. Usually we went outside and sat in the factory grounds. United Footwear had lovely grounds, beautiful lawns and flower beds and little winding paths and a little fish pond and that. A lot of the factories in Christchurch was like that, they was famous for their gardens and every year there was a competition to see whose was best. United Footwear won the prize two or three times. So that was nice. If it was sunny it was nice sitting on the lawn eating sandwiches we'd brought with us from home. But if it was rainy or cold we'd wish the factory had spent money on a decent cafeteria for us rather than chucking it round on lawns and flower beds so people driving past would think what good employers the bosses must be.

Anyway, during the tea breaks and the lunch breaks everybody would make up for lost time, they'd yak and yak till their jaws was sore.

'Silly, frivolous talk,' our forewoman said one day when we was all talking nineteen to the dozen about the latest film. 'You girls should discuss serious things, like the war, or politics.'

But life in that place was horrible enough without talking about things like that.

We used to sing a lot too, singing was good, it was something we could do over the top of the roaring of the machines. We'd

139

sing old music hall songs, and the latest songs from the radio, and sometimes we'd sing Maori songs too. There was a girl from Rapaki on our bench, her name was Whina, and she was a lovely singer. She taught us a lot of songs we'd never heard before.

Our forewoman liked the singing, sometimes she'd join in too. Actually she wasn't such a bad person.

'I'm glad you want to learn skilled work, Janet,' she told me one day when I said I'd like to work one of the harder machines. 'My father was a skilled man. It's not just the extra money you get from a skill, it's the dignity you get too.'

Well if any of the others had of heard her talking about 'dignity' they would of pulled faces, but I didn't mind too much. She was all right, Mrs Goodham. She was sort of motherly to us, a little round ball of a person, a wee bit up herself, but most of the time she meant to be kind. Like, she thought it was terrible the way we all called one another by nicknames. One day in the tea break I called out something to Hock.

'Hock!' I yelled.

And Hock yelled back.

'Yeah, Gin?'

Mrs Goodham sort of winced.

'Janet, please call her Ellen,' she said. 'I think Ellen is such a pretty name and Hock sounds so awful.'

Well I kept calling her Hock, but it was nice of Mrs Goodham to care about us, I thought.

There was only one time I had a real run in with Mrs Goodham. It was after I'd been at United Footwear a year or so. By that time I'd moved to a machine next to Whina, and between me and her there was two wooden boxes. Each machinist had a box like that to keep her work gear and sandwiches in.

Whina was a real dag; she gave Mrs Goodham a lot of cheek and of an afternoon if Whina had managed to get her quota done she'd sometimes just switch her machine off and sit and knit. One day I got my quota finished early too and Whina put down her knitting.

'Game of euchre, eh Gin?' she said.

Well I was a bit scared, but Whina took a pack of cards out

of her box and started dealing them out, and soon we was hard at it.

Mrs Goodham came down the aisle and caught us.

'Lazy little tarts,' she said. 'Where's your self respect? What do you think this factory is for? Don't you know there's a war on? The country needs our shoes, and all you two misses can do is sit here playing cards.'

It was a bit like Mum of a norwest day, but Whina just sat waiting till Mrs Goodham sort of wore herself out.

'You must be mad if you think we'd rather make shoes than play cards,' she said.

Mrs Goodham got really angry.

'There'll come a day when you girls won't be able to answer me back like that,' she said. 'This war won't last forever and the day it comes to an end you girls will be begging for work.'

United Footwear needed all the workers it could get. There was a shortage of labour cause of the war, like Mrs Goodham said, and our factory was what the government called a 'semi-essential industry', which meant workers couldn't be sacked, though they couldn't leave very easy either.

'One day the Japs will give youse Pakehas what's coming to youse,' Whina said.

Poor little Mrs Goodham was so shocked she just sort of goggled at Whina then walked away.

'I'm a Pakeha too,' I said.

Whina just laughed.

Apart from Mrs Goodham we didn't have much to do with anybody higher up in the heap. There was the office staff of course, but they never had anything to do with us and we never had anything to do with them. Except one girl, Moira Snodgrass.

Moira Snodgrass was a typist and for some reason all us machinists hated her. I don't know why, cause though everybody said she was stuck up, she didn't seem much different to the other office girls to me. But for some reason or other she'd been picked out for attention – all us machinists did everything we could to make her life hell. Like, when she went to the toilet. Her and the other office girls had to use the same toilet as us, so whenever

Moira Snodgrass needed a pee she had to walk right across the machine room floor in front of all us machinists. And whenever she did, we'd whistle.

Not a loud whistle, just a low, jeering kind of whistle. The first person to catch sight of her would start it, then the rest of us would join in. Moira Snodgrass would go red as red, she'd keep her nose up and wouldn't look at us, but her face would be all flaming red. Then the minute she came out of the toilet the whistling would start up again. Nobody would ever say anything, it was just us whistling and her walking past, red faced and stiff and silent.

Mrs Goodham would tsk and tut, but there was nothing she could do to stop us.

In the meantime the manager was looking down on us from a sort of glass booth up above us. That was his office, that glass booth. It was up high over the work floor, so he could look down and see everything, like God in an airship.

We had our ways of showing what we thought about that, of course.

The thing was, you had a sort of sixth sense about when his back was turned. We'd always be looking up to the glass booth, quick little looks, to see if he was at the window looking down at us, or if he was busy looking at some papers or turned away talking to a secretary or something, and whenever his back was turned one of us would stick out our tongue, or give him the fingers.

Another thing we did was, we all had these bags of french chalk, little bags of it which sometimes you had to put over the leather so it'd go through the machine. And sometimes when the manager had his back turned one of us would throw a bag of french chalk over the partition into the making room next door. Then another bag would come flying back from the men in the making room, and in half a minute french chalk bags would be flying in all directions. Then all of a sudden it'd stop. The manager would come across to the window and look down at us, and he'd see us all bent over our machines, whirring away, clouds of white dust filling the air all round us.

They couldn't say anything about it, they would of just made fools of themselves.

So that was one way we had of keeping our end up. It made us feel we wasn't just slaves. Though really it didn't make our life much easier.

Conditions at United Footwear was supposed to be 'among the best in the city', that was what Mrs Goodham told us. And as far as I know that might of been true, but if it was true all I can say is I'm glad I wasn't working somewhere else, cause from where we sat it wasn't anything to write home about. Like, the toilets, they was just bare concrete walls, like a prison, and to me they always seemed cold. The work rooms wasn't cold, I'll say that for United Footwear. There was big electric heaters hanging down from the roof, and big fluorescent lights too. So there was plenty of heat and plenty of light, in fact too much if anything. In winter you'd come in from a five degree frost and the factory would be like an oven and after an hour at your machine you'd be sweating so hard your armpits would turn all clammy and your head would be aching. And the light was a really bright white light, very hard and sort of sharp.

Worse than that was the noise. There was a lot of noise. If you turned up early of a morning you'd take off your coat and put your sandwiches in your soap box and sit down and yak to your cobbers. You'd be sitting there in the quiet, feeling good about your mates. Then all of a sudden at eight o'clock the whistle would go and the charge hand at the end of each row on the line would turn on the drive belts. And the noise, it was terrible. Ten machines on each bench, and they'd all start whirring, the belts between them would start moving and roaring and rumbling and shrieking.

But you got used to that too.

Well you had to, there wasn't anything you could do about it.

We had a union, it was compulsory to be in a union. We had to pay five shillings a week, that was what they called the 'levy', and there was this big levy book, but what it was all about I didn't really know. Nobody from the union ever came and talked to me and I never found out who my union person was. Most of us didn't think much of the union, cause we'd grown up listening to people like Mum say unions was just a way of keeping working people down.

'They'll talk themselves blue in the face about wages and conditions and that,' Mum always said, 'but it's just a bunch of smart jokers on the make.'

It was true too, our union was tied up with the Labour government.

'And it's the Labour government that got us in this bloody war,' Mum would say. 'And who's got to pay for the bloody war? Us, that's who. And who's going to make us pay? The unions and the bosses and the churches and the rest of them, that's who.'

So that was the way it was. There wasn't any point going to the union and saying we wanted better conditions or anything, cause that would foul up what the Labour government kept calling the 'war effort'. It was our job to shut up and put up, keep our heads down over our machines, and keep those boots coming for 'the boys'.

One of the worst things about United Footwear was there was hardly any perks.

'Make sure you pick up anything that's lying round,' Mum said. 'Slip it in yer pocket and bring it home. It's part of yer wages.'

I didn't really understand what she meant by saying it was part of my wages, so she got a bit aggravated.

'Might as well sit on yer head and use yer bum for yer bloody brain,' she said, 'for all the use it is. It's part of yer wages cause the bosses will make more out of you than you'll get back in yer pay packet, so it's up to you to take stuff to make up the difference. But don't get caught. And don't take anything that belongs to another worker, just stuff that belongs to the bosses.'

But there wasn't anything worth taking at United Footwear. Some of the girls took glue, or french chalk, or things like that. But that wasn't much use to anybody, there wasn't anything really worthwhile.

Mum knew that already.

'Thin pickings in a boot factory,' she said. 'Just take what yer can find.'

So I'd come home with a pot of glue every now and then, or some bits of leather, and once I even managed to smuggle a roll of toilet paper home.

'Good,' Mum said. 'If there's one thing I don't need it's paying out good money for useless kids to wipe their bums on.'

There was one perk the bosses organised for us, or it might of been the union, I don't know. Of a Thursday, that was pay day, we was all allowed to buy shoes cheap from the company. We'd get our pay packets and knock off and go next door to the warehouse where there was these mountains and mountains of shoes. I'd buy boots for the family, and I'd buy fashion shoes for me to wear to the pictures and to dances and that. That was a good perk, cause in the shops a pair of shoes would sell for two or three pound, but I'd get them from the warehouse for only seventeen or nineteen shillings.

So it wasn't all bad, working at United Footwear. The noise was terrible and the lights was too bright and the machines made my back sore and half the time I seemed to have a headache, but at least I got cheap shoes.

Of a night, after I'd got home and done my turn cooking tea and folding the clothes from the wash that day and mending some things and the rest of it, I'd go down to the bedroom and sit on the bed with Fag and try on my shoes. There'd be five or six pair under the bed, all mine. Some would be blue and some would be black and some would be red, some would have bows and some would have buckles. And me and Fag would slip our feet in and out of them, sliding them off and on, trying to decide which ones looked the nicest.

'This is a corker pair,' I'd say.

'Mm,' Fag would say. 'I think these are nicer.'

'Me and Hock,' I'd say, 'must have the best dressed feet this end of Moorhouse Ave.'

8

Nice things for the glory box

Ginnie

I worked more than six years at United Footwear. First of all at the rubbing down machine, then at a machine where I made the linings of shoes. After about two years of that I was shifted a bit further along the line to a machine that made a part of the actual shoe, not just the lining. Then after three years or so I came out of my time, I was a fully trained shoe machinist, and my wage was four pound twelve a week.

Four pound twelve a week, it seemed like a fortune.

It wasn't, of course. Most of the men working on machines at United Footwear got six or seven pound a week, quite a few even got eight. But four pound twelve was good money for a woman, and I liked having money, having a few bob to spare, the feeling that I could buy one or two little extras or give something nice to Mum.

Of a pay day on my way home I'd stop at a fruit shop and buy Mum pears. She was very fond of pears, Mum.

Earning a wage, paying for my own board, having a bit left over to buy things with, that seemed to make me sort of real. I felt as though I was a person who was doing something for the family, and doing something for herself. Mum still had two or three kids on her hands, Tots and Billie and that, so the money came in handy. It made me feel like I wasn't just a useless kid any more; I was a worker and I was a person in my own right. And it felt good.

After I'd been at the factory a while I stopped dreaming about being rich or beautiful or famous, I just thought about how to get onto a better machine, how to divvy up my wages, or how nice my new shoes looked. I started thinking that real life was just a matter of getting along from one day to the next. That was about what it amounted to, there wasn't any point thinking about what you couldn't have.

And I was all right. I was managing to get along.

Though it was hard walking past the shops with all the dresses and stockings and gloves on display in the windows, knowing you couldn't save up enough to buy them. You needed a bit of excitement in your life. Even if you didn't think you'd ever be rich or famous any more it was still nice to be able to put on some glad rags and go to a dance. And after a while I started to do what all the other girls did, I started to buy things on time payment.

Mum didn't like it, she said it was just a way for the shops to make more money out of us.

'Putting an iron on your shoulder,' she'd say.

She'd always said that, of course. She'd said that when Ruby and Frank bought their house in Avonside, and she'd said it every time Hock or Peggy bought a dress on time payment. But she'd been wrong, cause Ruby and Frank was rich now, it hadn't done them any harm buying on time payment, and Hock and Peggy and all the girls at work seemed to manage all right with time payments, so I thought I might as well buy one or two nice things too.

Working people who wanted clothes on time payment went along to Morse Order and Arnbell Order. First you went looking in the shops and when you found something you liked you took the price of it and asked the shop people to lay it by. Then you walked up to Morse Order or Arnbell Order and asked for a chit, a bit of paper with an order for the thing you wanted to buy. Then you'd walk back to the shop and hand over the chit. The shop assistant would check to see it was right, then she'd hand you the dress or whatever. And you'd pay it off at half a crown a week till it was all paid for, the cost of the thing and the interest on top.

Well I begrudged them the interest. But at least I got a few nice things.

Hats, like. None of us wore hats to the factory, hats was too precious for that, but we all liked to put one on if we was going out of a night. We called them 'beanies'. The first beanie I bought was a nice blue velour one, a royal blue it was and I thought it looked real good on my red hair. And I bought stockings too, rayon ones mostly, but silk stockings for a special treat once every two or three months. We didn't wear them to the factory, we wore socks there and kept our stockings for going out of a night. That was one reason we hated the office girls, they wore stockings and hats all the time, so they looked like little ladies.

One day Hock turned up in a pair of slacks. Most of the girls thought she looked real smart, but of course Mum just about hit the roof when she caught sight of them.

'Git them things off,' she said.

And away her tongue went.

'I've always bloody said the only thing youse tarts can ever bloody think of is getting inside a man's pants.'

And so on.

So we wasn't game to wear slacks again after that. Hock sold them to a mate on the beading machines.

I liked dresses. Not the old ones I wore to the factory but the nice new ones I bought on time payment from department stores. Once I'd got used to buying on time payment I tried to manage things so I always had at least two dresses for best, cotton dresses usually, 'polished cotton' it was called, cotton with a starch added. Polished cotton was nice. It wasn't exactly silk or satin, and I suppose the people in Fendalton would of turned their noses up at it, but I liked it, it looked sharp and smooth and smart.

'I might not have much of a face,' I'd say to Hock or Fag. 'But at least I look neat.'

And whenever I said that it always reminded me of Mum's sayings.

'We might be poor, but at least . . .'

A string of beads would of been nice too, just to finish things off, but jewellery was taboo, Mum thought jewellery was beyond the pale.

'Any tart who dangles beads all over herself is just showing yer she's a trashy item,' Mum always used to say.

So beads wasn't on.

I would of liked a few other things too. Like a magic spell to straighten hair, change the shape of my face, get rid of freckles, and lose weight. I always felt fat, though I wasn't really, it was just that I had a big frame, big bones like aunty Aggie had.

'Good child bearing hips,' aunty Aggie always used to say.

Which I hated.

I wasn't short and I wasn't tall, I wasn't beautiful and I wasn't plain. One day Eddie took a photo of me. He'd bought an old box Brownie second hand and he took a picture of me in the back yard. And when I saw the photo I was sort of surprised, I was quite nice looking really, nothing very exciting, but all right, sort of fresh and cheerful looking.

My freckles worried me a lot. I was always trying to scrape them off or bleach them away. Hock was the same, she had freckles as bad as me, so we used to worry about them together. Sometimes we'd go to the shops together and buy fuller's earth, then of the Saturday night we'd make facepacks. We'd spread it on our face and get in the bath, one of us at each end, and we wasn't supposed to talk or laugh, we had to keep dead still or the facepack would crack. We'd lie there in the bath looking at each other with dry mud smeared all over our faces and we'd start to giggle, then we'd laugh, and the facepacks would crack and fall to bits.

I was always struggling with my hair. In fact all of us was. The fashions in hair kept changing and if you wanted to keep up to the minute you had to twist and knot and wave and curl it the right way. We spent hours sweating over our hair. And mine was worse than most cause it was so wiry.

One year the fashion was to have your hair all wavy, so all us girls spent our pay packets buying butterfly clips, little metal clips, to make our hair wavy the right way. That was hopeless; my hair kept fighting back at me and I couldn't ever get the waves right. Then another style came in where you put the top of a silk stocking on your hair and you tucked your hair round it, and I thought I looked really good like that; it seemed to make my

149

neck look a little bit longer and the stocking held my wiry hair down.

Of course the main way of getting your hair to knuckle under was to have a perm. So every few months off I'd go to the hairdresser.

'Off to get yer hair tonged are yer?' Mum would say.

It was absolute torture getting your hair permed, but it was a thing we all did. The magazines and the films and the rest of it showed us what we had to look like, so off we'd go. We'd spend all day at the factory slaving away on the machines and then we'd spend another five hours at night paying money to have our hair screwed up with wire and sloshed with chemicals and baked and fried and bleached and dyed. The first bit, when they twisted in the rollers and put the solution on, wasn't as bad as the next bit when they put you under the dryer. They'd just shove you under – we was just factory girls so there wasn't any need to make a fuss of us – they'd just shove us under the dryer and turn it on really hot. Probably they turned it on hot to get us through quicker.

I used to get really scorched, scorched so bad the back of my neck would go all red and shiny.

'First degree burns,' Whina used to say.

She'd done a first aid course once, so she thought she was a bit of an expert on that sort of thing.

Me and Whina was quite matey for a while, but then I got shifted to another machine and my main friends then was the girls on either side of me, Monica Cohen and Violet McInnes. They was my first real friends, those two, they was the first people outside the family that I felt really close to. They helped make up for losing Fag.

I really missed Fag. Even though me and her had been so thick for so many years we hardly ever saw one another now. After she cleared out she said she'd come round and see me, but she never did. She hated Mum so much she couldn't bring herself to come back even for a cup of tea, and I didn't ever go and see Fag either, I was too scared of Mum.

So we drifted apart, me and Fag.

150

Which meant getting to be cobbers with Monica Cohen and Violet McInnes was good; it was what I needed. We was all mates together and we had some good times.

Violet lived with her family in a little old rented cottage in Sydenham. There was just the four of them, her and her sister and mother and father. They was just ordinary working class people, the McInnes family. I always felt a wee bit more at home with Violet than I did with Monica, cause of feeling that me and her was both on the same level, while Monica seemed a cut or two above us. Not that she put on side, it was just that she was very sort of dainty, very sort of ladylike. The Cohens lived in a big old villa in Linwood, the better part of Linwood near Avonside. Mr and Mrs Cohen owned their house, they must of had a few bob. Mr Cohen had been a cobbler. He'd had his own shop, though he'd sold it up since then and retired.

'I went to work at United cause I wanted to learn Dad's trade,' Monica said to me one day when I was visiting them.

Mr Cohen didn't look too happy about it.

'Working for wages in a factory,' he said. 'Far cry from cobbling on your own account. Bad wages and shoddy shoes. Those big factories have been the ruin of good work.'

I wondered what he was driving at by talking about 'good work'. As far as I could see the two words 'good' and 'work' didn't have anything to do with one another.

But he was old, so he had lots of funny ideas.

So anyway, me and Violet and Monica was a threesome. We used to sit at lunch together, and go out together. We went to the pictures a lot, and walked together along the river bank and that. Of a Sunday night we'd meet at the Edmonds Rotunda. That was nice, that big white rotunda, and the green poplars, and the river flowing past in a big slow curve. The evening sun would flash on the brass buttons and horns of the band, and that was nice too. But we didn't really go there to listen to music, we went to eye up the boys. There'd be lots of boys there, young jokers from factories and warehouses and that, hands in their pockets, fags hanging from their mouths, giving us cheek. Lots of other girls too, factory girls like us, all in twos and threes and fours,

151

arm in arm, walking round in our best cotton frocks, giggling and tittering and eyeing the boys up.

But the best place to meet jokers was at dances.

I really loved dances. We'd go of a Saturday night, me and Violet and Monica, and often we'd go of a Friday night too, and sometimes of a Wednesday night as well. There was a lot of cheap dance places for working people. There was the Caledonian, that we called the Cally, and there was the Latimer, and there was a place in Linwood, the Rendezvous, that was our main haunt. There was the Navy League too, where you could go and dance with jokers from the navy.

At dances me and Violet and Monica would sort of play games among ourselves. Like, we'd decide to all wear a white blouse and a skirt. Or we'd decide to all wear a dress with a cinch belt. And we'd make up different names for ourselves. Our surnames would all begin with S and our christian names would all begin with D. One night at the Rendezvous I was Dolores Sanford, another night I was Deirdre Sinclair. But most of the time I called myself Diana, cause I thought that was a really lovely name, I'd always liked it. When me and Fag had played games together as kids I'd always called myself Diana.

Diana. It sounded really glamorous, I thought. The sort of name somebody would have in Fendalton or up on Cashmere.

But most of the time I didn't go in much for that sort of play-acting, cause I'd sort of grown out of that, daydreaming and that, like I said. I looked back on the things I used to dream about and thought what a stupid kid I'd been, all those silly ideas about being rich, I had my head screwed on now, I could see the road ahead, I could see it clear as day. I was going to keep working at United Footwear, I was going to meet jokers at dances, I was going to find one I got on with, and I was going to marry him.

We was all looking to the day we got married. That was the only way out of the factory, as far as we could see. You either got married, or else you stayed on at the factory making shoes.

'The day some chap asks me to marry him you won't see me for dust,' Monica used to say.

'Yeah,' Violet would say. 'Me too.'

'No clocking in,' I'd say. 'Get up when you feel like it. Eat breakfast in bed, have a cup of tea and read a magazine.'

Well we knew married life wasn't really like that for working people, but when we thought about being married, having a husband, having babies, we pictured it the way it was in the movies and the magazines and the love stories. I'd think of Ruby's house in Avonside and see myself there – I wouldn't think about Sadie stuck in a hole with three screeching babies in Addington. We should of known better, me and Violet and Monica, we had mothers and aunts and that. We knew what their lives had been. They'd told us what to expect, but we hadn't listened to them.

'Things are different these days,' Violet would say. 'It's a welfare state now, we don't have to worry about being poor.'

'There'll be houses for everybody,' Monica would say.

So when I thought about being married all I could see was me and a baby in a nice little house, with carpet and a lounge suite and a brand new gramophone.

Fag

I was starting to get desperate.

Since leaving Tech I'd been working over the summer at Lane Walker Rudkins. I hadn't been able to find an office job, so I'd come back to the hosiery mill with my tail between my legs, and every time I sealed the celluloid over another pair of underpants I felt like I was sealing my dreams in there too. It was early in 1943, not long after my birthday, and Ginnie and I had just turned fourteen.

I've got to get out of this, I kept saying to myself down in the toilet at tea break. I'll go mad if I stay here much longer.

'Here's a job you can go for,' Mum said, shoving a torn bit of newspaper at me one day after I came home hot and tired and dirty from the factory. 'If it's office work yer after, here yer are.'

It was an advertisement for a typist at a legal office in town.

'Ruby saw it in the paper,' Mum said. 'She rung them up and jacked it up for yer.'

So it was Ruby, as usual, organising our lives for us.

'I don't know, Mum,' I said. 'I don't think my typing's good enough.'

Mum wasn't going to have any of that.

'You're to git up there Monday morning for the interview,' she said.

It was Grace and Grace in Cashel Street. Mr Grace from Cashmere was the senior partner, and when I discovered that I felt a bit better. He'll remember me, I thought, He'll remember me from that weekend Ginnie and I stayed up there in that house of his, he'll give me the job.

Monday morning I rang the bell at the office, hopeful and nervous and worried about my clothes, knowing I didn't look right, knowing I didn't look like an office worker, that I just looked like a working class kid from Phillipstown.

'I'm Miss Prisk,' the head typist said. 'Only three applicants. You might be in luck.'

Labour's scarce, I thought. It's the war. There's a chance I'll get it.

Miss Prisk sat me on a bench and got me to wait till Mr Grace called me in.

'Take a will, Miss Feron,' he said the minute I walked in.

I just about sank through the floor.

My year at Tech hadn't got me up to standard for that sort of job, I knew. And old Grace looked terrifying, nothing like the meek and courteous old gentleman who'd ignored Ginnie and I so politely that weekend up on Cashmere. Here he was four square in the middle of that big room, a big wide room with a big smooth desk, his back to two big windows opening out onto Cashel Street.

The *boss*, I thought. He's got the whip hand.

And I hated him.

Suddenly he started reeling off words. Words words words, half of them I'd never heard before, strange legal words, strange unfamiliar nouns.

'And to the Christchurch Liedertafel a bequest of . . .'

What the hell's that? I thought. The Christchurch Leederwhat?

But there was no time to think. He reeled it all off then suddenly came to a stop.

'Type that up in the outer office, Miss Feron,' he said. 'Then we shall see what we shall see.'

I spent an hour sweating over that will. Then when it was finished I took it in, and tried to smile at him, tried to look competent, as he reached out for it with a pink flabby hand.

'Miss Feron!' he suddenly roared out.

I scuttled a bit closer, wondering what the hell I'd done. My spelling's right, I thought. I checked it in the dictionary.

'*Commas*, Miss Feron!' he said. 'Commas! Commas in a legal document only when commas are stipulated, Miss Feron. A comma in the wrong place can entirely alter the meaning of a sentence, Miss Feron. A comma must be shunned, Miss Feron.'

I hated him even more.

Not that I said anything. I just sort of simpered.

'On the other hand,' he said, 'your spelling is impeccable, which is more than can be said for the other two young ladies who have favoured us with applications for this position. Consequently, Miss Feron, you may consider yourself in our employ.'

Thanks I don't think, I thought.

'Thank you very much, Mr Grace,' I said. 'I'll do my best for you, sir.'

But my best wasn't good enough and I knew it. My typing wasn't up to scratch, I could only manage forty words a minute and you needed a hundred words a minute to be any good in a law office. And my shorthand wasn't up to scratch either. So a life of misery started, worse even than Lane Walker Rudkins, because I just couldn't do the work properly. I had to struggle and struggle and skip lunch and stay on of an evening after the others, but even then I couldn't get the work done. It didn't take long for Miss Prisk to pick it up either. She saw I was having problems and came across to take a look at what I was doing.

'Never mind,' she said. 'I'll help you.'

She was a nice person, a tall, slim woman, very smartly dressed, very efficient, and sort of quick in her ways, the sort of person I wanted to be.

'Here,' she said. 'You'll save yourself time if you do it like this.'

But it was no good.

Just round the corner in Lichfield Street was the shop Ruby and Frank had bought themselves. A wholesale motor parts shop. I started dropping in there on my mail round, and if Ruby wasn't in earshot I'd have a yarn with Frank.

'It's horrible, Frank,' I'd say. 'Even when I come out to collect the mail I feel like a prisoner let out into the exercise yard.'

It was a comfort talking to Frank. He listened to my moaning and said things back to me about silver linings and lights at the end of tunnels and things like that, stupid things really, but very cheery and good natured. In the end I'd feel a bit better.

'Could you ask around and see if there's anything else going?' I asked him one day.

'Can't promise anything,' he said. 'But if I hear of something I'll let you know.'

Six weeks later he had some good news.

'Heard of something,' he said. 'Clerical job with a mate of mine. I rung him up about it. Go round and see him, and if you look sharp he'll take you on. It's an electrical supply place.'

Scholefield Electrical was a big shop in a row of tall brick buildings down High Street. My heart sank as I walked towards it – it was in a part of High Street where the buildings were old and fusty, topped with urns and terracotta gargoyles, with seedy little tailoring places and boarding houses and watchmakers on the second and third storeys. But Scholefield Electrical turned out not so bad. It had been 'modernised', it had a double frontage shining with yellow tiles and plate glass. Behind the glass were pyramids of electrical appliances. And up on the second storey was a big sign in neon.

'I've come about the job,' I said to a girl at the counter. 'Frank Morgan sent me.'

I liked Mr Scholefield from the start. He seemed easy going and friendly, and a bit diffident. He was dressed in a dark suit and tie, but it was obvious he didn't feel comfortable interviewing me.

'Hum,' he said. 'And . . . ah . . .'

After a while I found I was doing most of the talking.

'I can't type very fast,' I said, 'but I don't make many mistakes and my spelling is good.'

'She'll be right,' he said. 'Won't be much typing anyway. Sort of a dogsbody job really. Bit of typing, bit of clerical work. Selling things at the counter when there's nothing doing in the office.'

So we seemed to understand one another.

Half an hour later I was back at Grace and Grace, clearing out my desk, thanking Miss Prisk.

My instinct about Scholefield Electrical turned out to be right. It was an easy going place and Mr Scholefield was no trouble. He was only a working man himself. He'd started off life in Addington, left school at ten, and been lucky enough to be apprenticed to an electrician just at the time when the electrical industry took off. So he made money. He bought the shop, he added on the shop next door, and now there was me in the office, the girl selling out the front, and four or five men and boys in a workshop out the back. Every now and then his daughters came in to see their father. They went to St Margaret's College and they seemed very haughty and upper class. But their father was still just a working man. If something sticky came up in the workshop Mr Scholefield would take off his jacket, roll up his sleeves, and get stuck in.

I was so glad to have the job, so determined to make a go of it, that for three or four months I couldn't believe my luck.

I had my own little office, all to myself. It wasn't much, just a little room with a steel filing cabinet, a typewriter, a chair. But I liked it, I felt at home. Of a morning I'd pick flowers from gardens and put them in a glass in my room. And the secretarial work was easy, there was never any hurry. Mr Scholefield had such a slow train of thought it was easy to take down dictation from him. In fact he was so slow that after a while I started to prompt him.

'Umm,' he'd say. 'We are in receipt of yours of, umm, and . . .'

'We have pleasure in informing you,' I'd say, 'that the consignment . . .'

'Don't know why we keep doing this,' he said one day. 'You know better than me what's wanted. Why not just write them up as you think best and give me them in batches and I'll just read them over and sign on the dotted line.'

So that was what we did. And that was good, I liked that, writing letters on behalf of the boss, it felt as though I was a little bit a boss myself.

I liked other parts of the job too. Working on the invoices was interesting, I enjoyed that, making all the figures come out right. And I liked working at the counter out the front too, selling people what they wanted, passing the time of day with them. I felt as though I was in the world, that things were happening in my life.

But after a while I started to notice the months going by. Then more months. Soon it started to look like they were going to turn into years.

Things weren't the best at home either; Mum was worse than ever. She seemed to spend half her life finding ways to get my goat and the other half of her life moaning.

'Me bloody legs,' she'd say. 'Youse bloody tarts. This bloody war.'

The war was getting us all down, all the shortages and regulations, the rationing and the queues. There was a strange sort of atmosphere those last two years of the war, a sort of corrupt, deceitful atmosphere. The black market was doing a roaring trade, so there were always spivvy young fellows hanging round, buying and selling things on the sly. Sammie and Bobsie got involved in it, and Sammie got caught and ended up sitting in a cell at Paparua prison. It felt queer. All this conniving on the quiet, and then when you went along to see a film everybody standing up straight for 'God Save the King'. And the newsreels.

'Our boys doing their bit on the Italian front . . .'

It was all lies, we knew those fruity voices were telling us lies, but we sat there and listened.

The biggest bugbear was Churchill. Mum hated him. Whenever she heard his voice she saw red.

'Fat smarmy Tory bugger,' she'd say.

She'd scowl at his voice over the radio, and instead of giving the V for victory sign she'd give him the fingers.

So the dream of a glorious war was well and truly over. I wasn't Daphne de Feron, the belle of old Phillips Town any more, I was just Fag, living in the middle of curfews and black markets and ration books.

So what should I do? How was I going to escape?

'Night classes,' Nancy Wand told me. 'Night classes, that's the way to do it.'

Nancy had left school too, she'd found herself a job in a haberdashery shop, and she was as restless as I. Of a lunch time we'd meet together. We'd sit outside the High Street post office and eat our sandwiches and try to think of ways out.

'There's this really interesting course on book keeping,' she said. 'We could enrol in that. And after a couple of years we'd have qualifications.'

So we enrolled.

It was a disaster. I gave up after a week and Nancy gave up after a fortnight.

'How about modern poetry?' Wendy said. 'That might be more our style.'

But it wasn't.

'How about political science?' Nancy said a few weeks after we'd thrown in the towel over the English Romantic poets. 'There's a course at the WEA.'

But we set a record with that, I only lasted one night and Nancy fell asleep the third night and decided her best bet would be a language.

'How about this course in Maori?' she said. 'I'd love to be able to speak Maori. We could get jobs with the government as translators in the North Island.'

I had a sudden vision of myself sitting under a palm tree on a beach in the North Island, with a volcano smoking behind me and grateful Maoris in piupius giving me presents for explaining to them the ways of the white man.

We signed up for night classes at Tech, bought the textbook, went along to the classes.

'Tena koe,' we said. 'Tena koutou. No hea koe?'

'Let's go to a pa,' Nancy said after we'd been studying it a couple of weeks. 'We could go to Tuahiwi. We could talk to the people there, and they'll invite us into a whare to see how they live, and they'll be all pleased cause we're learning their language, and we'll become blood sisters to one of the girls in the pa, and when we die they'll have a tangi for us and throw photos of us into our graves.'

So come Saturday we got on our bikes and pedalled out to Tuahiwi. It was quite a distance, twelve or fifteen miles, but it was a lovely sunny day and we enjoyed it.

'Makes you feel really good, doesn't it?' Nancy said as we stopped at the Kaiapoi river to kick our feet in the water and eat some apples. 'Doing things for yourself.'

When we got to Tuahiwi we were a bit disappointed – no palisades or wooden statues, just an ordinary country township, little houses scattered along a dusty road.

We put our bikes down in the churchyard and walked across to a paddock where we saw some kids playing.

'Tena koutou,' Nancy said.

The kids burst out laughing.

'Kei te pehea koutou?' Nancy said.

They started rolling round on the grass, laughing and pointing at us. After a while it seemed a bit scary, there seemed to be something going on we didn't understand.

We started walking back to our bikes.

They were gone.

'God,' I said. 'What're they going to do to us?'

'It's all right,' Nancy said. 'It's just some kids. Look over there.'

Some boys were riding our bikes round, whooping and hollering at one another. Nancy started to chase them. They yelled when they saw her coming, but they laughed too, and after a while they let her catch them.

'Thanks,' Nancy said. 'Didn't mean to make fools of ourselves.'

So that was the end of Maori language month.

I was getting a bit down. If I couldn't stick to something at night school how was I ever going to get anywhere? But I always felt so tired of an evening. I didn't have the energy to sit over books and listen to lectures. And the teachers were so boring, they just droned on and on, just like the worst teachers at school.

'University,' Nancy said. 'We'll go to university. We'll save our

160

wages and go back to school full time and get through and go to university.'

So that made things easier. One day we'd go to university. And right now all we had to do was save our wages.

Not that saving wages was as easy as it sounded either. When I started at Scholefield Electrical I was only getting fifteen shillings a week and I never seemed to be able to put any of it aside. Twelve shillings went to Mum as board, and with the three shillings left over I had to find myself decent clothes to wear in the office. I wanted a suit, and found one in a shop off Lichfield Street, a nice red and navy check suit with a straight skirt made of wool, a 'classic' suit, the shop woman told me. I put five shillings down and got an order from Morse Order and took it home. But it took me months and months to pay that suit off, and then after that I needed a new seat for my bike. And after that I needed stockings. So what with one thing and another I never seemed to get ahead.

Then I cleared out from home, and that was the right thing to do, my finances took a turn for the better after that.

Hock and Peggy and Ginnie and I had been talking for ages about leaving home.

'Dunno why we just stick here taking it from her,' Hock would say. 'She doesn't own us. We should clear out.'

But none of us did anything. We kept handing over our pay packets, putting up with things, until a few months after I turned fifteen Mr Scholefield put my pay up to twenty-five shillings.

I felt so excited. Twenty-five shillings! After paying my twelve shillings board that'd leave me with thirteen shillings a week to spend or save.

'Right,' Mum said. 'Yer board's going up to a quid.'

So the battle started.

'I'm not paying a penny more than what I've always paid,' I said. 'It's my money, you can't just take it off me when you feel like it.'

Mum shoved a knife into a parsnip.

'Whose bloody money kept you fed and clothed and housed for fifteen bloody years, my lady?' she said. 'What's my bloody prize for working myself to the bloody bone for thirty bloody

161

years for fourteen useless bloody lumps of ungrateful bloody kids? What jer think I'm gitting out of . . .'

'I don't care,' I said. 'I want my own life.'

She started screaming all the things she'd been screaming for years.

'Yer a lazy bloody tart,' she said. 'When I think what I went through having you, to think I nearly died giving birth to you. Yer lazy. Yer dirty. Yer don't do yer share of work in the place. To think I nearly died giving birth to such a tarted up lazy bloody bitch.'

It lasted for days. I started to feel desperate.

Betty Leveret, the shop girl at Scholefield Electrical, came up to me one morning.

'Not looking too happy today, Daph,' she said. 'Trouble at home?'

'I'm going crazy,' I said. 'Mum's in a paddy and life's not worth living. If I knew some place to go I'd pack a bag and clear out.'

Betty Leveret was good natured, a bit of a fool, but she meant well. She gave me a pat on the shoulder.

'She's jake. There's an old lady I know of, family friend, she's looking for a boarder. I'll see if I can jack it up.'

All of a sudden my brain took a leap. I suddenly realised that, yes, I could actually leave, I didn't have to put up with Mum if I didn't want to, I could clear out and be free.

That afternoon Betty and I took the tram out to Spreydon to meet Mrs Childer.

'Her husband was a lithographer,' Betty told me. 'They saved a bit and when he died the house in Dunn Street was freehold. It's not much of a place, but it's a place, and it's hers. And she's a soft hearted old lady, so if you play your cards right she might leave something to you.'

Well I didn't like that sort of talk, but I didn't say anything.

She was right, it wasn't much of a place, just an ordinary cottage, a little narrow old cottage in a scungy street in the oldest part of Spreydon. But when Mrs Childer opened the door and I saw this little slight old woman with bifocal glasses, very old fashioned and quaint and gentle, I thought she looked lovely.

Then when she showed me into her sitting room I thought it looked lovely too. A little, low room with stiff, stiff old pieces of furniture, doilies on top of everything, framed photos on the wall, photos of her husband, her babies, photos of Queenstown and Wanaka. And in the grate there was a lovely fire, a good heaped up coal fire, lovely and warm and bright.

It was probably that fire that did it. I was so used to being cold in winter; Mum's meagre little handfuls of coal and heaped potato peelings.

'This could be your room,' Mrs Childer said, opening another door.

It was small, very cold, with lino on the floor and an iron bedstead. But it seemed nice, everything neat and nice. Nice sheets, a nice fresh coverlet. A chair and a little table by the window.

I could see myself sitting there with my books, studying for university.

And the idea of a room of my own. It all went to my head.

'Shall we settle it?' Mrs Childer said.

'That would be lovely,' I said.

'Fifteen shillings a week,' she said. 'All found, including washing.'

'The thing that's going to be nicest,' I told Ginnie that night as she sat with tear filled eyes watching me pack, 'will be not having to put up with a nagging old woman.'

Well it didn't take me long to find out that nagging isn't the only way life can be made a misery.

'Now that we've done the dishes,' Mrs Childer said next night after I'd moved in, 'let's go through to the sitting room and sit by the fire and have a nice chat.'

Mrs Childer liked to do one thing after another, each thing when it was time to do each thing, and then at the end of it all she liked to sit down and talk.

'I've had a long life my dear,' she said. 'Many memories, many memories.'

Oh my god, I thought. Spare me.

By the time a week had gone by I'd discovered that a nice cosy granny type of old woman like Mrs Childer was no easier to live with than a tough skinned old beetle like Mum.

'I'll have a nice hot breakfast waiting for you before you catch the tram tomorrow morning,' she told me. 'I'll expect you home on the first tram after five of the evening, and you'll find a nice hot meal on your plate, and we'll have that together, and then we'll do the dishes like we've done them now, and then we'll come through to the sitting room and sit by the fire and talk. Then about half past eight we'll make a nice cup of tea, and then after we've drunk that we'll get ourselves off to bed at nine so we'll be fresh for the morning.'

It sounded like the schedule for a day in Sunnyside.

'A good hearty breakfast for a working girl,' she'd say. 'Porridge and eggs and bacon and toast.'

'Now I don't pretend to be more moral than my neighbours, my dear,' she'd say at other times. 'Young people need to go out and dance from time to time. But I do like you to be back home by ten, so I can lock the door for the night.'

It was terrible. She was so kind and orderly and righteous.

'I'm a great believer in darning,' she'd say. 'Back in the early days of my marriage my husband's brother came out from England and was staying here with us, my husband was an Englishman, you know, my dear, not one of us. I was sitting in this very room, on this very chair, patching my husband's long johns and his brother said to me, "You can't be a colonial, colonials can't patch and darn as nice as that. When a colonial rips a thing he just throws it away and buys a new one." And I said, "Well I'm a colonial, and I'm proud of it."'

I heard that story a hundred times before the year was out.

She liked to tell me everything, Mrs Childer. She was like Mum, she had a sort of fixed ration of truths about the world, and she thought it was her duty to tell them to me.

'Now when you want to test the iron, my dear,' she'd say, 'you just spit on it like this.'

It was endless, an endless maundering monologue of homilies and anecdotes and memories, over and over and over again. I'd sit there trapped in the homely little sitting room by the cosy little fire, and I'd be thinking:

Out of the frying pan . . .

Or else I'd think I was going to go mad, I'd think something was going to go snap in my head and I was going to reach across to the poker and bash her skinny little skull in.

The Historian

When their school years ended and Fag and Ginnie found themselves 'entering the paid workforce', as government statisticians put it, the economy of Canterbury was based on industry and commerce. Farmers, landowners and many other people were unaware of this fact; they thought Canterbury lived off farming. They told the newspapers that Canterbury was a province riding on the sheep's back. Fag and Ginnie thought so too. Their teachers at school had taught them that Canterbury was the 'Empire's farm', that the fortunes of the town depended on the country and that the farmers and landowners deserved high incomes because they produced more wealth than workers and carried the burden of keeping the province prosperous. In reality three out of every four pounds of Canterbury's wealth came from the cities, not the farms. The economy was carried on the backs not of sheep but of factory workers, shop assistants, clerical workers and housewives.

By the time Ginnie and Fag turned sixteen an army of 18,000 women worked for wages in the city of Christchurch alongside 40,000 men. One out of every five women made clothes or footwear, bending over assembly lines in factories, turning out brassieres, rayon stockings, shirts, skirts, sandals, and underpants. Another one out of every five women earned a wage in the wholesale or retail trades, working as clerks or typists or sales assistants, banging on typewriters, thumbing through invoices, leaning on counters and rubbing their sore legs, frightened to take their shoes off for fear that the veins would swell up too much.

'Who is the factory girl?' asked an industrial psychologist in a 1947 report on *Girl Workers in New Zealand Factories*.

Factory girls, the industrial psychologist answered, 'tend to wear certain clothes, eat certain foods, live in certain parts of the town, speak in a certain way, obey certain social codes, feel certain fears from which a higher income might have protected them, know certain facts from which a higher income might have sheltered them, and acknowledge certain sentiments, feelings of inferiority, resentment, and submission, which are a result of the attitude of the higher-income groups towards them'.

Factory girls, the industrial psychologist went on to observe, disliked their work. They disliked having to 'clock in, to work all day, and never to stop work on their own accord'. They tried to escape from work whenever they could by 'lavatory-mongering', hiding in the toilets and sucking for a few furtive minutes on clandestine fags. 'The way they dash into the cloakroom when the closing signal is given,' the psychologist concluded, 'reminds one of prisoners suddenly released from gaol.'

In return for grinding out shoes, banging on typewriters and thumbing through invoices, women workers earned the lowest wages in the city. In the footwear industry 83 per cent of women workers got less than two hundred pounds a year. Of men in the industry, only 24 per cent got so little.

Men got better wages partly because they dominated the unions. Men dominated management too. And above all, men owned almost everything – most of the farms, most of the factories, most of the shops, warehouses, and workplaces in the province. United Footwear, for example, with all the lock, stock and barrel of the factory, the warehouse and machines, was the personal property of one man, a man called Stanley Norman Gabbatt, a man Ginnie never saw in her entire life, a man in a big house on Cashmere who spent the wealth she made for him on an unsuccessful courtship of the Christchurch Club.

'Bloody squatters,' he muttered to his wife, Gloria Gabbatt, one day after nobody but a hundred or so real estate agents, accountants, lawyers and industrialists had turned up for their black and white evening. 'I could buy or sell half them if I wanted.'

'Well, Stan,' Gloria Gabbatt replied, 'we can't make them come if they don't want to. It's a free country you know.'

'Bugger them,' her husband ardently replied, 'the stuck up bloody snots.'

Ginnie

When I turned sixteen I bought a glory box. I got it on time payment at Calder Mackays, a department store that sold cheap things. When I came home from work one day I found they'd delivered it and left it sitting on the front verandah at Moorhouse Avenue.

'Yer box is here,' Mum said. 'And yer needn't think I'm going to break my back helping yer git the bloody thing inside.'

Hock helped me drag it across the verandah and into a corner of our room.

It was made of rimu, stained dark and french polished. I lifted the lid to look inside and it was empty, and I felt sort of excited, and sort of scared.

After a while I managed to get some stuff into it, mainly linen, tablecloths, a few towels, and that. I tried to get something for it every week, but it seemed to swallow up stuff, that glory box, then come out looking as empty as at the start. I bought some things called supper cloths, stupid little bits of things that you was supposed to put on a side table when you served 'supper'. They was being advertised all over the place that year, so all the girls was buying them. And I bought flannels. And tea cups. And bread and butter plates.

But getting a glory box and filling it up was only half the battle. You had to get yourself a husband too. The problem was, there was a shortage of men cause of the war. There was always the Yanks, a few was stationed in town, but Hock warned me off them.

'Grubby sods, the Yanks,' she said. 'Stuffed up with clap.'

They seemed pretty thick sort of jokers too, the Yanks, small town jokers from the Ozarks who'd try to put across a big line like they was Clark Gable.

The girls who went after the Yanks got a reputation for being a bit dirty.

Dot Sewell, like, who when she was having her periods always seemed to smell bad. Everybody reckoned she never changed her pads, so one time somebody cut an advertisement for 'Modess' pads out of the newspaper and pinned it by her machine. Dot

Sewell didn't turn a hair, she just ripped it down, turned on her machine, and started working. ·

Girls like her seemed to think the Yanks was all right.

'There goes Dot Sewell,' people would say. 'She's mowed the lawn and dangling Yank bait.'

Mowing the lawn was what we said when we shaved our legs; and dangling Yank bait, that was what we said when somebody got their hair done in what the hairdressers called a 'pompadour'.

And if you didn't want to be like Dot Sewell you went out with local jokers. You'd have your hair screwed up into the latest shape, you'd put on your polished cotton dress, you'd turn up at the Cally or the Latimer or the Rendezvous, and after you'd paid two bob to get in you'd join the lines of girls sitting along the walls. The lights would dim and the band would start playing, Tommy Dorsey music, or Glenn Miller music, swing and big band and that.

Your foot would start tapping, and you'd sit there with a sort of hopeful smile on your face. You'd wait.

'The hicks aren't too thick on the ground tonight,' you'd say.

Hicks was what we called the men. A brown hick was a soldier, a blue hick was a sailor, and a mufti hick was a civilian. And while us girls was pretending to be Yvonnes and Cynthias and Dianas from Fendalton, the hicks would be trying to kid us they was all officers.

'I'm a captain in the army,' they'd say. 'I'm a flight lieutenant in the air force.'

But of course we knew they was all just privates or occasionally the odd sergeant. In fact when I think about it I never even danced with a sergeant, let alone a real officer. Even a sergeant was a cut above what a girl from United Footwear could expect to dance with.

If things went all right the hick would walk you home. You'd hang round outside the gate for a while, and if things seemed to be making progress the right way, there'd be a bit of kissing and cuddling. I quite liked standing at the gate doing that, it was like what you saw at the pictures. But I used to get a bit scared when the joker started to get all sort of hot and breathy.

'I'd better go in now or Mum might start yelling,' I'd say.

It worried me sometimes, I wondered why I was scared.

'I think I must be frigid,' I said to Hock in bed one night after a dance.

'No girl really likes it,' Hock said. 'But the hicks want it, so the trick is, make sure they pay for it.'

Things got worse after I broke the unwritten law one night and invited a joker inside for a late night cup of tea. I'd been at the Rendezvous and met this chap, Jim Farrier. He was a corporal and he seemed all right, though he wasn't particularly nice looking. He had a sort of squashed up face that made him look a bit like a flounder. But I was feeling fed up with Mum, she'd been carrying on about standing at the gate with jokers, so I'd decided I'd had enough.

'Mum doesn't like it when I stand out at the gate,' I said to Jim Farrier. 'Come inside and I'll give you a cup of tea.'

Well that was just to spite Mum, but it must of given Jim Farrier the idea I meant more than I did. When I sat down next to him with a cup of tea he started pashing me up like it was going out of style, pushing his tongue into my mouth and squeezing my tits really hard. I got sort of excited, though a bit sort of fierce too.

I didn't know exactly what was happening. He started pulling my skirt up. I kept tugging it back down again. Then in the end he got his hand up between my legs and started putting his fingers up me.

There was this sudden terrible pain.

'Argh,' I said. 'Shit.'

Jim Farrier looked sort of surprised, he pulled out his hand and there was blood on it. And before either of us could work out what to say next we heard a pair of heels clacking onto the back porch and the door opening and there was Peggy.

'Gidday,' she said, as though nothing unusual was happening. 'Tea still hot?'

Jim Farrier wiped his hand with a hanky. Peggy gave me a quick look. We talked for a while, then Jim Farrier said hooray and headed off home. I went to bed and wondered what it meant.

It had been horrible, I was sure about that. It had hurt.

169

'Think I'd better stay a spinster,' I said to Hock.

Then I met Cyril Callaghan.

Cyril Callaghan was lovely. The minute I first danced with him I seemed to turn all warm and sort of liquid and I thought *sex*. I knew that straight away. I wanted to have sex with him. He was in the army, Cyril, a private in the army, and he came from Phillipstown like me. And his face was so nice and gentle looking, his hair was soft and brown and wavy. He drunk a lot, mind you, he always took a hip flask to dances and as the night went on he'd get sort of droopy and heavy. But I didn't care, I tried to push that to the back of my mind cause he looked so nice and sort of soft, when he'd been drinking his eyelashes would sort of flutter down onto his cheeks. And when we walked home together I'd be hoping against hope that he'd do what Jim Farrier had done, or push me against a lamp post or something.

He never did though. I don't know what it was. I did my best to try to get him going, but half the time he didn't seem very interested. It might of been the drink. Often as not he'd be just about asleep by the time we got to the gate at Moorhouse Avenue.

And I didn't dare invite him in. Mum had found out about Jim Farrier coming into the kitchen, I think one of the boys must of told her, and the shit had really hit the fan.

'If you want to be a whore you can bloody git down the road to a whorehouse,' she said. 'But if yer intending to stay under this roof I'm telling you . . .'

Well anyway, there was nothing doing with Cyril. And in the end he let me down. We'd arranged to meet one night outside the gas works in Moorhouse Avenue. We was supposed to be going to the pictures. I stood there for an hour in front of the gasometers, a hot night in summer, I had lipstick and powder on my face, my hair up in a pompadour, and sweat trickling down my armpits.

'End of the big romance,' I said to Hock after I'd given up on him and walked back home.

'Plenty more where he came from,' Hock said.

But I went to the bedroom and cried.

After that I went out for a while with an air force hick, but

I didn't like him much. He'd take me walking of a night on the banks of the Avon, and of course we'd keep coming across people lying down having sex on the grass, all these shadowy figures sort of twined together and humping themselves up and down.

'What jer reckon?' he'd say.

I'd pretend I hadn't heard.

After a few weeks he sloped off and I never saw him again.

I went out with a real fly-by-night character after that. Ray Smith his name was, he was a clicker in a shoe factory in Sydenham, I met him at our works dance and I was quite impressed cause of him being a clicker. Clickers tacked down the linings in the soles of shoes and got good money. He had his hair slicked up in front and he had a little moustache.

'Like to go for a spin up Cashmere?' he said after the dance.

'Will your chauffeur be careful on the corners?' I said.

Cause I thought he was just having me on. But he took me outside and showed me a car, *his* car. Well I was in it in two seconds flat and we zoomed off down FitzGerald Avenue. He was the first joker I'd ever gone out with who had a car. In fact he was the last one too. And it wasn't just any old car – it was a sports car, a little Austin sports car with a canvas roof which he wound down.

'It's a warm night,' he said. 'Let's see the stars.'

And I thought, what a corny line, but I'd put up with anything to be driven somewhere in a car. So up the hill to Cashmere we flashed, past all the big houses lit up for parties, right up to Victoria Park, where we sat in the car and drank gin from a flask Ray Smith had. And we kissed, and I let him feel me up, and as we was doing it I was thinking about Mum, how her and the old man had gone up there on a dray years before to a works picnic, and how Mum had always told us the old man had ended up 'full as a boot'.

And there I was, sitting in a sports car drinking gin and being felt up by a clicker.

'You know he's married?' Monica said to me at the Rendezvous next night.

'Oh,' I said. 'No, I didn't. Well I'll scratch him off the list then.'

171

I was a bit scared of Monica. She thought it was important for girls to be nice and not to go too far. Well I didn't particularly care how far I went if I met a joker I thought I liked. I didn't think anything would stop me, but I wanted Monica to think I cared, so when Ray Smith came up to me a bit later I just said, 'Save it for your wife', and Ray grinned and walked away. Monica looked at me in an approving sort of way, like saying, that's right Ginnie, do things right.

But I felt a bit fierce, cause Ray had been good company.

'Your face looks a bit shiny Mon,' I said. 'You'd better go and powder it.'

The Industrial Psychologist

Another outstanding characteristic of factory girls is the degree to which their lives are absorbed by personal relationships. It is true that nearly everybody's life is dominated by personal relationships, but the lives of most factory girls are not only dominated but *absorbed* by this factor. This is partly due to the fact that their restricted education tends to isolate them from other interests, and their monotonous work, even if they like it, can hardly become an object of devotion. Moreover, repetitive work, even though it takes up the greater part of their waking day, leaves them free to daydream about personal relationships.

After all, when one considers that most factory girls spend anything from eight to twelve hours a day, enclosed in a single room, seated at a single machine, and performing a single operation, it is not surprising that in their leisure time they want and need, in contrast to their working day, informality, warmth, friendliness, variety, and entertainment.

The younger, unmarried girls have an all-absorbing preoccupation with the subject of marriage. This is certainly their main goal, to which everything else is subordinated. Very few girls have other outside interests, and they seem unaware of other possibilities. They therefore tend to regard factory work as a brief interlude in their lives, and whatever their attitude to the actual work itself or to the people in the factory, they want to be married and leave. They generally assume that they will be completely happy in their married lives and that all their problems will henceforth cease. They do not stop to consider that housework may be harder than factory work. Indeed, they do not even seem to think about housework. As for factory work, considered either as an alternative to marriage or in association with it, it just does not enter their calculations at all.

Fag

The men at Scholefield Electrical were always slinging off at me. Mr Scholefield didn't, he tried to be a bit of a father figure, but the men out the back would stare and make comments whenever I went into the workshop. And I had to go into the workshop, it was part of my job to take the men their cups of tea at smoko. If they saw me fidget, or scratch myself, they'd leer at one another.

'Ants in yer pants eh?' they'd say. 'Want us to give yer a rub down?'

At first I tried ignoring them, but that didn't work, they just got worse, so I started trying to answer them back saucily.

'You wouldn't know how to rub anyone but yourselves,' I'd say.

And they liked that, they'd laugh and say something else, and I'd have to quickly think of another answer back again. They thought it was a game, a bit of fun, but I hated it.

Just shut up, I kept thinking. Shut up and leave me alone.

Then after I'd been working for a while at Scholefield Electrical they started losing interest in that game. They didn't pay me quite so much attention. When I walked in they wouldn't stop talking among themselves – they'd just ignore me, just keep on talking. And it was horrible, it was even worse than when they'd slung off at me, because I discovered that they spent half the time talking about sex. Not love, not making love, but sex. They talked as though women were just things with holes for men to shove themselves into.

'She's always hot for it, that Doreen Glue,' they'd say. 'Half

173

the jokers at Alliance Electrical have been through her.'

It was horrible.

The men I danced with seemed hard and hungry like that too, or else they were just stupid little kids, young boys of seventeen or eighteen who were hopeless and clumsy and shy and tried to be what they called 'suave'.

It made me uncomfortable, hearing them say that, it reminded me that I had my own ideas about being suave too.

When in fact what was I?

A skinny clerk with scraggly hair and no bosoms who didn't even get her first period till she turned sixteen. And even when I did turn into a fully menstruating female, even when I'd dressed myself up in the smartest frock I could buy and had my hair permed and varnish slicked on my nails and lipstick on my mouth, I still felt as though I only barely passed muster.

At dances I'd sit there, waiting, hoping like hell somebody would ask me up, hoping like hell somebody wouldn't.

'Why is it always such a bloody struggle?' I'd say to Nancy Wand. 'Why does it always seem as though I'm in a tangle and that the more I try to fight my way out of it I find new strings tripping me up?'

Ginnie

One day I had trouble with my machine. I'd been at the Rendezvous that weekend and hadn't had any luck. And my stupid machine kept sticking. Blue smoke started coming out of it and the needle kept catching on the leather and going grrrr, grrrrrr. All of a sudden I gave a really vicious yank, pulled the leather out from under the machine, and busted the needle.

'Shit, fuck, hell,' I said. 'I wish there was a man that would marry me and get me out of this.'

9

Mister Right

Fag

'I'm eighteen,' I said to Nancy Wand, 'and I'm still stuck on the shelf.'

'You never know,' Nancy said. 'You never can tell what's coming round the corner.'

'Yes you can,' I said. 'The same old thing, that's what.'

A couple of men asked us up for a jitterbug.

We were at the Latimer, it was a Saturday night, and there hadn't been much talent. The two men who jitterbugged with us didn't look too promising either. They turned out to be West Coast miners in town for the weekend, so we got rid of them and went back to the chairs by the wall.

'See what I mean,' I said. 'On the shelf.'

'Never say die,' Nancy said. 'What about that chap over there, that tall dark chap? He looks nice, he might come over and ask me for a dance.'

'Looks all right,' I said. 'Looks a bit stuck up.'

He was slim and sort of tentative looking, wearing sports trousers and a tweed sports coat.

'He's been looking at us,' Nancy said. 'Bet if I give him the go ahead he'll come over.'

'Bet he doesn't,' I said. 'He doesn't look like the sort that dances with hoi polloi.'

'What's he doing here then?' Nancy said.

She started smiling in his direction and, when he saw her, pretended to be embarrassed, looked down at the floor, then looked back up at him again.

'He's coming over,' she whispered.

175

He stopped in front of us. Really very handsome, very nice looking, his hair very dark and his skin very fresh and smooth. And very polite.

'May I have this dance?'

It took me a moment to realise he was talking to me.

Nancy opened her eyes wide and I felt myself go red in the face. 'All right,' I said.

He took hold of me, the piano and sax and drums started playing, and we started scuttling round the dance floor together.

It was a foxtrot.

'This isn't the way the foxes trot in South Africa,' he said.

What? I thought. What's he talking about?

Then I realised it was a joke, he was saying silly things to have fun. So I tittered.

But then I felt scared, I couldn't think of anything to say, I couldn't talk like that; all I could do was grit my teeth in a smile and keep on foxtrotting. He was too polite, too well spoken; it seemed as though a tailor had come along and trimmed him off round all the edges.

'Were you in the war?' I said desperately after a while, thinking that at least war was something I could be expected to be ignorant about.

'Second Division,' he said. 'Infantry lieutenant. But these days I'm a public servant. Audit Department.'

A *lieutenant*, I thought. My god, a real lieutenant. But the Audit Department? What in Christ was that?

'Desk warming really,' he said. 'I was starting out at varsity when the war came along and my father wants me to go back. That's the way we're supposed to do things, one son gets the property and the others go into law or something. But I can't seem to settle down.'

I was absolutely bewildered. Mysterious, alluring words. 'Varsity.' 'Law.'

And what was that about 'the property' . . . ?

'You're from a farming family?' I said.

'Sheep,' he said.

A lieutenant! Who'd been to university! From a sheep-farming family!

This was my chance.

'Ashburton way,' he said. 'Near a little place called Alford Forest.'

'Oh yes,' I said. 'Will I have heard of your family's name?'

Trying hard to remember the names. The names of the *families*, the wool barons, the names in the gossip columns of the papers.

'Carrel,' he said, 'I'm Roderick Carrel. Roddie.'

Carrel! It *was* one of the names. I was dancing with a man from the gossip columns!

'I'm Daphne,' I said. 'Daphne de Feron.'

'Nice name,' he said. 'And do you work, or do you just dance?'

I laughed.

'Oh,' I said, 'I'm in the – electrical industry.'

And thank god he didn't ask anything more.

Things developed.

'I like talking with you,' he said over supper. 'You don't chatter and giggle the way most girls do.'

Then as he walked me down the steps of the Latimer it was almost too much for me, I was so keyed up and excited I was nearly hysterical, saying any desperate thing I could think of that might make me sound clever and upper class.

'I love this colonnade,' I said as we stepped down the stairs under the big white columns. 'It reminds me of Italy.'

'Italy is beautiful isn't it?' he said. 'When were you there?'

Which almost scared me out of my wits.

'In my dreams,' I said, quick as I could.

He laughed and looked at me sort of eagerly.

Keep it up, I thought. Keep on your toes, keep him guessing.

'Sorry about the car,' he said. 'Not much, but my salary's not much either.'

A little two seater Citroën, gleaming black under a street lamp like a chariot of luxury.

But I hadn't thought what it would mean, letting him drive me home. It meant we had to leave the glamour of the city behind

177

us and cross the railway into Sydenham, then darkest Addington, and finally Spreydon . . .

What would Daphne de Feron know about Spreydon? How would she even know such a place existed?

We stopped in Dunn Street.

Now what?

He opened my door for me, walked me towards the gate.

'Um,' he said.

My ears pricked up.

'Do you like walking?' he said. 'It's going to be a fine day tomorrow. Would you like to go for a walk with me?'

'That would be nice,' I said.

Oh prince of my dreams, I'd walk on my knees over broken glass for you.

By next morning I was so worked up I was in agony. He'd find out the truth about everything. He'd drive up and see Dunn Street in all its dingy detail under a horrible, naked sun. He'd see what I really was.

He'd make excuses. He'd go away.

I'd never see him again.

But when he did finally roll up in his little Citroën he didn't even raise an eyebrow.

'You look very nice,' he said, taking off his hat and smiling at me.

'Where shall we go?' I said after I'd twisted my fingers together and introduced him to Mrs Childer.

'Why not just stroll around the neighbourhood?' he said. 'It's all new to me, this part of town. Looks interesting.'

The last thing I wanted was to spend an afternoon stumping round Spreydon. But Roddie took charge and off we walked.

'Do many people own their own houses here?' he said.

'Oh,' I said. 'Some. I'm not really sure. Lots of them are just tenants.'

And as we walked past the rows of meagre little houses and the long blank walls of the factories and the warehouses, wandering through Spreydon up into Addington, along all the familiar old back streets and alleys, I started to see it in a new way, thinking how strange it was that to him all this seemed interesting, important, this dreary old stamping ground of South Christchurch.

I started to talk. I started telling him the truth about myself. How I'd been born in Spreydon and grown up in Addington and Phillipstown.

'And my name's not Daphne de Feron,' I said. 'It's just Daphne Feron, and most people call me Fag. And I'm just a dogsbody in an electrical supply shop.'

He laughed softly.

'Of course I didn't really believe in the "de",' he said. 'But I liked the way you told me about it.'

Which irritated me, I began to feel angry at him, this well groomed, well heeled man in his grey felt hat, walking round Addington like a psychiatrist visiting a mental hospital. So I started to try to shock him, I told him about the old man coming home smelling of beer and Sadie throwing stones at him, I talked about Mum nagging and bitching. And about my dreams, how I'd dreamed about getting an education, getting on in the world, and how I'd ended up banging a typewriter and selling radios in a shop in High Street.

Though somehow I felt I was betraying something, telling him things like that, telling him about Mum, and Sadie, and the old man.

But I kept on talking.

Roddie was very quiet and thoughtful. He nodded when I showed him our old houses in Kent Street and Braddon Street, and nodded again when I took him down Simeon Street to show him the place we were born, a place still full of yelling kids, a man sitting in his singlet on the verandah with a bottle of beer in his hand.

'Shut yer bloody gobs, youse bloody kids,' he yelled.

I poured it all out, I'd never tried to tell the story of my life to anybody before. It was strange, because all of a sudden I began to see that it *was* a life, it wasn't just nothing, as I'd always felt it was, it was a life story, and though it didn't exactly warm the heart to hear it, it was still something true, something real.

179

Until then it had never seemed real, not even the suffering.

'Working people have a lot to be angry about,' Roddie said. 'I think it's time things were changed. I've joined the Labour party. There's no reason why everybody shouldn't have a chance for a decent life.'

Suddenly I felt resentful again, I felt as though he wanted to take my life and pick up the whole of Phillipstown and Addington and Spreydon and put them in some filing cabinet in his brain, as though people like me were just some sort of problem for people like him to solve, as though the only reason he listened to me was to make sure I was the real thing, a real working class girl, who was unhappy.

'I don't regret it,' I said. 'It made me what I am. Mum made my life hell, but she knows things, she knows working people have to stick together.'

'Of course,' he said.

So I gave up.

'Well anyway,' I said, 'things are different now aren't they? Mum knows about the past, not the future. We don't all have to spend our lives in the same groove.'

Ginnie

World War Two couldn't last forever, though sometimes it felt like it would. Not long after I turned sixteen the Nazis surrendered and the Japanese looked like they was going under too.

'Yanks on top this time,' Mum said. 'Next time round it'll be somebody else. Same old story, and in the meantime us paying for it and gitting nowhere.'

Crowds of people went mad in the streets. The government and newspapers and the rest of them called it 'VE Day'. It was supposed to be celebrating 'Victory in Europe'. Then they dropped bombs on factory girls in Hiroshima and Nagasaki and they told us it was time to celebrate 'Victory in Japan'. At United Footwear the bosses gave us extra biscuits for morning tea and the loudspeakers screeched out 'patriotic songs'.

They gave me a headache, the patriotic songs.

'No work tomorrow,' Mrs Goodham told us. 'Everybody off for VJ Day.'

Standing at the tram stop on my way home I got bailed up by Ethel Stack.

'Exciting innit?' she said. 'What yer doing tomorrow?'

I didn't know Ethel Stack very well. She'd been in the machine room for a while and I'd run into her at dances and that, but that was about it. I was always a bit shy of her, she had a sharp sort of face and a quick tongue.

'Oh,' I said. 'Nothing.'

'That's no good,' she said.

'I thought I might wash my hair,' I said.

'That's no good,' she said again. 'Come round to our place, we've got a couple of boarders, and me and Mum'll be there, we'll have a few beers.'

I didn't want to say yes, I didn't want to go, though I couldn't think of any reason why.

'Men boarders,' Ethel said. 'Two jokers back from the war.'

That put me off even more. The last thing I wanted was to spend a holiday sitting round a kitchen table swilling beer and listening to a couple of drunk jokers tell yarns about the war.

'Nice jokers,' Ethel said. 'A bit quiet. One's called Bill and the other one's Jaz.'

Midday next day there I was, walking through Phillipstown to Mrs Stack's house in Nursery Road, wondering why I was going. I'd met Mrs Stack once before, she'd come to pick Ethel up from work one day, and I didn't like her. She struck me as a very brassy sort of woman, very hearty and jolly but fat and a bit slack looking. She looked like a brothel keeper, I thought.

But the house looked all right, old and small, but neat, with a little flower garden out front.

'Come on in,' Mrs Stack said. 'We've opened a flagon.'

It wasn't as dirty as I'd been expecting. The front room Mrs Stack took me into was quite tidy looking, there was a bay window and a lounge suite.

'This streak on the sofa is Bill Moffet,' Mrs Stack said. 'And the other joker over there is Jaz Smith. This is Ginnie, gents.'

I felt all sort of awkward, and I wished she'd told them my real name.

'Let's take the weight off,' Mrs Stack said, taking her own weight off all of a sudden, falling onto a bulging chair and making a sound like a big fat 'chuff'.

'Like a beer?' Ethel said.

'Oh,' I said. 'Um, no thanks. I've never really drunk beer, only gin.'

Mrs Stack gave Ethel a quick little look and Ethel sort of screwed up her nose.

Shit, I thought. How can I get out of this?

'Lemonade instead?' Jaz Smith said, picking up a glass.

'Um, all right,' I said. 'Thanks.'

And I decided I quite liked Jaz Smith.

After a while me and him ended up talking together while the others started playing poker.

'We've only just got back, me and Bill,' Jaz said. 'Time to get back into harness.'

He wasn't a kid, Jaz Smith, he was in his late twenties, a fairly small joker, sort of compact. His hair was wiry and sandy and his face was nice, I liked looking at it, it was tanned and friendly and moved a lot and there was little fine lines round the eyes and mouth.

A grown up person, who knew what was what.

'What's Ginnie short for?' he said after a while. 'Virginia? Marjory?'

'It isn't short for anything,' I said. 'It's the colour of my hair. My real name's Janet.'

'Wouldn't call your hair ginger,' he said smiling, 'I reckon I'd call it auburn.'

And of course I liked him even more for that.

'How about your name?' I said. 'What's Jaz short for?'

'James,' he said.

'That's a nice name,' I said.

And he looked at me in a quiet sort of way.

He had a bullet shaped head, Jaz Smith. I liked it, it looked sort of dependable, a reliable sort of head. And his eyes was really lovely, lovely brown eyes, very bright and sparkling and merry.

'Tucker time,' he said, nodding at Mrs Stack, who'd just stood up and was heading off to the kitchen.

There was a big heap of food waiting for us on the kitchen table, and a big, red faced, hearty looking joker standing behind a leg of mutton.

'Dig in before it gits cold,' he said.

I'd heard about him before, his name was Max something, he was a cook at a pub in Addington, and him and Mrs Stack lived together.

I was a bit shocked, being in the same room with two people that 'lived together'.

'Two four six eight,' Mrs Stack said, 'bog in, don't wait.' So we bogged in, and it was good food, lots of it too.

'Now we've plastered up a few cracks,' Mrs Stack said, 'let's git ourselves down town and see the parade.'

It was like a madhouse, that VJ Day in town. Me and Mrs Stack and Ethel and Max and Bill and Jaz rode in on the tram and when we got out in Cathedral Square it was packed tight with people, screaming and yelling and singing and dancing, shoving and pushing us along. The parade, which was why we was all supposed to be there, sort of fell apart as the afternoon wore on and all the laughing and singing started turning into swearing and vomiting, glass getting smashed and fists starting to fly, people falling into gutters, women with smudged faces crying on lamp posts.

'Let's duck in here,' Jaz Smith said to me. 'Quieter in the pubs than on the streets.'

He steered me into a hotel, the Oxford, a place in Victoria Square.

'A beer,' he said, handing me a glass. 'You look like you need it.'

I had a sort of confused awareness of being in what seemed like a film set, a film set in a movie about people drinking in a pub. It was the private bar, smooth wood panelling, brass fixtures, cigarette smoke, and leather and beer.

I'm inside the Oxford, I thought, drinking beer with a joker I hardly know.

'It's a weird day isn't it?' I said. 'I don't know whether I like it or hate it. But this beer tastes nice.'

'Best to take it easy,' Jaz Smith said. 'Don't drink it too quick.'

But before I knew it the beer was all gone.

'I wouldn't mind another one,' I said.

Jaz Smith looked at me a bit doubtingly.

'Well,' he said. 'If you're sure.'

He started telling me how good it was to be home.

'Not that it really is home,' he said. 'Me and my brothers and sisters was born in Timaru. There was six of us all told, but the two girls got infantile paralysis, they died when I was just little, and my brothers are up north working in the bush somewhere. When I left school I went up there too, but the south suits me better so I came back down here and got a job, linesman with the P and T, that's the Post and Telegraph Department. Hanging lines on poles. Then the war came and I got called up, and while I was away Mum and the old man passed away. I'm going . . .'

'Um,' I said. 'Would you excuse me for a minute . . .'

I ran to the toilet and was sick. The mutton Max had roasted for lunch and the pudding Mrs Stack had steamed and served to us with custard came out all mixed up with bile and beer.

I felt terrible, dirty and trembly and ashamed. I mopped my face with bits of toilet paper and poked at my hair in a mirror.

'Oh shit,' I said to my reflection. 'He'll think I'm just a pig.'

And I couldn't face him again. I crept out of the toilet round the back way, pushed my way through a crowd in the public bar, and got out onto the footpath.

Now what was I supposed to do?

The street was still like a madhouse, filled with yelling and screaming people.

'Think I need a breath of air too,' a quiet voice said behind me.

And of course it was Jaz Smith; it was like he was my fate.

So he took control, Jaz Smith, he got hold of my arm and steered me to the trams. He bought us two tickets and walked with me down the aisle.

'This is the best seat,' he said. 'Right in the middle. Won't rock you about too much.'

What a nice joker, I thought.

He started talking, nothing in particular, just talking about this and that, and I felt comfortable, relaxed and comfortable and somehow warmed up inside.

Maybe he's the one, I thought. Mister Right.

Though it was a bit of a come down if he was. He was only an ordinary working class joker, after all, with a head shaped like a bullet.

Maybe he is Mister Right, I thought again. And if he isn't, well, maybe he'll do. I'm getting sick of waiting.

But that was a bit premature, cause after he'd walked me home from the tram stop to our place in Moorhouse Avenue he shook my hand and said hooray.

'Off to the Coast tomorrow,' he said. 'Starting work there for the P and T. I was starting to tell you about it in the pub. Thanks for a nice afternoon. See ya.'

Tell me the old old story, I thought.

Fag

'Pop was never very free with money,' Roddie would say when he told me things about his childhood. 'Don't get the idea I was cossetted.'

But he was just showing his innocence, of course, the innocence people from his world always have about money, not understanding that the way he talked, the way he carried himself, the sort of easy confidence he always seemed to have, made it clear he'd woken up every morning and been tucked into bed every night with the soft rustling kiss of pound notes. Even the name he gave his father, 'Pop', was proof that he'd grown up in the cosy world of money where father is Pop and mother Mummy, where mouths are fed with beef and lamb, venison and pork, where nice little boys like Roddie, little, kind, cheerful children, run around big old houses, echoing big rooms, with tall trees and wide green lawns visible through the windows, sedan cars in the garage and cakes in the pantry.

'The privileged don't know they're privileged,' I said.

He looked surprised, then smiled.

'That's part of the problem is it?' he said. 'They think they're just ordinary and that everybody lives like them?'

'Let's not talk about politics,' I said. 'Let's go for a spin.'

So he'd kiss me, and we'd get in his little car and zip down Ferry Road to Sumner or New Brighton, we'd walk along the sand and eat ice creams on the pier. Or we'd zoom up the hill to Cashmere, we'd eat scones and drink cups of tea at the Sign of the Takahe and then walk on up to the summit. It was wonderful up there on the hills, it was so vast and airy and free, it was as though Christchurch was just nothing, just a flat strip of unimportance down below, and up above it a great big bowl of blue air, a huge luminous silver sky. And it was so nice to be with Roddie. He was so easy and congenial, he'd talk if he felt like talking, and he'd be quiet if he felt like being quiet.

'I'd like to meet your mother,' he said one day. 'What do you say to dropping in there and saying hello?'

He didn't like my answer.

'Give her a chance,' he said. 'She's probably mellowed quite a lot since you left home.'

'You can't mellow a pickled onion,' I said.

He smiled, then looked guilty at having smiled, then started talking about something else.

'Look what I've got,' he said one afternoon two or three months after we'd first met. 'Tickets for a ball.'

He waved some yellow pieces of cardboard at me and my stomach went cold.

'A ball,' I said. 'I've never been to a ball.'

But after a minute of fear and another minute of calculation I was panting to go. And I went. Not without a struggle. For a while it seemed I'd never manage to rake up a frock and some gloves and some shoes and all the other bits and pieces I'd need to appear on the dance floor at the Wentworth. But in the end I did it. The frock I borrowed from Ruby, which was galling

because it meant Ruby got a chance to bail me up for an hour
or so telling me off about not going home to see Mum. But as
I stood there in front of Ruby's mouth, watching it open and close,
I thought, well at least I've got the frock. Then after two weeks
of ripping seams open and pinning them up and stitching them
tight again I found myself twirling round in front of Mrs Childer
in the sitting room at Dunn Street.

'You'll be the belle of the ball dear,' Mrs Childer said. 'Your
waist is so trim and your frock looks just lovely.'

The belle of old Phillips Town.

The frock was satin, a beautiful glowing white satin.

'White muslin was the universal costume . . .'

And it was long, it swept the floor. It was the first long frock
I'd ever worn and it was wonderful.

'You look beautiful,' Roddie said after handing me a little posy
of freesias to pin on my frock.

I fell in love with myself as I stepped into the Citroën, my satin
skirts whispering to me softly. And when we walked into the
Wentworth ballroom from the street it seemed to almost hit me
in the chest. It was so big, so enormous, a gigantic high room
which just seemed to sparkle. So much light, so much colour, the
whirling frocks of the women.

Roddie took my hand and put his other hand on my back and
steered me onto the floor.

Don't fence me in.

The band played it, and I hummed it, and I thought, that's going
to be my song, that's what it's all about.

'I just want to dance and dance and dance,' I said.

When we walked over to a punch bowl a woman in yellow silk
and pearls came up and smiled at Roddie.

'So this is your mysterious little friend,' she said.

She talked to him across me, treating me as though I was a joke.
Then, just as I was seething with hatred of her, she turned and
sort of switched on a smile at me, lined up all her teeth in two
little rows close to my face.

'It's lovely to meet you at last,' she said. 'We've all been dying
of curiosity. I hope you have lots of fun.'

Other friends of his came up not long after, and then some more, and they all seemed to treat me the same way. They either looked right through me, as though I wasn't there, or else they talked to me in a sort of sickly sweet voice they obviously kept for kids and sick people and workers.

Roddie started to get angry.

'They behaved just like this when I joined the Labour party,' he said. 'When something unthinkable happens they just seal their minds up. They just pretend it's not there or they laugh at it.'

'It doesn't matter,' I said.

'Of course it does,' he said. 'But I hope that won't stop you from marrying me.'

'What?' I said.

I understood him all right, and of course he'd said what I wanted him to say, but somehow I felt listless, I didn't want to hear him saying things. I seemed all of a sudden to be uninterested, I felt that somehow something had gone wrong, that I'd wandered off somewhere and got lost.

'Will you marry me?' he said. Just like the movies. 'I love you very much.'

'Oh,' I said. 'Well all right.'

He smiled and kissed me, but looked a bit quizzical too.

'You're sure?' he said. 'You don't exactly seem to be leaping for joy.'

'Is that one of the conditions of acceptance?' I said.

But then I felt sorry, he looked hurt, and suddenly I felt as though he was very young, that he was just a little inexperienced child and I was an old, worn out woman.

'I'm very happy,' I said. 'I've been happy ever since I met you, and it's all because of you.'

So he smiled again, and I felt guilty again, as though I'd played a trick on him. And scared, as though I didn't want to depend on words for my happiness.

Over supper he told me all the plans he'd been making for us, how he wanted us to go down south to Timaru, where there was a job in the Audit Department.

'I don't really feel at home in Christchurch,' he said. 'I'd like

188

to be closer to the country. And it'll be nice down there for you, you keep saying how much you hate your life here. Timaru will be nice, a nice friendly little city where we can live a nice quiet life.'

I wasn't excited by the thought of living so far away, but I pretended to go along with him.

'It'll mean shifting away from your family,' he said, a bit thoughtful. 'You might not like to lose touch with your sisters.'

'I can get along without my sisters,' I said.

He took hold of my hand.

'My salary with the Audit Department wouldn't be much,' he said. 'But we could be comfortable enough on it. And we could buy a little house, I've got a scrap of money I inherited from an aunt.'

The band struck up and we started to dance again.

'I'll go and see your mother tomorrow,' he said. 'Ask her permission. Do the right thing.'

I just about choked.

'She'll have your guts for garters,' I said.

He laughed.

'I'm sure she's not as black as you've painted her,' he said.

It was autumn, a yellow autumn afternoon, and because it was warm Mrs Childer and I worked in the little garden at Dunn Street, pulling up weeds and clipping back bushes. Then we put our feet up on the front verandah and had a cup of tea.

'Roddie's late,' I said.

'Probably having a nice yarn with your mother,' Mrs Childer said.

'Probably lost his nerve and decided not to go and see her at all,' I said.

But just as I said it he turned up in his grey felt hat.

'Whew,' he said, sitting down on the verandah and shaking his head. 'Goodness gracious me.'

I laughed.

'We've got her consent at least,' he said. 'That's the main thing.'

Mrs Childer handed him a cup of tea.

'She's had a hard life,' Roddie said. 'You can see it in her face. No wonder she looks on the worst side of things.'

'What exactly did she say?' I said, though I wasn't sure I wanted to know.

'Oh,' he said. 'Nothing much really. Just told me a few home truths, that sort of thing.'

Now I was sure I didn't want to know.

'Poor old thing,' he said. 'What she needs is someone to love her.'

'She's not a poor old thing,' I said. 'She's an interfering old bitch and let's drop it.'

So we dropped it.

'Now it's settled,' he said after eating a couple of Mrs Childer's pikelets, 'you'll have to come down to Alford Forest and meet my parents.'

And of course I made excuses, and of course it was useless, so one evening in May I found myself sitting next to Roddie as the little Citroën flashed between dark trees and paddocks, heading for Trecarrel. Trecarrel was the name of 'the property'. Trecarrel, Alford Forest. It was a sort of incantation Roddie had taught me over the last few months. He'd smiled at me and told me all about it, about the walnut trees and the orchard, the family porcelain and the family history, about sleeping on 'pallets' on the verandahs in summer and about skating on the lake in the garden in winter. Trecarrel was an 'old property'. It was 'one of the original runs'. It was named after the family's 'old place in Cornwall'. It was a place where 'Pop' sailed out in a Buick to sit on padded seats at the offices of the county council, the hospital board, the agricultural and pastoral association. It was the place where 'Mummy' dispensed light and grace, kisses and vol-au-vents.

It gave me the creeps, the thought of all that land, all those empty spaces with nothing but sheep and the Carrels and their money.

'See those lights?' Roddie said. 'Alford Forest. Soon be home.'

It was like all my childhood dreams, all my fantasies about Cinderella and the goose maiden, when Roddie turned off the road up a long dark avenue. Then a big lawn, white under the moon, and a long house lit up like a liner about to sail off on an ocean cruise.

'Welcome home,' Roddie said, and gave me a kiss.

I felt terrified.

The front door opened onto a yellow hallway and three black figures appeared against the light. I wanted to die. I clutched my handbag fiercely and stepped up to meet them. As they came towards me they passed under a light and turned from black to grey. A man, tall and erect in a dark suit. And two women, two slim women, one young, one ageless, both with their hair piled up on top of their heads, pearls around their necks, tweed skirts, loose knitted tops.

And all so polite, horribly, horribly polite.

'So lovely to meet you at last. Pleasant run from town? I'm sure we shall all be such friends. But my dears, you must both be famished . . .'

Walking down a high hall, under an arch like something from a film set about Imperial Rome.

A discreet female whisper.

'If you'd like the bathroom . . .'

And yes, I would *love* the bathroom, cavernous and frighteningly marbled though it turned out to be, but I couldn't stay there forever, though the bath looked opulent enough to sleep in, if you padded it up with some of those fat towels . . .

I stiffened my back and stalked out into the dining room.

And wilted. A dim and glowing and endless dining room. Blue walls and red carpet and a big round table heaped up with white and blue vases, plates, tureens.

How can I get out of here? I thought. What the hell am I doing here?

They were like well painted and very well oiled machines, those people, they seemed to move and talk like very subtle robots. And it was terrible the way they *discussed* things. They wouldn't just talk, say what they'd done, what they thought, how they felt. They *discussed* things. They'd say, 'It seems to me that . . .' And then they'd say, 'or perhaps on the other hand . . .' And then somebody else would say, 'I take your point, but . . .' And then another person would laugh and say, 'Oh, apropos of that, I imagine . . .'

Though they were doing their best, trying to include me in the conversation.

'Do you like the country, Daphne?' Mrs Carrel said.

'No,' I said.

Mrs Carrel gave a very quick little look round the table, something I wasn't supposed to see, something she probably didn't even mean to do, because next she laughed a little and looked somehow apologetic.

'I'm sure you'll get to like the country in a while', Diana said. 'Town is nice, I always have such fun when I run up to Christchurch and go shopping or partying, that sort of thing. But there's nothing like the country, I just love the country.

Diana was Roddie's sister, very slim and pretty, with little teeth in neat white rows like beads on the bodice of a wedding frock.

There were brothers too, two brothers who were 'up at the Lakes for the shooting'.

Wherever 'the Lakes' might be. And whatever 'the shooting' was.

'Seed cake in your honour, Roddie,' Mrs Carrel said.

She turned to me.

'Roddie just adores seed cake, it's been his favourite since he was a tot.'

Everybody smiled, and everybody simpered, and I wanted to scream.

It was a succession of horrors all weekend.

'Daphne,' Mrs Carrel said to me in a mild, friendly voice after lunch the next day. 'People will be coming for afternoon tea. We change our dresses.'

I ran to my bedroom and panicked. I only had one outfit with me, my 'classic' suit, and I was wearing it.

The 'people' came. They were facsimilies of the Carrels, a whole Bentley full of them, and then a Rover filled with more. They sat around in wicker chairs on the verandah, drinking tea and talking. And after a while some of them strolled onto the lawn and started to play croquet.

Croquet!

Mr Carrel found me hiding in a corner in the drawing room.

192

'Ah,' he said. 'Studying the family tree? Glad you're interested. Bit of a hobby of mine, genealogy.'

'Yes,' I said. 'Um.'

I hadn't even noticed that on the wall next to me was a big chart spiked with coats of arms and names in gothic script.

'De Carrel of Trecarrel,' Mr Carrel said. 'If you look right down there you'll see Roddie's name. Roderick Alban Carrel. You'll see where the Alban comes from if you look up here in this corner, an old Norman name, first borne by Sir Geoffrey Allebone. Carrel itself is Cornish of course, first one to carry it was Hugues, follower of William the Conqueror, took the name de Carrel when he got the manor of Trecarrel. Now if you follow this line down here . . .'

And on and on and on.

Carrel, de Carrel, Trecarrel, I was getting hypnotised.

At last the weekend was over and we were in the Citroën again, speeding down the dark country roads.

'My god,' I said.

'Wasn't as bad as that,' Roddie said, 'was it?'

'All my dreams come true,' I said.

'What?' he said.

'Forget it,' I said.

Ginnie

One warm windy day in spring me and Tots was scrubbing down the front verandah at Moorhouse Avenue when a shadow fell across us. I looked up to see a bullet headed joker smiling down at me.

'Gidday,' he said. 'Been transferred back over here. Coast was a bit wet. Thought I'd look up old friends.'

It was Jaz Smith, of course. It was over a year since VJ Day and I'd forgotten all about him. But I must of been glad to see him, cause Tots just took one look at me and was on her feet.

'I'll go and make a brew,' she said.

So there he was again.

He took me out to the pictures that Wednesday, then we went

out for a walk Friday night. He picked me up after work and we ate sandwiches on the river bank and walked along the avenues. Then he came round Saturday night to take me to a dance, and I introduced him to Mum.

She didn't look at him, she just rested her chin in the crook of her hand and squinted.

'How do,' Jaz said.

'Make sure you git her home before twelve,' Mum said.

As we was walking along Ferry Road he stopped under a shop verandah.

'Got something important to say,' he said. 'You probably won't want to come to the dance after I've told you.'

As usual, I thought. Something gone wrong as usual.

'I'm married,' he said.

'Oh.'

'Happened over on the Coast,' he said. 'But she started going out with other jokers on the sly. When I found out, she didn't care. She said she wanted to have a good time while she could. So I left her.'

'That's all right,' I said.

And he looked really grateful, really happy.

'The thing is,' he said. 'I like you, Gin.'

'That's all right,' I said again.

Cause I liked him too, I believed him when he said his wife had done the dirty on him, I didn't think he'd of been the sort who'd of done it to her.

The dance that night was a Labour party do. It was in a public hall over the hill at Allandale, and after we'd jitterbugged a while we went outside for a walk in the domain. He held my hand and I felt really nice, sort of soft and warm and happy.

We lay down together under a big tree and started pashing.

'You really tempt me, you know,' Jaz said.

'Mm,' I said.

'It's all right though,' he said. 'Nothing's gonna happen, I'm a married man and till I'm free nothing's gonna happen.'

But of course something did happen. We started pulling our clothes up and getting carried away. And it was good, it was really

194

good. I was surprised I was enjoying it so much, cause I'd been a bit scared since that night in the kitchen with Jim Farrier, but this was different, this was really good.

I feel good cause it's Jaz, I thought.

Then there was this strong sort of shuddering feeling come over me, I felt sort of strange and happy. Somehow all of a sudden I felt like I was a big white sheet flapping in the wind on a clothesline.

Well it was an orgasm of course.

'Christ,' Jaz said all of a sudden. 'Quick! I've got to get out of this.'

What's he talking about? I thought.

But he didn't 'get out of it', he just started sort of trembling and then he started shoving and then he shuddered and shook a lot of times.

So that's sex, I thought. Well I can do with some more of that.

'If we end up having a baby,' I said, 'and it's a boy, we'll call him Allan after this place.'

Which must of scared the shit out of Jaz. But he didn't say anything, just lay there with me under the tree and mumbled nice words.

'When I'm free,' he said a few weeks later, 'will we get married? I'm going for a divorce. It'll take a while, but when it's through I'll be free.'

'All right,' I said.

And I was happy. I loved Jaz.

Somebody cares about me, I was thinking. At last somebody cares about me.

And I needed that, I needed it more than ever as the months went by, summer and then winter and then spring again, cause I felt lonely at home, and all sort of deserted. The day Fag got married was terrible, I was the bridesmaid, but I felt really morbid. I kept going to the toilet out the back to cry. Fag seemed to be in a daze too – at the end she just gave me a quick peck.

'See ya, Gin,' she said.

And that was the end of it.

Peggy got married a month later. She married Arnold Gee, a

195

brewery worker she'd been going round with for a while. Then a few weeks later Hock ran off to the registry office with a joker who worked as a builder's labourer. Suddenly the house at Moorhouse Avenue seemed all sort of empty. There was still some of the boys there, but the girls had all gone, all except Tots, who was working at a clothes factory.

'When your divorce comes through,' I told Jaz, 'we'll make a real little home together.'

But of course it wasn't as straightforward as that.

'I think I'm pregnant,' I told him one night as we was walking down Colombo Street to the pictures.

Jaz looked sort of strange for a minute, then he burst out laughing.

I thought he must of gone nutty.

'I feel really happy,' he said. 'I've always wanted a baby.'

I started to cry, I felt so relieved, I'd been dreading the idea of telling him, I'd been thinking he'd be scared off and clear out back to the Coast and leave me up shit creek all alone and only Mum to go to.

He took charge of it all, Jaz did. He rang up a doctor next morning and made an appointment for us, for Mr and Mrs Smith, and he told me what I had to do, that I had to take a urine sample with me, and he laughed at me when I went all red in the face. And he held my hand as we walked along FitzGerald Avenue to the doctor's rooms. And in the other hand he held the bottle of pee in a brown paper bag, it was in a lemon essence bottle Mum had just used making bath buns for aunty Millie.

The doctor was a bit bossy, a bit offhand, the way doctors usually are. But he did the things he had to do.

The 'results' was 'positive'.

'Next step,' Jaz said, 'is to talk to your mother.'

We found her at the kitchen sink with a wet rag round her head. She was peeling potatoes.

'We've got a bit of news,' Jaz said. 'We think it's good news, but you might think different.'

Mum put down the potato knife and scowled.

'How many other people know?' she said.

I felt really fierce with her, really hurt, I wanted to cry. All she cared about was whether anybody else knew.

'Nobody,' Jaz said. 'I can't marry Ginnie yet, I'm married to somebody else and the divorce will have to come through.'

'Fine bloody kettle of fish,' Mum said.

'We'll live together till the divorce comes through,' Jaz said. 'We'll get a flat somewhere. And we'll have the baby and when we're through the wood we'll get married.'

She looked at him, and she didn't believe a word of it.

Fag

'No family lined up in rows in some silly church,' I said. 'The registry office will do. We can just nip in, sign up, and nip out. Ginnie can be the witness. Then we can just jump in the car and head off to Timaru.'

'Fine,' Roddie said. 'If that's what you want.'

I was reckoning without Ruby.

'A car's just pulled up, dear,' Mrs Childer said, very anxious and a bit scared, two or three days later at Dunn Street. 'A woman's got out, she's coming up the path.'

Ruby, busting through the door with a big square black handbag, marching into the sitting room, taking possession.

'Things have changed since Mum was young,' Ruby informed me. 'There's no need these days getting married in back yards and that. Times are changing, some of us Ferons are gitting on in the world. Things are looking up.'

It was horrible, of course, it was like a record player turned up very loud playing my own old tunes back at me.

'I thought you always wanted a white wedding,' Ruby went on. 'You was always talking about it enough when you was a kid, white weddings and wedding breakfasts and rows of bridesmaids and that. What's come over you now?'

'Oh well,' I said. 'Um.'

'There's a Presbyterian minister up Beckenham way says he'll marry you,' Ruby went on. 'It's just a matter of slipping him a couple of quid.'

The only thing I dug in my heels about was my dress.

'I don't want to wear white,' I said.

Ruby eyed me up and down.

'Something in the oven?' she said.

'I just don't want to wear white,' I said.

I wanted to wear something special, something I liked, something I felt was my own.

I went along to a little shop in High Street, not a smart shop, not a shop for people like the Carrels, but a nice neat little place that sold nice neat little things. I riffled through the frocks they were selling off the peg. I tried some on, a green one, a gold one, and in the end I chose a blue crêpe one, a lovely frock I thought, with silvery beads across the bodice.

'I'll be able to wear it afterwards,' I told Roddie that evening. 'When we go out to parties and dances.'

'It's pretty,' he said. 'I'm looking forward to seeing you in it.'

Then he turned serious.

'I've had a phone call from Pop,' he said. 'Offering to help us. He means money.'

'Oh,' I said.

Shocked at how eager I was for him to accept.

'Turned it down of course,' Roddie said. 'We'll do things on our own, won't we darling?'

I smiled and said something friendly, but I hated him. What right did he have to decide things for me, what right did he have to turn down good money? I wanted to scream at him. But I didn't, I just sat there, and let him kiss me.

'One thing I've always wanted to do,' he said, 'is work on things with my own hands. Not just buy things, but make them.'

I asked him what he meant.

'Furniture,' he said. 'Odd jobs around the house, that sort of thing, like a working man.'

And then I just felt tired. What did he know about working with his hands? What did he know about my family amd me? Do people like us spend our whole lives working just so people like him can play carpenter?

'That'll be handy,' I said.

Next day on my way out to lunch from Scholefield Electrical I caught sight of a man walking towards me, an oldish man I couldn't remember having ever seen before. But somehow he looked familiar. He was a labourer, I could tell that, and funnily enough the more I looked at him the more he reminded me of Eddie and Sammie and Bobsie, the same sort of face, same sort of build, only with a mop of flaming red hair on top, shaved up the sides.

'Dad?' I said.

He stopped in his tracks.

'Well well well,' he said. 'If it isn't my little girl Hock.'

'No I'm Fag,' I said.

'Little skinny Fag?' he said. 'Well well well, the years roll past and youse kids grow up and what does that mean about the old man? Due for the glue factory I suppose.'

I felt bewildered. Here I was standing on the footpath with him, I'd been longing for him ever since I was a kid, and now here he was. And I wasn't feeling happy, I wasn't feeling angry, all I felt was embarrassed and, when I started to think about it, bored.

'Are you down here for good?' I said.

'No fear,' he said. 'Wind blew me in this morning. Back up to Kaikoura tomorrow.'

'I'm getting married,' I said.

'Well bugger me days,' he said. 'Little Fag a bride, eh? Well I'll be buggered. Hang on a minute, you'll need a present from your old man.'

'Oh,' I said. 'No, it doesn't matter, don't worry.'

'A pitcher,' he said. 'I'll buy yer a pitcher.'

I was so confused I didn't know what he was talking about. A jug? I thought. Does he mean a jug? Then I saw a sign over the door he was leading me through, Bellevue Picture Framers.

'Any pitcher you like,' he said.

I looked around to see what I could find for two or three pounds.

'Sky's the limit,' he said. 'Git in while the going's good.'

I saw a painting I liked, a watercolour of Christchurch from Cashmere, yellow and blue.

199

'That's nice,' I said. 'How about that?'

'She's jake,' he said, poking round in his pocket and pulling out a roll of dirty notes.

He seemed blank all of a sudden, he didn't say anything more, just paid for the painting, watched it wrapped in brown paper, then kissed me on the cheek.

'Love to yer mother,' he said, and was gone.

The last thing Mum wanted was a message of love from my father.

We got married on a sunny Saturday in July. I was nearly eighteen and a half years old. Roddie was in his mid twenties. The church was pretty, a little colonial church at the end of an avenue of big bare trees off Colombo Street.

Frank Morgan stood by to 'give me away'.

'Hope you have a happy life,' he said to me that morning. 'He's a good man and if the two of you stick together you'll be on top of the world, like Ruby and me.'

I wasn't sure I wanted to end up like Ruby and Frank, but I tried to smile.

'Cheer up,' Frank said. 'Not a funeral you know. That's what they always say at weddings, it's not a bloody funeral you know.'

The wedding service was ridiculous, of course. The Ferons felt uncomfortable, wriggling and squirming in their seats. And the minister muttered on, mouthing all the formulas.

Oh get on with it, I thought. What the hell are we doing in a church anyway?

But when it came to the vows I listened, I listened to them carefully and thought to myself, yes, I mean this, this is the real thing, I'm going to make a good job of this marriage, not like Mum and the old man.

' . . . to love, honour and obey . . .'

The word 'love' pulled me up a bit.

Making love, I thought, tonight we'll be making love for the first time. That'll be nice, it'll be nice when we get to the hotel and get into bed. We'll make love.

The Dainty Inn on High Street did a regular line in wedding breakfasts. Ruby had arranged for us to have the five bob one;

200

five bob a head for sausage rolls and triangular sandwiches, round pies, fluted jellies, dishes of fruit salad and ice cream. There was a 'head table' with places set aside for Roddie and I and, lined up on each side, 'best man and bridesmaid', 'groom's parents', 'bride's parents'. Except of course that there wasn't a bride's father. For a moment I thought I should stick the painting of Christchurch on the empty seat where the old man should have been sitting, but then Frank Morgan came to the rescue and sat down in it himself.

'This is a happy day for me,' Roddie said at the start of his speech. 'The first of many happy days . . .'

I felt lonely, I felt as though somebody was missing. Who was it? Not the old man, I didn't want him. And not Nancy Wand, she'd gone up north and said she was never coming back. Not aunty Aggie or aunty Millie, sitting side by side and exercising their jaws down at the bottom of the table. And not Mrs Palto, who bustled up to me after the breakfast and planted a wet kiss on my cheek.

'Ach, you vill be happy now,' she said. 'I saw you born and I hope to see you with a baby of your own. But don't forget your mother, Daphne. Her life has been hard. She did her best by you.'

But I didn't want platitudes from Mrs Palto.

Who was it I missed?

The Carrels were there, doing their duty, drifting into the Quality Inn with a nonchalant air as though they spent all their lives going into cheap little tea shops down the wrong end of High Street.

'Call me Pop,' Mr Carrel said.

'That would be lovely,' I said. 'I'd love to.'

No more able to call him 'Pop' than the prime minister.

Mrs Carrel was wearing grey silk, a few diamonds, and a little hat of white velvet.

'Welcome into the family, Daphne,' she said.

Mum stalked up in a limp frock of blue cotton, a navy blue straw hat rammed down over her skull.

'I hope yer not expecting me to pay for this bun fight,' she said.

I looked at Mum, her little pinched face and tight little gestures, and I was frightened to realise I still wanted her to love me.

'It's all right,' I said. 'I thought Ruby told you. Roddie and I are paying.'

'Hmph,' she said. 'Wish you both well then.'

And off she stalked again.

'Funny isn't it,' Ginnie said coming up to me, 'Mum and you both wearing blue.'

I was horrified to realise it was true, Mum's limp cotton frock was just a shade or two darker than my own lovely dress with its silver beads and padded sleeves.

'Mrs Carrel,' Roddie said to me. 'Time for us to be off.'

Mrs Carrel? I thought. She's his mother . . .

And for a moment or two I was confused. It was as though I was Roddie's wife, and his mother, and my own mother too, Mum in a limp blue frock.

'Next stop, Federal Hotel,' Roddie said as we pulled out from the kerb.

It had always been my dream to get inside the Federal Hotel, ever since Ginnie and I had read about the Stevenson-Merbrook wedding.

'Veil of tulle and beautiful old lace. Blue cloques with slit bodices caught by silver and pearl clasps.'

Ever since the days we'd gone up town to collect Mum's maintenance and, stopping to rest outside the courthouse, looked across the quiet green of Victoria Square, past the statues and the fountain, to see the facade of the Federal Hotel looking back at us with disapproval.

Now the door of a room in the Federal Hotel closed behind me.

We'd had our experiments, of course, Roddie and I. Up on the hills in the shelter of a pine plantation, or in a sandy hollow between clumps of marram at New Brighton, snuggling down and fumbling around and getting ourselves steamed up.

'We'll save the best bit for later,' Roddie had always said. 'For when we're alone together.'

And now we were.

'It's nice,' I said to him after we'd been going for a while. 'It's a pity I'm so darned tired.'

And half an hour later, while Roddie snored and snuffled on the pillow alongside me, I lay alone there in the dark room, awake and wondering.

I lit myself a cigarette.

Inhaled.

Exhaled.

PART FOUR

10

Wives, mothers

Fag

It was an adventure, spinning across the plains with Roddie, frost crackling on the windscreen, woollen rugs warm round our knees, a thermos of hot tea snug between us, our eyes fixed on the Alps in the distance.

'Mum's never been this far west in her life,' I said. 'And she's never been as far south as Timaru, and she's never been as far north as Kaikoura.'

'Things will be different for you,' Roddie said. 'Sky's the limit. Aren't the mountains beautiful!'

And they were beautiful, the Alps. Pink and distant when we first set out from the city, white and looming as we drove closer to them. White and looming, big and blank, then bigger and blanker, taller and wider, till suddenly somewhere about Bealey they seemed to fill up the whole world and I felt frightened.

Roddie took breaths of the hard mountain air as we drove along.

'Marvellous,' he was saying. 'Puts things in perspective, being in the mountains. Helps you see clearly.'

Which frightened me even more.

'They don't help me see better,' I said. 'They block things out, if you ask me.'

But he wasn't asking me, he just looked at me with friendly unbelieving eyes.

What's wrong with me? I wondered.

The whole honeymoon was like that. It was all just too lonely and big, all those high white mountains and green wet forests and black deep lakes. And the glaciers. Big and cold and careless, like all the 'scenery', all the 'vistas' Roddie kept talking about.

'Beautiful landscape and friendly people,' he'd say. 'What more could you ask?'

We'd be buzzing along through a forest and we'd come out at a hotel and Roderick would stop.

'This do, d'you think?'

And of course I'd say yes.

And inside would be people. Friendly, chatty, busy little people. Australians, Americans, English, North Islanders. Waitresses in white aprons, a publican with a red face, a landlady with hair permed into steel wire. 'Cosy,' Roddie would say. 'Friendly.'

And he'd walk through all the horror of it, oblivious.

At one place after dinner people drank whisky and laughed and sang around a piano. Roddie and I sang a bit too, and drank whisky, then sat down and talked with 'the other Canterbury couple', a fussy old man and woman nursing brandy and pursing their lips in a corner.

'Ordinarily, my dear,' the woman said, inclining a pair of gold-rimmed glasses at me, touching the back of my hand with her fingers, just the tips of four thin and blue little fingers, 'ordinarily we prefer not to stay at this – this quality of hotel. But . . .'

She raised her fingertips a moment then dropped them again, as if from exhaustion.

She wanted an accomplice, she was as frightened as me.

'I'm so homesick,' I whispered. 'All I want to do is get back to Christchurch.'

'Oh yes,' she said, excited, ecstatic. 'Dear Christchurch, the Avon, the Cathedral. And the people, the nice people.'

She bent a little closer.

'Have you noticed, my dear,' she confided, 'how nobody else ever seems nice the way Christchurch people are?'

I hated her then, I hated the Avon, and the Cathedral and the nice Christchurch she was talking about. She was just as much a stranger to me as the Australians, the English, the North Islanders getting drunk on gin. Roddie.

Well that wasn't a comfortable thought. I looked away from the woman, behind her. And saw the Alps through a big picture window, the Alps gleaming white and terrible under the moon.

There was a sudden silence. Everybody stopped talking, looked towards me.

I felt terrified, I felt as though they were all about to turn on me, as though somehow they'd realised I was an outsider and were turning on me to kill me. A little girl came running towards me. A blue satin ribbon in her hair, a little posy in her hands. She stopped in front of me and thrust the posy out.

'Oh,' I said. 'Thank you. That's nice.'

The landlady stood. Smiled a big, motherly sort of horrible smile.

'A little posy to welcome a bride,' she said.

I just about shredded the flowers to pieces as I sat there, trapped on the sofa, while they all grinned and clapped and drank a toast.

'To the honeymooners,' they said.

'Why can't they damn well leave us alone,' I sort of hissed at Roddie.

He was surprised, he looked puzzled.

'They're trying to be kind,' he said. 'They're nice friendly people.'

Next morning was our last.

'Can't wait to get back,' I said as we headed up the Otira. 'Can't wait to start our new home.'

He could understand that, he approved of that, so he reached across and squeezed my hand.

And it was nice, I loved him, I did want to set up a home with him, he was my friend, he was being good to me, I could trust him.

'Welcome back to the big smoke,' he said as we drove in that afternoon through the western suburbs.

He was being sarcastic because of the smog. It was absolutely cold and still, the air, and the smog was a dirty yellow stain for miles above us. But it didn't worry me. Smog was part of the place, I'd never known anything but smog. And as we drove in through the western suburbs that afternoon I felt that I'd never loved Christchurch more, never been so sure it was my home.

Not that it was any more. Next morning Roddie and I set off for Timaru.

The Historian

'TIMARU, SECOND CITY OF THE PLAINS', was what they called it. A town of twenty thousand people, a town of undulating streets, brick and tile bungalows, gardens and hedges along the long swelling ridges of South Canterbury downland. Caroline Bay, the 'playground of South Canterbury', a crescent of smooth sand and calm water, backed by warm cliffs and the dome of the Hydro Grand.

A working class of wharfies and clerks, bank tellers and shop girls. And factory hands; one out of every four Timaru families depended on wages from manufacturing.

A middle class of shopkeepers and 'professional men', retired farmers and factory owners.

An upper class of 'old families', Rhodeses and Elworthys, Rollestons and Studholmes, landowners and lawyers.

A Labour member of Parliament, because most people were workers. A 'Tory' city council, because in Timaru as in most places power meant money. The town had always been governed by what its historian called 'men . . . associated with finance and big business'.

Timaru grew larger, more 'prosperous', more comfortable every year. The Timaru Yacht Club marina was enlarged, the gardens along Caroline Bay grew more and more colourful, more and more convoluted. Every summer twenty thousand people drove down to this 'Riviera of the South' to unload their picnic baskets and sunbake their hopes on the sand of Caroline Bay.

Fag

When we reached the top of the hill and started driving down through all the houses and saw Caroline Bay in front of us, I thought what a nice town it looked. The bay looked so lovely, so nice and clean and gleaming. And the whole town seemed like that, very clean and orderly, everything very solid and substantial. And it made me feel a bit inferior, reminded me who I was, Fag Feron, somebody who'd been just dragged up any old how in the back streets of South Christchurch.

210

So the town made me feel angry. It looked so handsome, so smug.

It's just a little hick town, I said to myself. Not a real city, not like Christchurch.

For the first few months I went into myself. Roddie worried about me; he couldn't understand what was happening, but he was kind and patient and nice. And in the end, when I found I was pregnant and I started having terrible mornings feeling sick and miserable and helpless, he wiped up the vomit and smoothed back the hair from my face.

'Bound to be a place on the market soon,' he said. 'Just a matter of time.'

We hadn't been able to find a house of our own, so we'd had to board in a stuffy little bungalow with the Meeks. The Meeks were farming people, what Roddie called 'small farmers'. They'd retired from their farm and come down to Timaru to spend their last twenty years playing bowls at Caroline Bay, and though they were nice to us, very nice, I was desperate to get out.

'Last place I thought I'd find myself,' I said. 'Trapped in a bungalow with an old man and an old woman and two hundred china cats.'

'It's the war that's done it,' Roddie told me. 'And the depression before that. There's been about fifteen years of houses unbuilt.'

Sometimes I felt like suggesting that he ask his father to do something. If he let 'Pop' pull a string we'd be in a house in ten minutes.

But of course Roddie wouldn't dream of that.

'What we want is a nice little place,' he'd say. 'Something we can pay cash for. Some place I can potter round in, teach myself a bit of woodwork.'

A couple of months into my pregnancy I was standing in a shop, sizing up some nylon stockings, when I overheard a woman talking to the shopkeeper.

'A coupla places,' she was saying. 'Down Circuit Street. Public Trust's putting them on the market.'

I grabbed the woman and interrogated her, got the details, ran

211

down to the Audit Department and burst in on Roddie.

'There's a place on the market,' I said. 'Two places. You're to ring this number, I got it from a woman.'

Roddie rang.

'Yes,' he said to the voice on the other end. 'Mmm. I see. Yes.' While I tore out my hair.

The houses weren't officially on the market, it turned out. They were to be on the market the next day, but the person Roddie was talking to wouldn't give the address. Roddie asked to have a word with somebody higher up. The somebody higher up turned out to be from one of the 'old families'. He'd been to school with Roddie. They got chatting. Soon the address and all the rest of it came out and Roddie was told he could go and have a look at the houses that night so long as he took care not to be seen.

That night after dark we walked very slowly up and down Circuit Street, eyeing up the houses. Two cottages, very old, very small. Half an acre of overgrown land. They were like Addington houses. The whole street reminded me of Addington, a working class street, old cottages, a few workshops, and a pub on the corner. So it felt reassuring to be there, to see that even in smug little Timaru there were places like Addington or Sydenham or Phillipstown.

'Well they're not very nice,' Roddie said. 'I was hoping they might have one or two nice features, a bit of a verandah or a bay window or something.'

'Yes,' I said. 'But they look quite neat don't you think.'

'Suppose so,' he said. 'Pretty old. What do you reckon?'

'Let's buy them,' I said.

Suddenly everything was exciting. The bustle of meeting lawyers, bankers. Handing across the money for the houses. Shopping for furniture. And summer, a lovely warm December.

'Thanks so much,' I crowed at Mrs Meek the day we shifted out. 'You've been very kind and I've had a lovely time staying with you.'

Roddie raised an eyebrow.

When we took possession that morning it was a bit of a shock, but I soon bounced back. The garden was a wilderness, weeds about a yard high. And the house, after we'd pushed open the back door, turned out to be a succession of small and dark and dirty little rooms. Two little rooms out the front, a passage down the middle, a kitchen out the back and then off under a lean-to a tiny little scullery and dingy little bathroom. The barest, dirtiest looking place I'd seen for a long time.

Roddie stood in the kitchen and looked a bit desperate.

'I don't know . . .', he said. 'Perhaps we're a bit game taking this on.'

'Oh it's lovely,' I said. 'A lovely, nice little old cottage, I'm going to plant flowers in the garden and I'm going to make this kitchen really cosy, a nice old fashioned cosy kitchen.'

In fifteen minutes I was down on my knees scrubbing grease and dirt off the floor, a bucket of hot soapy water beside me, a jam pan of extra water steaming on the coal range.

'Now I know what you mean,' Roddie said, 'when you talk about being a worker.'

And he was right. It was damned hard work those first weeks in Circuit Street – the place was so filthy, everything was so rough – but I was happier than I could remember having ever felt before.

After we'd cleaned up we had to spend the next few weeks fixing up the place next door, the second house, which was let to a family of tenants. The tenants had been renting from the Public Trust and wanted to stay on, but their roof was leaking and their rooms were a bit shabby.

'They need a new roof,' Roddie said. 'And new wallpaper inside.'

'Mm,' I said.

It seemed miraculous to me that all of a sudden I wasn't only a 'home owner' but actually a landlord too. All of a sudden I was a Mrs Moneygall, a Mrs Stevenson, a Lady Pelf. And I was starting to feel the way they felt too.

'Shouldn't we get ourselves comfortable first?' I said. 'Why should tenants live better than us?'

Roddie looked a little indignant.

'They're our tenants,' he said. 'We have to do the right thing by them.'

Not that the tenants were grateful to Roddie for doing 'the right thing', of course. They were working people and they didn't exactly love landlords. Their name was Spade, and Mr Spade was a labourer, a big fat beer swilling labourer who worked in a builder's yard down in the port. Mrs Spade was a fat little woman with ginger hair and ginger eyelashes. I'd see her all day long in her back yard, waddling in and out with her washing. I took a dislike to her, and I'd grit my teeth of an evening when Roddie and I were sitting over our dinner and we'd hear her yelling out from her back door.

'Tea time, youse kids. Come and git yer tea.'

It wasn't that there was anything particularly unusual about the Spades, they were just ordinary working people. It was just that I wanted everything to be nice.

And it was, it was starting to be nice. Roddie bought himself some carpentry tools. He was very determined and excited, and he blundered round with the saw and hammer and screwdriver, stopping up boards, putting up shelves. He wasn't much good at it, but he enjoyed it, rolling up his sleeves, spitting into his palms. And after a while he got better. Mr Spade came in and gave him a hand, taught him a few tricks.

They took the coal range out one weekend, heaving and shoving. Then on the Monday a lorry drove up and unloaded a shiny new electric stove.

It was marvellous, that electric stove. I stood in front of it, looking at the gleaming white enamel, the sparkling chrome, the black knobs and levers.

'That's just the start,' Roddie said. 'We'll do it in stages. We'll build out from the kitchen, we'll add on a new bathroom, hang some nice wallpapers, put down a carpet . . .'

I spent hours with the new furniture, the lounge suite of brown hessian, the bedroom suite of blond rimu, the dining suite of oak. I shifted each piece about, squinted at it from all angles, inched the sofa a little further to one side, the bow fronted bedroom cabinet across to another side.

And it was wonderful.

Our home. Our cottage home.

The Carrels came down for a visit, arriving in state one afternoon with a car full of 'little presents', 'old things from home we've no earthly use for'. A pressure cooker, brand new, untouched since Mrs Carrel a day or so earlier took it out of its box so she could pretend to us it was just an 'old thing'. And saucepans. And a wine table. And linen, beautiful crisp white linen with a little C for Carrel monogrammed in each corner. And a gravy boat, and forks. And a copy of the family tree.

'I've been knitting one or two things for the baby, Daphne dear,' Mrs Carrel said after her first sherry.

From then on every second week a parcel would arrive for 'Mrs R. A. Carrel', a brown paper parcel which, when I slit the string, would pop open to expose a warm little bundle of lovely creamy soft things, jackets and bonnets, cardigans and bootees.

Roddie took me up to Trecarrel for family Christmas.

Singing carols by candlelight in the drawing room. Hanging tinsel on a monstrous fir tree in the entrance hall. Hiding presents in the garden for the children to find. Pulling crackers, and squealing with delight. Chatting, and laughing.

'Oh my dear!'

'What a darling.'

'The *sweetest* little thing.'

'Daphne dear,' Diana said to me, taking hold of my hand and running me across the room to where a tall man about thirty years old hid like a shark among a seaweed of glossy curtains. 'This is Maxwell. I'm sure you'll both like one another, and of course you're going to be brother- and sister-in-law.'

Maxwell Urquhart and Diana had 'announced their engagement' a few weeks earlier.

'We won't be anything to one another, actually,' he said. 'The spouse of an in-law is no connection, under law.'

'Really?' I said. 'How interesting.'

Diana smiling at us both, holding both our hands.

'Daphne worked in a legal office once,' she said brightly.

Maxwell sort of sneered, but didn't say anything. After a while Diana and I crept away.

'He's so far up his nose he can't see the bloody ground,' I said to Roddie that evening as we went for a walk together in the home paddocks.

'Look at that lovely sky,' Roddie said.

So I took the hint and shut up.

Next morning, coming back by myself from another walk through the paddocks, I overheard two voices filtering through a hedge.

'Of course,' the first voice said, 'his people aren't exactly . . .'

I recognised that voice, it was Miss Fitzroger, a terrifying woman built entirely out of ramrod and pearls, she was what the Carrels called the 'maiden aunt' of the family.

'His father was a schoolmaster,' the other voice said. It was Mrs Carrel. 'A state schoolmaster down Dunedin way or somewhere. But he's dead, one can say that for him. The mother too.'

'A schoolmaster,' Miss Fitzroger said, with a sort of theatrical sigh. 'Still, these days . . .'

'Yes,' Mrs Carrel said. 'These days young people marry as they please. Look at Roddie . . .'

Tinkling laughter.

'Dear little Daphne,' Miss Fitzroger said. 'I'm so fond of her already. I must say she has a certain *piquancy*. I find it very refreshing. She reminds me of a little watchful rat.'

A rat! Me, a rat!

'Maxwell Urquhart, on the other hand . . .' she added.

'Yes?' Mrs Carrel said.

'Maxwell Urquhart, on the other hand . . . More of a . . .'

'Bulldog, dear?'

'I rather think yes,' Miss Fitzroger said, ending the conversation with a neat little clink which I supposed was the sound of a tea cup returned to its little bone china saucer.

This was the first time I discovered that there were some people who thought they were superior to schoolmasters. And who even thought they were superior to lawyers, because Maxwell was a barrister and solicitor, he was practising in Ashburton, and when I'd first heard about it from Roddie, memories of old Grace swelled up in my head and made me feel as though I was going to burst

216

with indignation every time I saw Maxwell Urquhart marching around the grounds.

It was hot that summer. Roddie and I spent evenings strolling along Caroline Bay, strolling along the crescent of sand then going up to the Hydro Grand to sit at a big window drinking whisky and soda and watching the ocean turn pink below us. Pregnancy seemed to suit me, the more pregnant I got the more my skin seemed to grow smoother and soft, my hair sleeker and glossier.

I was starting to feel like a lady.

And I *was* a lady. I was a householder, a ratepayer, a wife, a mother. I had tenants, I had soft skin and a husband from an 'old family'. I looked at the fashion magazines, I saw that Italian princesses and Hollywood stars were changing their hair styles, they were giving up curls and going in for a new 'classic' look.

Right, I thought. No more perms.

I let my hair grow longer, I put a bottle of expensive tint in it to turn it from mouse to 'auburn'. I dragged it back from my forehead and knotted it behind me in a little low chignon in the nape of my neck.

I bought myself a pair of sunglasses. I strolled along Caroline Bay with a husband on my arm, a baby in my womb. I dreamed.

Axminster carpets. Frigidaires.

Ginnie

The day I left home Mum gave me an old frying pan.

'Here,' she said, shoving it at me. 'You might as well have this.'

Though she didn't say goodbye.

I felt good about leaving home. I wanted to be with Jaz, I was glad we was having a baby, and I was glad I'd seen the last of United Footwear.

'No sense both of us working,' Jaz said. 'Best for you to build up your strength.'

Not that I was fading away exactly, in fact as the baby got bigger I put a lot of weight on round the belly, and I started putting it on in other places too. I was worried I'd end up really fat.

'More for me to cuddle,' Jaz said.

We went to live in Palmers Road, a long straight road lined on both sides with little jerry built bungalows sort of plonked down one after the other on top of sandhills out North Beach way. We'd seen it advertised in the paper and went out on the bus to take a look at it. It was pretty awful, a fibrolite house, very small, cramped and grubby. It belonged to a family called Brown. He was a labourer with a broken nose. His wife was really skinny, with scraggly sort of hair and a tongue that could take paint off a tram. And there was five kids, five wild, dirty, sad eyed little kids.

'We can do better than that,' Jaz said to me in the bus on the way home.

But we couldn't.

'It's all right,' I said. 'We can manage.'

So we shifted our stuff in. A little table we'd bought, just a wee wooden table. And a bed, that we bought at a second hand shop in Phillipstown. It was a good thing we didn't have much, cause there wasn't much space to put it. We only had one room, that was all, one little dark room that never got any sun.

'You can use the kitchen and bathroom,' Mrs Brown said, 'when I'm not using them.'

Me and Jaz got a shock when we walked into the bathroom the first day after we arrived. The bath was full up with coal. I'd heard about people using baths to keep coal in, but I'd never actually seen it before. Well we got a shovel and dug all the coal out, scrubbed the bath, filled it up, and had a good soak. And the funny thing was, Mrs Brown shoved the kids in there that night and gave them all them a bath too. So what they'd done to get clean before that I don't know.

I think she was sort of cowed down by her old man, Mrs Brown. He spent most of their spare money on beer and the horses. And instead of taking it out on him she took it out on the kids.

She was really terrible to those kids. She used to swear at them, and slap them, really belt them. The oldest one, a girl called Suzy, really got the abuse.

'Shut yer face,' Mrs Brown would scream. 'Stop yer whingeing, you little bastard.'

Mrs Brown had had Suzy before she got married, and that poor kid was treated terrible.

I couldn't stand it. One day Jaz came home and found me crying.

'Best we can do is have lots of kids ourselves,' he'd say, 'and make sure they're happy.'

That made me feel a bit better, but sometimes it was hard keeping my spirits up. I felt lonely, sitting in that little box of a room. I'd just sit there on the bed, and knit. And look out the window. And all I could see was lupins and fences. It was cold too. Winter was coming on, there wasn't a fireplace, we couldn't afford an electric heater, and in the end I spent half each day in bed just to keep warm. Of a weekend when Jaz was home we'd spend most of the time in bed too, talking, and drinking cups of tea, and having sex. Sometimes we'd put on our shoes and go for long walks along North Beach, looking out to sea and talking about the baby.

I got lonelier and lonelier.

The house got colder and colder.

'She's flogging our milk too,' I told Jaz. 'Half the time when I go to get the billy from the gate it's empty. I bet she's taking it.'

'She' was Mrs Brown. I was starting to really hate her, I found it hard even to say her name.

Mum came out to see us one Sunday afternoon.I made some scones and she sat there eating them, then she bitched on as usual about Sadie and Ruby and Hock and that, but she squinted pretty hard at Mrs Brown too. Then she went home.

Peggy knocked on the door next morning.

'Mum's been talking to me,' she said. 'Says this place is terrible and you look worn out. And she's right. Come and live with me and Arnold till you find some place decent.'

I nearly burst into tears, I was so grateful.

Peggy and Arnold had been lucky after they got married, they'd managed to get hold of a house in Moorhouse Avenue just a few doors down from Mum's. It was an old villa, a solid old place with just Peggy and Arnold rattling round in it.

'We pay the same rent Mum does,' Peggy said. 'So if we go

halves you won't have to pay much more than what you're paying already.'

It was lovely being back in Phillipstown again. The shops and streets and factories, Mum just down the street, Peggy to talk with and share things with. Peggy was pregnant, not as far on as me, but putting on beef like me. And the house was good, nice and roomy. Me and Jaz had a bedroom to ourselves, and a big front room, that we called the 'lounge', though of course it was just a bare room really, cause we didn't have any furniture to put in it. And a big kitchen, with a coal range. And a wash house with tubs and copper and that out the back, which me and Peggy shared.

We got really close, me and Peggy. She taught me to see the funny side of things.

Like, one day Mum came down for tea. I gave her hogget and spuds and a lettuce salad. She ate them up and didn't say anything. Then a couple of days later Peggy came running in, laughing her head off.

'I've just been talking with Mum,' she said. 'And she said, "Ginnie can make a good salad. She's shaping up pretty good".'

And for some reason Peggy thought this was really hilarious. She stuck her fists up like a boxer and started sparring with me.

'You're shaping up all right Gin,' she laughed. 'You're shaping up for the fight.'

I started laughing too, I didn't know what she was talking about but I started laughing and laughing, and soon we was both dancing round the kitchen cuffing one another and laughing till tears streamed down our cheeks.

I got on good with Arnold too. He was a little joker, Arnold, he looked a bit like a rat. He had brown skin and dark brown hair and a ratty, wiry build, and a great big nose. But he was hard working. He'd been in an engineering works before the war, then after the war he worked at a brewery for a while, then he left and got a job labouring at a rubber place, a big new factory that made all sorts of rubber things.

One day he came home with a brown paper bag.

'Flogged these today,' he said.

Peggy ripped the bag open and pulled out a fistful of condoms.

'Bit late for these,' she said, patting her belly.

'I dunno,' Arnold said. 'Must be something we can use them for.'

'We can have a party,' Peggy said.

So me and Jaz and Arnold and Peggy took the condoms and blew them all up and tied knots in them and strung them from the ceiling, so they looked like balloons, and we opened a flagon of beer, and we played euchre and sang songs together.

And it was good, I felt really happy.

Jaz made me feel happy, he was so sort of good to me, he was the sun and moon for me. It wasn't that I thought he was a film star or anything, it was just that I knew I could trust him, that he'd always look after me. And it didn't matter that he was still married to that other woman, I never worried about her.

'To think you've done this before with her,' I said one night after we'd been having sex.

'It was never like this,' he said. 'The times I was with her, it wasn't anything like this.'

And that was all I needed, I was happy with that, I didn't want to know more.

One night we was up town together when Jaz gave me a squeeze.

'That's her,' he said.

I saw this little blonde woman scurrying through Woolworths in a brown overcoat. And I was glad I'd seen her, to see she was just an ordinary person, just like me, to find I could see her without hating her or even caring very much about her.

It was a performance getting the divorce though. It cost money, and it took ages, and in the meantime Jaz was paying maintenance. Every week of a pay day we'd sit down together at the kitchen table and I'd open up the packet. I'd give Jaz five shillings for his beer and smokes, though often as not at the end of the week he'd give me two or three shillings back again. Then we'd put aside the money for the rent, and the money for his wife, and ten shillings for our savings, and I'd keep the rest and run the house on it for the week.

We was quite proud about our savings. By the time the baby was born we had nearly twenty pound in the Post Office.

In some ways it worried me not being married to Jaz. I was cagey about it with my old friends from work. In the end it seemed easier just to stop seeing them than try to explain what was going on. So after a while Monica Cohen and Violet McInnes and them just sort of slipped out of my life.

Mum was always nagging too, of course.

It wasn't that she really cared about me and Jaz not being married, it was just that it gave her an excuse to pick on us. When she was in a bad mood she'd sit in the kitchen bitching and bitching.

'Shacked up shameless as a bloody whore.' she'd say.

Jaz quite liked Mum.

'She's a battler,' he'd say. 'She's a real battler.'

'Yeah,' Peggy would say. 'Just wish she'd go and battle somebody else.'

Mum didn't do any knitting or sewing for our babies. Well she couldn't really, not with her arthritis and her bad eyes, but one day she turned up with a couple of little winceyette nightgowns.

'Saw these in Calder Mackays and bought them for youse,' she said, tossing them down like they was red hot.

Well that made me feel all soft and soppy. She *does* care, I thought, the tough old thing. But then a week or two later, when me and Peggy went down to Mum's for a cup of tea, it turned out she'd been expecting us to give her some money.

'I've been real hard up lately,' she said. 'Those baby gowns cost nine and six each.'

So for the next few weeks me and Peggy had to put aside money till we had the nineteen shillings to pay for the gowns.

'Tt,' Mum said, taking the money.

Another day I turned up at Mum's to find her cooking a big pot of beef stew. I really loved Mum's beef stew, it was a real luxury, and sometimes she drew some of the liquid off for beef tea. Seeing the stew steaming there I felt really hungry.

'Can I take a cup of that to drink?' I said.

Mum looked at me in horror.

'Never drink beef tea when you're having a baby,' she said. 'If you drink beef tea the baby will be so big they'll have to take it out *in parts*.'

Peggy tried to give more practical advice, but she didn't know much more than me. We was both sort of floundering round in ignorance, and the doctor I went to every few weeks didn't tell me anything about what to expect when the baby started to come, he just poked things up me, and mumbled, and scribbled things down on bits of paper.

'I've booked you into a nursing home,' he told me one week. 'Good clean place in Linwood. Nurse Macnulty runs it.'

But he didn't suggest that me and Jaz go down there to have a look at the place and meet Nurse Macnulty.

Me and Peggy tried to work it all out by getting books from the library.

'How will we know it's time?' I said. 'That's what worries me, how are we supposed to know it's starting?'

'Well,' Peggy said. 'We'll get a few stomach pains, like you're getting already, but harder. That means the baby's coming.'

'How much harder?' I'd say. 'Sometimes they're quite hard already. How are we supposed to tell the difference?'

And so on.

Then one Monday morning early in October I started getting these terrible pains, really terrible pains like nothing I'd never dreamed of before. I started yelling, I couldn't stand it, I was terrified.

'She's jake,' Peggy said. 'It's the baby coming. Keep still and I'll try to time the pains.'

'Timing the pains' was something we'd read about in one of the books. But Peggy wasn't as confident as she pretended to be and after fumbling round for a while she gave up.

'Christ,' she said. 'How're we supposed to bloody do it? Git her into a taxi, Jaz.'

So the nightmare began.

Nurse Macnulty's was an old house in Worcester Street. The minute we got out of the taxi this little barrel of a woman came busting out the door to meet us. It was Nurse Macnulty.

'Thank you, Mr Smith,' she said. 'You can get away to your work now. We'll look after her.'

I started crying.

'Don't go away,' I said to Jaz.

'Now, now,' Nurse Macnulty said. 'No nonsense. No need to waste your husband's time. It'll be a long time yet before the baby comes.'

Oh my God, I thought. A long time yet!

The pains was already so horrible I seemed to go black every time they came.

But that didn't worry Nurse Macnulty, she was too busy taking all my clothes off, getting me into a bath, shaving me with a safety razor and a sort of cold blue jelly. Then she pulled a gown down over me, a white, stiff, sort of hospital gown with a slit at the back, and she pulled some white stockings up onto my legs, then took me to a bedroom. It was a white empty room with a bed, which she made me climb onto. Then she tied two pieces of knotted sheet onto the end of the bed.

'Now when you get a pain,' she said, 'just pull on those.'

Then she left.

And I thought, what the hell is happening to me!

I was still fairly sane at that point, so for a while, between the pains, I was able to look round the room. It was a very plain room, varnished boards halfway up the walls, and everything else just painted white, white curtains across a bay window, white sheets on the bed.

I needed a pee. I found a po under the bed and sat down on it. I squeezed and squeezed and tried to pee, but nothing came out. Then the door swung open and there was Nurse Macnulty.

'You naughty girl,' she said. 'Get back into bed.'

She had a poke and prod at me.

'Hm,' she said. 'Enema.'

I didn't know what an enema was. She led me down to the bathroom and got a sort of syringe out of a cupboard.

'Stand in the bath,' she said. 'Now, lean over.'

She started sticking it up my bum. And I thought, this is it, I'm going crazy, it's a madhouse, what the hell is she doing to me?

224

When we got back to the lying-in room she patted my shoulder.
'Now let's have some good pains,' she said.

And walked out.

And shut the door behind her.

Then I really did go insane. It was that door shutting on me, leaving me there all alone, locked up and trapped and alone. And the pain, hours and hours and hours of pain. The room got dark, night must of been coming on. I heard the phone ring, and I heard Nurse Macnulty answer it.

'Oh no, Mr Smith,' she said. 'There's no good coming around. Nothing will be happening this side of the evening.'

Nothing *this side of the evening*. And in the meantime I was screaming and yelling and swearing with pain. Everything going black, then red, then black again.

'Who's Jaz?' I heard Nurse Macnulty say to the doctor later, much later. 'She keeps calling for Jaz.'

'Her husband,' the doctor said.

'Hm,' Nurse Macnulty said. 'Common sort of a name.'

The baby was born just after midnight. I can remember giving one last almighty scream just as it was born, because I thought, this really is the end, I'm just splitting in two now, I'm dying, I'm splitting apart and that's all there is to it. I'm dead.

But of course I wasn't dead, I was a mother.

11

The cottage homes of Canterbury

Ginnie

After three weeks at Nurse Macnulty's it was time for me to go home. Jaz came in a taxi. Nurse Macnulty dressed little baby Allan up in some things I'd knitted, she gave him a pinch on the cheek, and handed him to me.

'He's a fine little Cantabrian,' she said. 'And you're a natural mother, my dear.'

That was one from the book, it was the first human thing she'd said to me.

But she was right, he was a nice wee boy and things was going good. My milk had come down no trouble, baby Allan didn't have any problems feeding, and he soon got really chubby. He'd been a good sized baby from the start and by the time we took him home he'd put on about two pound more. And he was really nice looking, he had great big black eyes and black hair.

Peggy came running out when we turned up at Moorhouse Avenue. She was wearing an apron and her hands was covered with flour, she'd been baking a big tea for us, a big roast tea with hogget and dumplings and steamed plum pudding.

'Glad to see you back, Gin,' she said. 'You're looking good.'

For the next few months I was really happy. Allan kept growing bigger and stronger and happier, and I loved looking after him. I loved cuddling him up to me, a little warm thing. And I loved seeing Jaz with him too. As soon as Jaz came home from work he'd pick him up and cuddle and kiss him, lie down on the floor with him and smile and carry on. Peggy and Arnold played with him a lot too.

We felt a bit guilty though, me and Peggy. Nurse Macnulty

had told me it wasn't good to cuddle babies too much.

'A pampered baby is a spoiled baby,' she'd said.

But it was hard keeping our hands off him, he looked so nice and cuddly. And it was hard trying to stick to the feeding routine too.

'You're to feed him every four hours,' Nurse Macnulty had told me. 'No more, no less.'

But a lot of times he'd start crying for milk an hour or two too early, and I didn't know what to do. I'd try and try to just sit there, looking at the clock, trying to wish the hands to move round so I could pick him up and feed him. Then in the end I'd sneak into the bedroom, poor little Allan would be all blue with crying, and I'd pick him up and give him what he wanted.

But I felt really bad about it, I didn't want to spoil him.

The Plunket nurse backed Nurse Macnulty up. She came to the house regular for the first few weeks and sort of inspected everything, then after that I had to go down to the Plunket rooms and have Allan weighed and checked up.

'This baby's getting too much attention,' the Plunket nurse said. 'He'll grow up a cry baby.'

But I kept doing the things I wasn't supposed to, I broke all the Plunket rules. Me and Jaz even had baby Allan in the bed with us most nights, and of course that was something that was absolutely forbidden in the Plunket rules, though we didn't know why.

Then it was time for Peggy to have her baby. She went away one morning and came back three weeks later with a nice wee baby girl.

'We're calling her Margaret,' Peggy said when I went up to visit her. 'After Mum.'

Mum didn't seem very interested though. She was only a few doors down the street but she hardly ever dropped in to see the babies, and if she did come she'd just give them a quick once over, then forget them.

'Well you can understand it,' Jaz said. 'She's had enough babies for anyone. Can't expect her to go to town over two more.'

But it got me down. I'd hoped that being a grandmother would make Mum a bit kinder towards me, but she hadn't even visited me at Nurse Macnulty's. In fact nobody had except Peggy, and once I got home I hardly saw any of all those brothers and sisters of mine. Eddie put his head round the door once or twice, he was still living with Mum, but I never saw the other boys from one end of the year to the next. And the girls wasn't much better. Ruby was too busy being rich. Fag was down in Timaru, of course, and Tots was away too, she'd gone up to Hanmer Springs to work as a maid. So apart from Peggy, the only sisters I ever saw was Sadie and Hock, and they was both up to the eyeballs in babies and didn't have time for more than the odd cup of tea on the run.

Then things started to go wrong with Peggy. It was to do with little baby Margaret, she sort of looked a bit funny. There was something a bit unusual about her, but at first me and Peggy never said anything about it to one another.

Then one day Mum was having a cup of tea in the kitchen, watching Peggy feed baby Margaret.

Mum put her cup down.

'There's something wrong with that kid,' she said. 'Take her to a quack.'

Peggy didn't say anything. But her and Arnold looked all sort of strained and worried, their tempers started to get a bit short, and Arnold started taking it out on us. Like, he'd come home tired from work and find me and Peggy having a cup of tea and the two babies sitting on the floor. Allan would be chuckling and gurgling, but Margaret would be just sitting there quiet and still. Arnold's face would sort of stiffen.

'Look at youse tarts,' he'd say to me and Peggy. 'Sitting round with your hair in curlers and your feet in bloody slippers. This place is like a bloody brothel.'

Then Peggy went all silent. Some days she'd spend a whole afternoon not saying anything. Then she'd say something bitchy. I'd sort of shrink up inside and feel like crying.

One day we was in the wash house, doing the nappies. I was busy with a load of stuff in the copper.

'How long will you be with that?' Peggy said.

It was the first thing she'd said since breakfast, and all of a sudden I felt really angry with her. Right, I thought. I'll give her a dose of her own medicine. So I didn't say anything, I just kept possing.

Well all of a sudden Peggy turned on me in a black rage, she threw me against the copper, really hurled me against it, so my bare leg fell on the hot metal.

I just screamed, my leg felt like it was on a hotplate.

Then I ran, I ran out of the wash house and into our bedroom and shut the door and cried and cried and cried.

Peggy never came to knock on the door and say something, like I expected her to, she just stayed away. And she never met my eye or said anything about that, ever.

In the end it was the Plunket nurse who took control.

'She needs to go to a doctor,' the Plunket nurse said. 'She doesn't respond the way she should.'

'She's a mongol,' Peggy said after she came home next day from the hospital. 'She's a mongol and she'll be dead in five years.'

All I wanted was just to put my arms round Peggy and cry, but Peggy kept her distance. Her jaw was fixed sort of tight. She wouldn't cry, she wouldn't look at me, she wouldn't let me help her.

Arnold went sort of berserk when he found out that night, he yelled and screamed at us all and then disappeared.

'They don't want us,' Jaz said that night in bed. 'We better see if we can find some place else.'

'It's probably for the best,' Peggy said when I told her next morning.

I felt really sad those last weeks. Things had been so good with Peggy at the start, her and Arnold had been so good to me and Jaz, and now we was breaking apart with bad feelings all round and nobody saying anything about them, nobody trying to work things out. Of a night Jaz would cuddle me, tell me things would look up, that we'd get a nice little place of our own. But I still felt bad. Anyway we didn't have a hope of getting a place of our own, all we could find was rooms, or a flat if we was lucky.

Every morning we'd look through the ads in the paper. Jaz would get on his bike and follow some of them up, but the places would always be gone before he got there. Then he'd have to pedal like mad so he could clock in at work by half past eight.

'We'll put in for a state house,' Jaz said.

But it turned out we wasn't allowed to, we wasn't legally married so we wasn't entitled to a state house.

'There's always transit housing,' Jaz said. 'We could try that.'

Transit housing was what they called the camps out on the edge of the cities where working people could go if they couldn't find houses. We caught a bus and looked at the camp near Wigram aerodrome one Saturday, and it was terrible. It was like a prison camp, it was just rows and rows of prefab cabins, with a wash block at the end of each row, and dirt tracks in between. And a lot of worried looking women.

'I'd rather live in a tent,' I said.

'Me too,' Jaz said.

But it was too cold for camping, not to mention the fact that we didn't have a tent anyway. It was the middle of winter, and we was getting desperate.

'There's a place in Barbour Street,' Jaz said one morning.

'*To Let*', the paper said. 'Barbour Street, one room, use of bathroom.'

Barbour Street was just round the corner. Jaz jumped on his bike and was off.

'We've got it,' he said, walking back into the kitchen half an hour later.

'Whoopee,' I said.

'Um,' Jaz said. 'Don't get your hopes too high. It's not the Clarendon.'

'Oh,' I said. 'Oh well, it can't be worse than staying here.'

Which was a rash thing to say if ever there was.

It was deep winter when we shifted to Barbour Street, deep winter of 1949. It was an old house, a real old, square, wooden place that once had a verandah across the front, which the landlady had pulled down. The landlady was slightly mad, she was a short little woman with black heaped up hair and a string of beads and a fast tongue. She kept reefing off about how she was going to do this and going to do that to the house, make it fit

230

to live in. But she never did. She just talked, and took our money. And there was three families in that house. There was us, in our room on the cold side of the house. Then there was another young couple with two babies in a room on the other side. Then in the front was a Mrs Willey, well she called herself Mrs Willey, though there wasn't a Mr Willey on the scene, in a couple of rooms and a porch. Out the back was a kitchen with a gas cooker, which we all had to share, and a bathroom with a gas water heater. Out in the back yard was an old railway carriage off its wheels; an old alcoholic joker rented that, but we never saw much of him.

Our room was really small, we could only just manage to squeeze our bed into it, and we couldn't fit a cot in at all, so Allan had to sleep in his pram. That had its advantages, mind you. Of a night if Allan started crying Jaz could just stick his foot out from under the blanket and rock Allan back to sleep. He got quite expert at that.

Mrs Willey hated Allan crying. She'd bang on the wall.

'Stop that kid screaming,' she'd yell.

She made life difficult, Mrs Willey. She was a little wee sour faced woman with straight yellow hair, cut real short, a hairclip shoved in one side.

'Too many bloody adults in this bloody dump without bloody kids as well,' she'd say.

And it was dirty, that place in Barbour Street. It was hard to keep clean. One morning when me and Jaz sat down to our breakfast I was just about to eat a spoonful of porridge when Jaz looked at me sharp.

'Hold on,' he said. 'Look.'

I looked at the spoon and saw little dark lumps in it.

'Mouse dirt,' Jaz said.

'Mice must of got in the porridge packet,' I said.

I went over to the shelf to have a look.

'It's in the flour too,' I said. 'And the sugar.'

After a while that sort of thing got a bit hard to take. Me and Jaz started looking at newspaper ads again.

'How about a bach?' Jaz said one Saturday morning.

He'd found an ad for a 'seaside cottage' at Brooklands.

231

'It's a long way out,' Jaz said. 'Way out past Stewarts Gully. That'll be why it's cheap.'

Well I didn't even know where Stewarts Gully was, so it was all double Dutch to me. But I liked the sound of it, a seaside cottage, it sounded nice, it'd be nice to be near the beach again, there'd be sand and seagulls. And we'd be able to go for walks together again too, which would be good for me, cause I was pregnant again.

So Jaz got onto his bike and went to see the joker that owned it.

'Said we'd take it sight unseen,' he said when he came back a couple of hours later. 'The owner looks all right. His name's Phillips, he's a carpenter, says he built the bach out of bits he picked up round about.'

'It sounds lovely,' I said. 'Our own little house.'

'And we can git married before we go out there,' Jaz said.

'Aw,'I said. 'Yeah. All right.'

The divorce had come through, it'd taken all our savings but it was through now and we was free to get married. But I didn't particularly want to get married, I was quite lukewarm about the idea, there didn't seem much point. We was happy enough. Getting married would just be a big fuss about nothing. I'd have to buy myself a frock. I didn't want to be bothered with things like that.

'Let's do it some other time,'I said.

'First thing next week,' Jaz said. 'It'll make your mother happy.'

'Huh,' I said. 'The day I see Mum happy I'll see Ballantynes go bankrupt.'

That weekend Tots turned up.

'I'm back home with Mum,' she said. 'Walked out on the job at Hanmer Springs. Boss kept putting his hands where he shouldn't.'

It was nice seeing Tots again, she'd grown up since I'd last seen her. She was very tall and skinny, with wild sort of fair hair that she shoved back from her face. When I told her me and Jaz was going to get married, she grinned at us both.

'I'll be your witness,' she said.

So come Monday, me, Jaz and Tots got onto the tram and went

into town while the neighbour with the two babies looked after Allan for us. I felt quite sort of excited as the tram rattled us into town, me in a cheap little blue linen suit I'd bought on time payment from Calder Mackays, Jaz in his demob suit, and Tots wearing her black maid's uniform disguised as an afternoon frock. But the registrar at the registry office in Hereford Street didn't seem very interested. He just stood in front of us and droned on for a while, then got us to sign some bits of paper, then told us we was married.

As we started walking down the stairs Tots pulled out a packet of confetti and chucked it all over us.

'Here comes the bride,' she sang. 'Fair, fat and wide. See how she wobbles from side to side. Here comes the groom . . .'

We started giggling, me and Jaz and Tots, and started laughing. We stood in that narrow stairway laughing and laughing, till the tears was streaming down our faces.

Fag

When Roddie turned up at Timaru Hospital to see me after the baby was born he looked like the man in the Lichfield shirt advertisement.

'Hello darling,' he said, kissing me on the mouth. 'You look wonderful.'

He was lying of course, I looked a wreck, I was bruised and battered and groggy. And looking at him standing there with a silly smile on his face, a silly bunch of roses in his hand, so safe and clean and male and intact and stupid, I hated him.

'I've seen the baby,' he said. 'Looked in at the nursery window. A nurse held her up for me. Prettiest little thing I've ever seen.'

'Mm,' I said. Hating him, hating his stupid fatuous words.

'You're tired,' he said, putting his hand on my cheek. 'Poor darling.'

He came to see me next day too. Carnations this time, pink carnations.

'I've decided,' I said. 'I don't want to have any more babies.'

Roddie looked very hurt for a moment, and I was glad. Then

233

I felt guilty. Then I felt angry, because I saw him wipe out the pain and make his face bland again.

'Whatever you think best darling,' he said.

Another kiss.

'Nothing wrong with little Pamela is there?' he said. 'Everything going well?'

That was part of the problem, everything *was* going well. Pamela on the breast, my milk gushing down. The perfect mother, the model child.

When I got home I looked at myself in the long oval mirror on the bedroom door.

'God,' I said. 'I look like a cow.'

Standing there with my hands on my waist, frowning into the glass, determining all over again never to have another baby, I suddenly remembered Scarlett. I was Scarlett again, the belle of old Phillips Town.

'Yo waist jes done got bigger, Miss Scarlett. And dar ain't nuthin ter do bout it.'

'There is something to do about it,' thought Scarlett as she ripped savagely at the seams of her dress to let out the necessary inches. 'I just won't have any more babies.'

It was a help, becoming Scarlett again, becoming the belle of old Phillips Town. It gave some sort of dignity to all the fumbling with rubber and plastic, the condoms and diaphragms and the rest of it, that followed. Our sex life had already got mechanical enough without technology interposed between us. Making love with Roddie had turned into a sort of twice weekly ritual of kissing and cuddling, Roddie whispering, me starting to breathe more heavily, methodical strokings with his finger, 'does that feel good, darling?'

A nice comfortable orgasm.

Then his turn.

Roddie on top of me. In and out. In and out. 'Oh darling, I love you so much.'

'Oh, oh, oh.'

But if making love didn't seem to offer much in the way of excitement any more, there were other things, other roles to try.

Being a mother, for example. I actually enjoyed being a mother, once I'd got back home from the hospital. Pamela turned into a little soft cheeked thing with big soft eyes, and I just melted over her. It was wonderful to have something so vulnerable and small and trusting, something that needed me absolutely.

Roddie had suggested naming her after a female Carrel.

'Constance is nice,' he said. 'My mother's mother was called Constance. And Prudence is nice. And Virginia.'

'I'd like to call her Pamela,' I said.

He agreed straight away, smiling, but I was too embarrassed to tell him why I wanted her to be Pamela, that it was the fantasy name I'd given myself when I was a kid with Ginnie.

Pamela Constance Carrel, we called her.

And I loved her.

Another exciting thing was that my skin and hair stayed glossy and soft even after the pregnancy was over. In fact after my waist had tightened up again I realised I'd suddenly become very good looking, you could even say beautiful.

I turned more eagerly than ever to the idea of being glamorous.

It was a good time to be interested in glamour, because it was the time of the 'New Look', a style Dior had launched a few months before our wedding. I'd heard a bit about it when I went shopping for my wedding frock, I'd seen it in the papers and the glossy magazines, but I hadn't really believed it would come to anything and I'd chosen a wedding dress in the old style with sharp, pointed shoulders and hardly any bust and the skirt not much lower than the knee. But the New Look was all over the place now. It started to turn up in the movies, in the shops and then, after a while, on the backs of the Carrel women.

And wasn't I a Carrel woman now? Couldn't I be fashionable too?

I sat in the circle and watched Myrna Loy and Cary Grant in *Mr Blandings Builds His Dream House* and I thought, oh it's just like Roddie and I, we're like Myrna and Cary, we're building our little dream house, and we love one another. And doesn't she look lovely in that little soft surcoat with that tipping of leopard fur?

Eva Perón was even more exciting than the movie stars. There

235

were pictures of her in all the newsreels and the magazines, and she was the living embodiment of the New Look, and when I saw her, so cool, so elegant, I wished and wished I was a blonde.

I started an account at Ballantynes.

At first it seemed incredible, me, Daphne Feron, walking into Ballantynes. Millinery and silk and satin. Assistants dressed in black, like countesses in mourning, simpering and saying 'Of course, and will that be all?' in reply to my 'Charge it.' I spent hours at the cosmetics counter, trying on new lines. I went to a furniture shop and ordered a chiffonier, and after it was delivered to Circuit Street I draped it with tulle and heaped it high with bottles and jars, mirrors and little brushes. Sometimes, stooping to look at the clutter of glamour reflected in the chiffonier mirror, I felt incredibly rich, as though all my little cut glass bottles were jewels strewn in front of me.

I got scientific about my appearance. I plucked and pencilled like Lana Turner, I depilated and waxed and polished like Grace Kelly, I put on lipstick with the expertise of Elizabeth Taylor.

I even thought, for a month or two, about really going blonde.

'You don't think,' Roddie said carefully, 'you look nice the way you are?'

So I gave the idea up. Not without regrets.

I strutted on stilettos. I garotted myself in a tight wasp waist. I loved that narrow waist, that new style with its low sloping shoulders and surging wide skirts. It seemed so romantic, it was like the crinoline, it was like Scarlett and Lady Barker. 'White, the universal costume.' And, like Scarlett and Lady Barker, I laced my ribs into a knot, I stuffed my breasts and behind with foam rubber and nylon. A new style of brassiere, ferociously wired so my breasts stood up and stuck out. Pads on my hips to make my waist look narrower. Fifteen denier nylons, dark and sleek. And my first evening dress, a wonderful wonderful dress of whispering blue silk, wired tight onto my back so my shoulders emerged bare and white above. And below, on thin steel hoops heaped up with five taffeta petticoats, my skirts ballooned and surged, curvetted and swished.

Elegance cost money, of course, and sometimes that worried

236

me. Because though Roddie was born a Carrel, at the moment he was just a clerk. His family kept offering him money, but he kept turning it down.

'We'll make our own life,' he kept saying.

In the end it was Feron money that helped us out. Morgan money, rather.

'Not many motor parts places down here,' Frank Morgan said one evening when he and Ruby came to dinner with us.

Frank and Ruby were on holiday, it was summer and they'd been staying in a motor hotel at Queenstown. They were in the money, Ruby and Frank. They'd just bought a second shop, taken on some more employees. Ruby dressed as though she was planning to corner the market in semi-precious stones.

'Can't say I've really thought about it,' Roddie said.

'I have,' Frank said. 'There's an opening here for somebody. The garages and stock and station agents only sell motor parts as a sideline. There's an opening for somebody to specialise.'

'How do you mean?' Roddie said.

I wasn't really listening, I was trying to stop myself yawning while Ruby kept explaining to me how I should go and see the Remarkables. Frank talked on about specialising, cutting costs, taking lower margins, underselling the others. Roddie didn't say much in return, just nodded, looked thoughtful.

A week or so later he came up to me.

'Might run up to Christchurch for a day,' he said. 'If that's all right with you darling. Have a word with Frank.'

Within another couple of weeks we were in business.

'We'll have to take it slowly,' Roddie said. 'Can't expect to have an easy first year.'

Roddie left the Audit Department, bought a van, stripped the inside, fitted it up with shelves and drawers, had it painted blue and gold.

CARREL WHOLESALE MOTOR SUPPLIES LTD, it said.

The idea was that Roddie would go up to Christchurch every month or so and buy motor parts, brake linings, carburettors, petrol fittings, tyres, that sort of thing, and that Frank Morgan would give him a loan, let him have stuff on credit, teach him how to buy, help him choose the best stock, introduce him to wholesalers. Then Roddie would load up the van and head off into the countryside. He pinned maps of South Canterbury all over the kitchen wall and divided them up into 'sales territories'.

He was full of confidence, very cheerful and bouncy.

'All this debt,' I'd say. 'How are we ever going to pay it off?'

'No need to worry,' he'd say. 'I know all those farming people, they all know me. Nobody else is offering them service like this, door to door deliveries, on the spot purchases.'

It helped that he was a Carrel, half the people in South Canterbury looked up to that name. It helped that it was 1949. Business was booming, there was a new sort of exuberance, there was money to be spent, there was a boom. And the motor industry boomed more than most. Big new rubber factories opened up in the cities, big car assembly plants in the North Island. Farmers were scrambling to buy tractors and trucks and cars and motor parts. Within a few months we had the Reidrubber tyre agency, a South Canterbury monopoly over their tyres. Then we got other franchises too.

Soon we had accounts all over the country, hundreds of pounds under our name with firms in Auckland and Wellington and Christchurch.

Ginnie

We was supposed to to be all efficient the morning we shifted out to Brooklands. Jaz left early, the carriers came and picked our stuff up from Barbour Street, then me and Tots walked to town with Allan. We was supposed to catch the bus to Brooklands. Well we found the bus, and got on, and played with Allan and yakked with one another. In the meantime shops and offices and houses went past. Then we got out into the country, it was all paddocks and that, all sort of lonely looking.

'Stewarts Gully,' somebody said.

And the bus stopped at this little straggly row of houses and pine trees.

'Brooklands must be the next stop,' I said.

238

The bus set off again. Pine trees, paddocks, more pine trees. Then we stopped, but there wasn't a shop or house or anything, just paddocks.

'This can't be it,' I said. 'Must be the next stop.'

So we stayed on board and the bus got moving again. More paddocks, more trees, a river.

Then rows and rows of houses started going past.

'Looks nice doesn't it?' I said. 'Lots of houses and streets and that. It's just like a city.'

'I think it is a city,' Tots said. 'I think we're back in Christchurch.'

And she was right, we'd gone all the way there and back, and that lonely stop where all you could see was paddocks must of been Brooklands.

'She's jake,' the bus driver said. 'Stay on board.'

We felt quite stupid, the way the bus driver grinned at us, so this time we made sure we kept our eyes peeled and looked hard out the windows. And it seemed very lonely, very big and lonely to me, very empty. But quite nice too, sort of refreshing in a way, no more streets, just grass and sky.

Jaz was waiting for us. We got out and all walked together into Brooklands.

Brooklands was mainly baches sort of scattered round a wilderness of sandhills and lupins and pine trees. It was nice. The lupins and pine trees smelled nice, and there was a domain with big old gnarled macrocarpas, and a great big lagoon just out the back of the little house Jaz stopped outside.

'What d'you reckon?' he said.

It was just a little place, a bit funny looking, made of fibrolite, grey fibrolite, with maroon coloured window sills, sitting in a sandy paddock.

'I like it,' I said.

When we walked inside it seemed like the cabin of a little ship, or what I would of imagined the cabin of a ship would of looked like. Everything sort of small and compact, with things fitting into one another. There was a little sunny room I decided to call the dining room, and next to it there was a kitchen, just a cupboard

239

practically, with a little wee electric cooker not much bigger than a soap box. Stuck onto the back of the kitchen was a bathroom, with a galvanised iron bath, and a wash house, with a copper and two pumice tubs. A bedroom opened off the dining room, quite nice and sunny. And that was it. A little sun porch out the front, and a pump out the back. A handpump it was, there wasn't any running water in the kitchen, I'd have to go out and pump water by hand. And none of the doors and window sills and cupboards quite fitted right, there wasn't any way you could close anything properly, so the wind blew in through cracks and chinks.

'It's pretty basic,' Jaz said.

'We'll be right,' I said. 'We'll manage.'

And really I quite liked it. It was much better than Barbour Street or Palmer Road, it was a whole house just for us, we could do what we liked and be by ourselves as much as we liked, and nobody could stop us.

'It'll be like a holiday,' I said. 'I'll be able to sit in the sun and get a tan.'

'Wish I was married,' Tots said. 'This is real nifty.'

We shifted our things round, putting them in place. Me and Jaz had gone off to Calder Mackays and bought some stuff on time payment: a wooden table and four kitchen chairs, a sofa, and a duchesse. Everything very plain, the cheapest ones we could find. I had my glory box of course, and there was our bed and one or two other bits and pieces from Barbour Street, but nothing much.

'It's real sunny inside isn't it?' I said.

'Better than the Bay of Islands,' Jaz said.

Not that he'd ever been to the Bay of Islands. But it really was sunny, and I felt sort of excited, it was as though we'd made the right move at last, things was starting to come right. We fried some eggs and bacon for tea, and sat in the dining room, and felt like we was home.

Then the sun dropped down behind the Alps and the house suddenly got cold.

'Christ,' Jaz said. 'I'm freezing.'

We put our jerseys on and huddled round another pot of tea

240

and tried to play poker. But it was so cold our hands started to turn blue.

'It's these fibro walls,' Jaz said. 'They're too thin. But we'll get some wood tomorrow and have a good fire.'

There was a little brick fireplace. We all looked at it, and tried to imagine flames crackling inside it.

The landlord, Mr Philips, came out to see us next day. Which was nice of him, we thought. He came puttering up in a little old black Ford, a sort of square black box on wheels. And the minute I saw him I liked him, he was just working class like us, I felt sort of comfortable with him.

'Sorry about the pump,' he said when I went outside to get some water for a cup of tea. 'I've been trying to get hold of an electric one. When I find one I'll stick it in for youse. And if you want firewood there's going to be some pines felled out Spencerville next weekend. People can go and take what they want, branches and that. If you want I could give youse a ride over there with a trailer.'

It wasn't just talk, he turned up next Saturday with a trailer, and him and Jaz went to Spencerville and got a load of branches. Next day Jaz and Tots cut it up with a crosscut saw. I wanted to do some sawing too, but Tots wouldn't let me.

'Your job's to keep us in scones,' she said.

Tots left us the week after that. She found herself a job in a clothes factory in Christchurch and took her suitcase into town on a bus one morning. Me and little Allan waved her off at the bus stop, then I went home and cried. All of a sudden I felt really alone, really stranded. But there wasn't any use crying, there was Allan to be looked after, and sewing to be done for the new baby. And tea to be cooked for Jaz.

Thinking about Jaz always made me feel better.

He was such a good person, Jaz was, I felt really good about him, a sort of really strong, trusting, sharing sort of feeling. I depended on him now. He was the main thing in my life, he was the one person I could trust.

It was hard for him, living out at Brooklands, cause he was still with the P and T and had to get into the yard in town every day to work. There was a bus early of a morning, he could of taken that to town, but we couldn't really afford it, the tickets wasn't cheap.

'I'll bike,' he said. 'Keep me fit.'

So he did, he biked. He got up at sparrow fart every morning and made us our breakfast and kissed me and Allan goodbye then got onto his bike and pedalled off through the fog. Then he'd turn up again at seven o'clock at night, looking really tired, really worn out and cold and tired. I used to feel terrible, seeing him like that. On nights when the dunny had to be emptied it was even worse. The toilet at that place was just a wooden dunny with a can, and there wasn't a night cart or anything like that, you just had to dig a hole in the sand and lug the can across to it and pour it out, then you had to fill the hole in with sand. The hole had to be deep, cause if it wasn't the turds would sort of float up to the surface again. So once a week Jaz would come home from work and have to dig the hole before he had his tea. That was really terrible for him, I thought, to have to do that on top of everything else.

One day I decided to get in first. I put the tea on and fed Allan, then while the tea was cooking I went out and dug the hole and buried the stuff.

'No need to empty the can tonight,' I told Jaz after he got home and went to pick up the shovel. 'I've already done it.'

Jaz looked really unhappy.

'You shouldn't of done that,' he said. 'Not with another baby on the way.'

'It's all right,' I said. 'It was easy enough. It's just digging sand.'

Which it wasn't easy, it was hard bloody labour. The digging gave me blisters on my hands and made me feel sort of faint. After I'd done the job I had to lie down with my feet up for half an hour before the lights in my eyes would go away. But from then on I dug the hole every week. Jaz didn't like it, but he couldn't stop me.

Another problem was that nothing in the house really worked properly. Like, windows kept getting stuck, and handles kept coming off things, and electric sockets came loose.

242

'It's the Labour government,' Mr Philips said one weekend. 'They've stopped us buying overseas, they've handed it all on a plate to the factory owners in Christchurch and Auckland and their stuff's all shoddy.'

'Think the Tories would of been better?' Jaz said.

'They'll soon have their chance,' Mr Philips said.

And he was right. There was an election not long after that and Labour lost and the Tories got back in. It was the first time the Tories had been in since I was a little kid, and I felt sort of scared. Jaz sat up on election night and listened to the radio, but I went to bed early. Then when I woke up next morning he was there with a cup of tea for me, and he was looking sort of grim.

'The bosses are back on top,' he said. 'They was on top under Labour anyway, but things'll be even worse for working people now.'

I felt like there'd been some sort of catastrophe. Then when me and Allan got the bus that afternoon and went into town to visit Mum she made me feel worse. Uncle Jim Hay was there, he was drinking a cup of tea and talking with Mum about the election.

'Hard times coming,' Mum said. 'Soon be back to rock bottom.'

It all seemed so terrible. Mum had hardly ever had a good word to say even for Labour, so what was it going to be like with the Tories back in? I thought it was going to be like when I was a kid again, soup kitchens and Salvation Army handouts and clothes parcels in the schools.

I felt really guilty too. I hadn't registered to be an elector, Jaz had asked me if I had, and when I'd said I hadn't he'd told me half the problem for Labour was working people was so slack about voting.

'Well what's it matter?' I said. 'It's just politics.'

'Everything's politics,' Jaz said.

I didn't vote, and Labour lost the election, and I sort of felt it was my fault.

'Right,' I said to Jaz after I'd got home from seeing Mum. 'I'm going to learn about politics.'

And that Monday I got on the bus to Christchurch again and

went to the public library and got a big stack of books on politics and took them home. And when it was time for Allan to have his afternoon sleep I put him in his cot, made myself a cup of tea, sat down in the sun at the kitchen table, and opened one of the books. It was called *The Provincial System in New Zealand*.

I started to read.

'New Zealand is today as closely unified, alike in feeling and politically, as any of the nations of the Commonwealth, and it has always been politically one.'

Well, that was interesting, and the sun was warm, and my cup of tea smelled nice, and I could hear the lupins popping and crackling outside.

'In all new countries there is a tendency to dispersion . . . Its effects, though not negligible, were less important than the special circumstances . . . The first external trade done by New Zealand . . . dependent on Sydney capitalists . . . It seems probable . . .'

I started to feel sort of sleepy. The book was interesting, but it was sort of hard to understand, the words and sentences and that. So after I'd read three pages I closed the book and finished my cup of tea.

I'll just read a few pages at a sitting, I thought, and get into it gradual.

Two weeks later I took the books on politics back to town and got out some love stories instead.

After a while it didn't seem to make much difference, the Tories being back in. Things was the same as they'd been before. In fact they was better if anything, cause summer was coming on, the weather was getting hot, and Brooklands was coming into its own. I planted some flowers in our yard, not much, it was hard to get things to grow cause it was so sandy, but I put in some marigolds and that, and they looked nice and bright. And out the back we put in spuds and carrots, cabbage and silverbeet. And Jaz came home from work one day with some turnip seedlings.

'Joker at work gave me them,' he said. 'Got them from some other joker that works in a nursery out Belfast way.'

We put them in and watered them and watched them, and in

the end they grew into real monsters, big huge fat looking things.

Jaz split one open.

'Taste that,' he said.

It was horrible, all sort of sweet and sticky.

'I reckon they must be sugar beet,' Jaz said.

So we turfed them out, we couldn't do anything with them, they was too big and coarse.

As the season came on I started bottling things. I bottled carrots and beans and baby potatoes, then one Friday night we caught the bus to Belfast and bought a couple of cases of plums and apricots and I bottled those too. We used old beer bottles. We cleaned them with soapy water and set them out on the kitchen table and then Jaz would soak some string in kerosene, heat it up and whip it round the necks of the bottles. The top would come off nice and clean and give us a preserving jar.

It was good, that summer. The new baby was giving me good strong kicks in the belly, and I was feeling good, really good.

Weekends were extra good, cause Jaz would be home and he'd do the washing and look after Allan and that, so I could put my feet up and have a rest. And we went for walks. We'd walk for miles past the lagoon and through the pine plantations and along the beach. We'd sit on the sand till the sun set, we'd eat sandwiches packed in an old biscuit tin, and we'd boil up tea on an old primus, and when we got home of a night we'd be all sunburnt and sandy and happy.

But then autumn started to come on, the days started to get shorter and the house started to freeze up again of a night.

'Like me to bring the trailer out again?' Mr Philips said one day when he came to see things was all right.

So next Saturday him and Jaz went and got more wood from Spencerville and we gave him a beer and then on the Sunday morning me and Jaz went out into the yard and looked at the pine branches lying there in a big tangled heap.

'Joker down the road might give me a hand,' Jaz said.

'I'll do it,' I said.

And I did. Jaz tried to talk me out of it, but I stuck to my guns and we spent most of that Sunday on the crosscut saw, grinding and squawking our way through the heap of branches.

Two days later the new baby was born.

It wasn't anything like as bad as the first time. I knew what to expect now, so that was a help. And instead of going to Nurse Macnulty's chamber of horrors I went to Essex Hospital, which was a big old brick place in Linwood, a real rabbit warren of a place, but I felt comfortable there cause the women was all just working people like me. The nurses let me have a drug too. Once the pains started getting really hard and I started tensing up and yelling, they gave me a needle.

'This is twilight sleep,' they said. 'It'll relax you.'

It was absolutely marvellous, that drug. I just sailed off into space and didn't really come back to earth till it was all over, I was in the delivery theatre, and there was this baby crying. And it was mine.

'You've had a son,' the midwife said. 'He's a real All Black.'

A real big lump of a little boy, he was, he weighed nine pound twelve and the doctor gave me a great big cut to help him come out. And when he stitched me up again he had to put seven sutures in to get me back together.

Sadie came in to see me, trailing kids and complaints behind her. When I told her I'd had seven stitches she sort of opened her eyes wide.

'Shit,' she said. 'A bloody chaff sack only has eight.'

12

Who's got the key of the door?

Fag

I didn't want to think about the fact that I was turning twenty-one. It seemed too final, irrevocable, being twenty-one. It seemed as though it was the end of something. Definitively the end. As though what I was by the time I got to twenty-one was what I was always going to be, that there weren't going to be any more chances.

My brain seemed like a movie projector, a defective movie projector, running back over my past life, mixing up all the scenes, getting everything out of sequence, going backwards instead of forwards, unspooling jerkily, winding up again suddenly. And instead of me as a climax – me, Eva Perón, Cinderella, a slim and stylish young lady stalking in stilettos up Stafford Street or down Caroline Bay – sometimes it seemed as though the climax wasn't me at all, that I was just the foetus, the embryo, and that the real person who grew out of me was a skinny little kid smoking dock leaf cigarettes in the back yard at Kent Street.

Or a flat chested typist in an impatient hunch listening to a maundering Mrs Childer in Dunn Street.

Or a fidgety tart in a threadbare blue gym frock, gazing up with admiration at Miss Lightowler.

Or the belle of old Phillips Town.

Kent Street; Braddon Street.

Simeon Street.

Mum.

Me.

What was I? What the hell was I?

'Can't be bothered making a fuss about it,' I said to Roddie.

'Why don't we just have a quiet drink here at home?'

'You sure, darling?' he said. Looking at me with soft eyes. Too carefully, too gently.

'Yeah,' I said.

'If you're sure,' he said.

Though in the end he persuaded me to 'go out'. Which in this particular instance meant getting in the Citroën and buzzing up the hill for dinner at the Hydro Grand. My skirts crackling as we walked over to a little table for two. Stiff white linen. A view of the sea. But I didn't want to look at the sea, the sea was grey and soft that evening, a strip of grey silk stretched thin from one end of the world to the other.

'Let's sit over there,' I said. 'Looks cosier.'

Stuck up against a column. My stilettos digging into the carpet. Elbows tight against my waist.

Drawing off my gloves.

Twiddling with my pearls.

'I do like this place,' Roddie said. 'Bit fusty, but the view's everything.'

'Fusty!' I said. 'To me it's the most opulent place in the world.'

Roddie laughing softly.

Disbelievingly.

'Here's to you, darling.'

And we drank a toast, Roddie and I, just the two of us. We clinked our whisky glasses together, and drank a toast to me in Black Label scotch.

'Best years ahead of you,' Roddie said.

I wanted to throttle him, of course.

Ginnie

'You're only twenty-one once in your life,' Jaz said. 'We'll have a party.'

'But,' I said.

Cause I could think of about fifty reasons why we shouldn't have a party. Like not having enough room, not having any

248

money, not having any way of getting anybody out to Brooklands. And not really wanting to make a fuss either. I didn't really think I was important enough to have a twenty-first birthday.

'Where there's a will,' Jaz said.

So we had a party, the first party me and Jaz ever had. Jaz jacked it all up, he got on the blower at the P and T and rung up the people that had phones, Ruby and aunty Millie and Mrs Palto and that, and told them all about it. And he biked over to Sadie's and told her what was up, and he went to see Mum about it too, and aunty Aggie. And he went to see Peggy too.

'What did she say?' I asked Jaz that night.

I was really scared of asking Peggy to come to the party. I wanted her to come, I wanted her to come a hell of a lot, but I was scared she'd say no.

'Said she could do with a party,' Jaz said. 'And she's bringing sausage rolls.'

And it felt like barbed wire suddenly sort of unwound from round my stomach.

Finding ways for people to get to Brooklands was tricky, but Jaz organised all that too. He arranged for Ruby and Frank to take some people in their Chev, and for Sadie and Curly to take some in the little old Prefect they'd just bought. Eddie had a car too, an old heap he'd picked up from god knows where, but it had four wheels that moved if you was lucky, so he brought Mum and Tots and Billie out, and he picked up aunty Aggie and brought her out too. Jaz organised for everybody else to come in a couple of taxis. That cost a lot, but with everybody sharing the fare it didn't work out too dear. So in the end it was quite a big party, there must of been about thirty people, all jammed into our little fibro bach.

I baked things for it, pies and buns and cakes. And we put on beer for everybody, we got a keg from the pub at Belfast. And everybody brought things too, so it was a real feast, enough food to sink a ship.

Eddie brought the old gramophone from home, and some new records, so we played those all night and sung and danced.

Mum sung too, just like the old days at Moorhouse Avenue.

She sat herself down on a chair in a corner and nursed a shandy all night, and sung and muttered.

'Happy birthday, Gin,' Peggy said.

I found it hard to say anything back to her, I was too sort of choked up, cause I was really happy to be friends with Peggy again, even though neither of us said anything about why we'd had the row in the first place. We just took one another as we was, and carried on like nothing had ever gone wrong.

'Fag's the only one of us missing,' Hock said a bit later.

It was typical of Hock to say that. I could see Peggy and Tots was thinking it, but they didn't say anything, cause they must of known I didn't want to think about that. But once Hock had pointed it out everybody started talking about it.

'Lady Carrel's too high and mighty these days to have time for the likes of us,' Sadie said.

'Trouble with her,' Ruby said, 'she's out of touch with the way things really are. All those Carrels and that, they've had their day.'

Tots stopped the talk by going outside with Jaz and coming back in with a great big pink cake. That was a real surprise to me, that cake. Jaz and Tots had kept it a secret. They'd bought it from a shop in town and Tots had iced it. The icing wasn't quite the way Tots had planned it to be; like, there was all these blobs and bumps round the edge which was supposed to be roses. But she'd managed to write my name on top, Ginnie. And there was twenty-one candles. And when everybody went quiet and looked at the candles sort of flickering like little fairies I felt my throat go all sort of dry and lumpy.

'Who's got the key of the door?' everybody started to sing. 'Never been twenty-one before.'

I gave Mum the first slice.

'Hmf,' she said. 'You've had the bloody key of the door ever since you cleared out to shack up with that Jaz Smith.'

And I think she was quite enjoying herself, for Mum.

Fag

I found it hard to believe how easy it was to make money. Not that I really understood how much money we were making, but I understood well enough we were making it. And then not long after my birthday Roddie told me it was time to expand the business.

'I've had the idea of turning next door into a shop,' he said. 'Mrs Spade's just been talking to me. Says she and her husband and kiddies want to leave, been offered a state house. So that'll fit in with us nicely.'

'What about money?' I said. 'Won't it take money?'

'Had a chat with old Lomax down at the bank,' Roddie said.

Within a few weeks the Spades had gone and a gang of men had starting ripping out the insides of the cottage next door. The back rooms got turned into a warehouse, the front rooms into a shop, and the yard got covered over with concrete.

'I'll have to give up my country rounds now that we're expanding,' Roddie said. 'I'll need to be here on the spot. I've found a chap to do the rounds for us. Good steady chap. Won't knock the van about. Used to work for us up at Trecarrel.'

I was quite excited by the idea of a shop. Shops had always seemed glamorous to me, places where men wore suits and women wore nylons, places where transactions took place over smooth shiny counters, places where cash registers tingled, papers riffled. I'd been looking after the invoices and typing our correspondence ever since we'd got started. Now I envisaged taking a larger role.

Running the office.

Managerial functions.

'I'll be able to help out in the shop,' I said.

'I've been thinking,' Roddie said. 'We can afford to pay somebody else now. I've never felt happy about the way you've felt you had to work for the business, darling. You've never complained, but I know there're pleasanter things you could be doing.'

'Like what?' I said.

Roddie was a bit startled.

251

'Well there's little Pamela,' he said. 'And the house. And your pretty flower garden . . .'

Then he stopped, seeing my mood.

'No sense paying good money for somebody to do what I can already do for us,' I said. 'I can do the paperwork, I'm good at counter hopping, I know how to keep accounts.'

'It's starting to get a bit big,' Roddie said. 'Perhaps it's time to get an accountant.'

'The turnover at Scholefield Electrical was much bigger than this piddling little outfit,' I said.

And though Roddie murmured a bit more, I won. I paid a woman to come and look after Pamela of a morning and at nine o'clock prompt I'd step out the front door in a neat little suit and walk into the shop through a new glass door. I'd serve customers at the counter. I'd answer the telephone. I'd take down orders. I'd type, I'd draw up the accounts, I'd drive the Citroën to the bus depot and the railway station to collect consignments.

And it was hopeless, and Roddie was right.

'I can't keep up with it,' I confessed one evening over my third double whisky.

And in my tiredness and disappointment I found time to resent the way Roddie showed no sign of triumph but just murmured, and nodded and kissed me.

Within a week we had a brunette busy banging the typewriter in the back room of the shop, and an accountant taking our books away to an office in Stafford Street. I gave vent to my feelings by going out on a spending spree.

'Oh yes, moddom,' they told me at Ballantynes. 'That style looks gorgeous on you, moddom, just gorgeous. And really not at all dear, considering the quality.'

'I'll take it,' I said.

Then upstairs to eat milles feuilles.

I went on a home and garden craze too. I'd already transformed our garden. I'd planted and planted and planted, not just the flower garden Roddie praised me for, but a shrubbery too, and one or two little saplings, a beech, a maple, which were now turning into nice young trees. So whenever we looked out our

252

windows now we saw leafy green branches wave back at us where at first the only sight had been Mrs Spade's brassieres and Mr Spade's underpants flopping about in the easterlies.

And garden furniture.

'The well appointed garden,' I read in a magazine, 'should be no less well appointed than the dining room or hall. And the basis of its appearance, as in the dining room or hall, should be elegant and appropriate furniture.'

I bought a cast iron table, painted green, which sprouted a striped umbrella. I bought cast iron chairs to go with it, and a cast iron bench to put under the branches of the baby maple.

When spring brought out the flowers, Roddie and I would sit under our sun umbrella, drinking our whiskies, smoking our tailor mades, leafing through magazines.

The house had been added to by that time too. A new wing had been run up at the back, and two or three walls had been taken down inside, and everything had been relined and rewired and repainted and repapered. A new sitting room, with sliding glass doors onto the terrace where the garden furniture now stood. A new bathroom, shining with chrome. And whiteware, new whiteware. A washing machine, a clothes dryer, a refrigerator. A vacuum cleaner. A radiogram. And a toaster, a pop-up toaster, with a little dial which let me choose every morning whether I wanted my toast 'light', 'medium', or 'dark'.

Dark toast.

The words seemed so strange and exotic and rich, I felt like a queen every morning, sliding in my two slices of white milk loaf, catching them as they popped out a minute later.

The most wonderful thing of all was the new carpet.

'Oh look,' I said to Roddie over instant coffee and dark toast one morning. 'That carpet's for sale, that carpet I was showing you at the DIC last time we were in Christchurch. They're having a sale and they're selling that carpet. Oh it's not fair, it's such a beautiful carpet and they're going to sell it.'

I shoved the newspaper advertisement under his nose.

'Shall I go up and get it?' he said. 'Have to go up to Christchurch this week anyway.'

'Oh yes,' I said. 'Get it for us. It's a wonderful carpet. It's a beautiful carpet.'

I was on tenterhooks all day, pacing backwards and forwards, imagining how the carpet would look in the new sitting room, imagining how terrible it would be if I couldn't get it.

'Got it,' Roddie said that evening as I met him by the car. 'They're going to send it down. Here's a swatch.'

I burst into tears.

'Oh it's so beautiful,' I said. 'How can anything be so beautiful?'

It was the colour called 'fawn', a lovely colour, I loved saying its name, a soft quiet deer-like name. And there was a pattern sprigged across it, a pattern of little golden kowhai blossoms.

'I'm not tired,' I said to Roddie the night after some men had come to lay it. 'I'm going to stay up with a book.'

He gave me a kiss on the tip of my nose.

'Night darling.'

And once he'd gone, and I'd prepared myself by drinking a scotch, I took off my shoes, slid off my stockings, and walked in my bare feet on the new carpet.

'Mm,' I said to myself. 'This is heaven. I've died and I'm in heaven.'

The Historian

'What is the meaning of human history?' the Archbishop of Canterbury asked twenty thousand people towards the end of that year.

His audience, gathered in Cathedral Square to celebrate the centenary of Canterbury, murmured a little restively. What was the point of questions like that? But the Archbishop wasn't offended, he had no intention of letting anybody answer but himself.

'We inherit history,' the Archbishop observed. 'We make it for a few years, we hand it on. Why? To what end?'

He paused, and the audience once again was a little restive.

'History,' the Archbishop announced in triumph, 'has a purpose and a goal and a place in the personal purpose of God.'

254

So that was easy, it turned out that the answer was easy after all. And the audience, relieved, gratified, a little bored, coughed for a moment, a multiple spasm of the polite little 'hems' which a Canterbury audience uses to signify that it is . . .

What?

Acknowledging? Accepting?

Pretending?

'Canterbury offered thanksgiving,' the morning paper announced next day, 'in a great centennial service at which the Archbishop of Canterbury, whose predecessor one hundred years ago blessed the pilgrims on their departure from England, was present to preach the sermon to send the province into its second century with the same benediction. Christchurch was an enormous open-air cathedral with city streets forming the nave and transepts. There, a vast crowd from all stations of life gathered to thank God for the blessings of a century. From a pulpit over the west door of the Cathedral, the Archbishop of Canterbury spoke of the simple faith of the pioneers and the needs of today. Then, with the sunshine gleaming on the primatial cross of the See of Canterbury, he gave his blessing to the huge congregation, silent below the lofty Cathedral spire.'

Fag, sitting in front of the cathedral with the rest of the Carrels, giggled halfway through the benediction. Then, after noticing the calm eyes of Mrs Carrel senior looking across at her, took it out on Roddie.

'This is pathetic,' she said. 'What does the stupid old goat know about anything?'

And then, sorry for Roddie, tense with the struggle to fight down her giggles, she ended up with a violent headache.

'I'll stay here,' she told him in a darkened room at the hotel later that afternoon. 'Go and enjoy yourself. I'll be fine.'

Mrs Carrel senior glanced at him as he joined her and the others in the vestibule.

'Poor thing,' Roddie said. 'Headache. That hat she was wearing was so tiny, it didn't shade her at all.'

Mrs Carrel saw temptation coming and, after a brief struggle, succumbed.

'But it was such a lovely little hat darling,' she said. 'Worth a hundred headaches I'm sure.'

Her son merely smiled, seeming not to notice.

They drove off to the bishop's palace, where servants in black uniforms slid about on a lawn serving strawberries and ice to the guests at the archiepiscopal garden party. Diana in silver and yellow ran up, smiled, kissed them, held their hands.

'Maxwell wants to meet his nibs,' she laughed. 'Can you do the necessary, Daddy?'

'I'm sure the Archbishop would be as honoured to meet the newly elected vice-president of the Canterbury Law Society as I would be to effect the introduction for him,' Mr Carrel said, nodding and smiling at Maxwell Urquhart, who stood like a stump beside Diana.

'Stuck up bunch of bloody snots still won't say a bloody word to me,' observed Stanley Gabbatt, managing director of the newly incorporated United Footwear Company Limited, as the Carrels walked past him on their way to shake hands with the Archbishop.

'Shut up, Stan,' Gloria Gabbatt replied. 'I crawled up half the backsides in town to get this invitation, so don't you spoil it for me.'

Ruby Morgan, driving her beige Chevrolet past the entrance to Bishopscourt, felt faintly superior.

'Silly tarts with their noses in the air,' she told her friends over bridge half an hour later. 'Wouldn't know a good time if it was halfway up their fanny. They think things are just going on the same and that nothing's changing. But they're out of touch, things are modern now.'

Margaret Feron, sitting in the yellow chair in the kitchen at Moorhouse Avenue, was fiddling with the dials on her wireless.

'. . . the meaning of human history?' she heard. '. . . a purpose and a goal and a place . . .'

'What's bloody happened to *Sing me the Old Songs*?' she muttered. 'Can't bloody find it anywhere on the stupid bloody dial.'

On the following day a crowd of a hundred thousand people

watched a procession two miles long wind through the city streets from Latimer Square to Hagley Park. The Prime Minister dedicated the new Christchurch International Airport. Crowds cheered and screamed at a river carnival, a fireworks display, a military review. The Royal Musical Society sang Bach and Brahms, the National Orchestra played Beethoven's *Ode to Joy*.

'We have inherited a dream,' a politician declared. 'And what has become of the dream?'

And the politician, like the Archbishop, knew the answer.

'The dream,' he said softly, 'has become reality.'

Fag

Now that I was affluent and elegant and all the rest of it I started to have a 'social life'. The magazines told me I needed one, and now I had one. For the first time in my life I found myself able to lounge over a whisky on a Saturday afternoon and say to Roddie, 'Oh gosh, do we *have* to go and have drinks with the Wildes tonight as well as the Spencers? Can't we skip one of them?'

'Better go to both,' Roddie said. 'We don't want to hurt anybody's feelings.'

I'd pour myself another drink, and sigh.

'Suppose you're right,' I'd say. 'But it's a bit of a bore.'

And swallow my whisky.

I was drinking rather a lot actually. I drank whisky before meals, and glasses of cold beer under the sun umbrella of an afternoon, and whisky and tonic and Pimms and vodka when we went out to places for drinks or people came to our place for drinks, squeezing into our cottage, laughing and chattering, drinking and smoking. Alcohol and nicotine were important at those parties. When people said 'come round and have a drink' they meant it. They didn't mean 'come round and have a talk'. They meant *drink* – they put it away like it was going out of style.

Percy Spencer, for example, he was our accountant. I don't think I ever saw him dressed in anything less than a lounge suit and a glass of scotch. And his wife Valerie, she was always very chic. She was a rival to me as far as high fashion went, but she drank too much too.

One night at their place I was a bit worried; it was a hot night, and I was worried my make up would be getting streaky so I slipped into the bathroom to look in the mirror. I never did find out if my nose was shiny or not, because the minute I turned on the bathroom light I saw Valerie Spencer lying in a heap on the black tile floor, her shoulders white and bare in her low cut dress. Around her in a big jagged circle was her frock, a yellow silk frock. And she was crying, just crying quietly and hopelessly, in that gleaming naked bathroom.

She turned round to look at me, her shoulders seeming very thin and scrawny under the hard light.

'I can't stand it any more,' she said. 'Why are we here? What's it all about?'

But I didn't want to hear people saying things like that. The last thing I wanted to think about was anything like that. I shut the door and walked away.

We knew lots of people in Timaru, Roddie and I. Every time I walked down Stafford Street, swinging my skirts, stopping to look at my ensemble in the shop windows, people would nod and smile and wave, nice people, prosperous people, people who looked like me.

'It might be nice to have a real friend,' I said to Roddie in bed one night. 'Not just party friends. I miss Ginnie sometimes. And the rest of them too, Peggy and Tots and that.'

'Natural enough,' Roddie said. 'Making real friends takes time.'

'I need a sort of best friend,' I said. 'A sort of sister.'

'I'll be your best friend,' Roddie said.

So that was that.

But it wasn't too bad really. It was a nice life. It was a lovely life. When had my life ever been anything like so good?

A storm blew up from the south halfway through January and cooled the air down in a hurry. After a day or so of it I began to think it was too cool if anything, and that I'd had enough, thank you, it could start getting hot again. On the Saturday afternoon Roddie and I, sitting over cups of coffee, looked through the glass doors out onto the terrace and talked glumly about how many leaves the storm could be expected to strip off the maple.

'Mind you,' Roddie said. 'A southerly in the middle of summer reminds you not to take things for granted.'

I hated it when he said things like that, I don't know why. My brain would seem to go black, I'd seem to suddenly feel as though everything was a trap, that his homilies and adages and little tags were something that could trap me and kill me.

So I didn't say anything, didn't look at him. Sipped my coffee.

The phone rang. Roddie answered it.

'It's your sister,' he said. 'Ginnie. Says she and Jaz are staying at the motor camp.'

We bundled ourselves into the car and drove out there. It seemed such a dreary day, the sky was as cold and grey as a stone and the wind was blowing cold off the sea. And the motor camp, it was even drearier than the day, rows and rows of little wooden huts surrounded by black pine trees.

We drove up and down the huts, going slowly, splashing through puddles. A watery ray of sunlight came out and we saw Ginnie and Jaz, lit up on the verandah of a hut.

'Poor things,' Roddie said.

I hated him for saying that. My heart seemed to close up against him and leap out at Ginnie. I felt as though I was going to cry. She looked so poor. Her hair was hacked short like a prisoner, her clothes were threadbare, and on her feet she was wearing a pair of old sandshoes. Jaz looked just as bad, his face was rough with stubble, he obviously hadn't shaved, and he was wearing black fingerless mittens.

'Look at the boys though,' Roddie whispered as he stopped the car.

He was right, the two little boys looked warm and well cared for, bundled up in jerseys and tam-o'-shanters. Two little pink cheeked boys, holding tight to Ginnie, looking up at us with shy smiles.

Ginnie was shy too.

'You're looking good,' she said.

'You too,' I said.

'Come in and I'll make us a brew,' she said.

When she stood up I saw she was pregnant again.

My god, I thought. Count your blessings, forget about the old life, there's nothing there for you. Just look at poor Ginnie.

You don't know you're living.

Ginnie

It was hot, that summer at the end of 1950. I don't know if it was hotter than summer usually is, but to us it seemed absolutely boiling. At midday when the sun got up high it was terrible. The lino on the sunny side of the house would be that hot it burned you if you touched it. Even at night the house would still be stinking hot. Me and Jaz would sleep with no clothes on, wishing for a bit of a cool spell.

Come January we decided to have a holiday.

'We could get on a bus,' Jaz said. 'Head off somewhere.'

'We could go south,' I said. 'I'd like to see Timaru. I'd like to see Fag.'

So we filled a cardboard suitcase and got on a bus and headed south. The weather packed up on us though. Trust our luck. When we wanted it to be cool it was hot, and when we wanted it to be warm it was cold. But it didn't worry us really, it was too exciting being off on a holiday. And it was especially exciting for me. I'd never been further south than Sockburn before, so I felt like I was heading into the unknown. And then when we got to Timaru it looked really nice, a nice town, very sort of solid and rich looking.

We got out of the bus and walked to the motor camp. Which was nice too, the motor camp, it reminded us of Brooklands. Pine trees and cabins. It was fairly basic, but that didn't worry us, we liked it, it was a bit of an adventure and anyway we was used to things being basic.

'I'm scared of seeing Fag though,' I said to Jaz.

'She won't eat you,' Jaz said.

Last time I'd seen her was the day she got married, at the Dainty Inn.

I walked down to a phone box and rung them up.

'Gidday,' I said. 'It's Ginnie. How are you, Roddie?'

Roddie was all friendly and nice. He told me him and Fag would come out and see us. My stomach felt all fluttery, but I didn't say anything to Jaz, I just made us a cup of tea and we went out and sat on the verandah of the cabin with Allan and Jimmie and told them stories and waited. It'd been raining, it was a grey sort of day, but it wasn't too bad, we didn't mind.

Then we saw their car coming, splashing through the puddles, and I could see Fag's face inside, sort of pale and distant.

She waved.

I waved back.

And she was a stranger. When she stepped out of the car and came across to kiss me I felt like I was being visited by the royal family. She was wearing this big long flowing rustling skirt, it was all sort of fashionable and expensive. And she had a little short jacket on, and a little hat with a veil, and gloves, and stockings. And her face was made up all careful and precise like a mannequin in a shop window.

She was very friendly, there was even tears in her eyes. She talked and talked and talked. She made us come back to their place for a meal.

'I wish you'd sent us a line to let us know,' she said. 'I would've cooked something special. But it's lovely you're here, I've really missed you.'

'Come and stay with us,' Roddie said. 'We'd like to have you.'

'Yes come on,' Fag said. 'It'd be really nice, all of us together.'

Jaz looked like he was going to say yes, so I got in first.

'It's all right,' I said. 'The cabin's all right. We don't want to put you out.'

Course they tried to talk us out of it, but I stuck to my guns. Then we went and had a meal with them, and played cards and talked till late, and Roddie drove us back to the motor camp. Next morning they drove us down to Caroline Bay. We had a picnic lunch and then when it was time for us to get back on the bus Fag burst into tears.

'Come and see us again,' she said. 'Come and stay with us.'

And I cried too, but somehow I felt like I was crying cause it was like there wasn't a Fag any more. I felt like I'd lost Fag forever, that there wasn't a person there any more, just clothes and money and alcohol. I felt like she'd died.

And all that was left was a cardboard cutout of Princess Elizabeth.

Or Lauren Bacall.